THE
Pleasure
TRAP

Also by Niobia Bryant

Mistress Series
Message from a Mistress
Mistress No More
Mistress, Inc.

Friends & Sins Series
Live and Learn
Show and Tell
Never Keeping Secrets

Strong Family Series
Heated
Hot Like Fire
Give Me Fever
The Hot Spot
Red Hot
Strong Heat

Make You Mine
Reckless (with Cydney Rax and Grace Octavia)
Heat Wave (with Donna Hill and Zuri Day)

Published by Dafina Books

THE
Pleasure
TRAP

NIOBIA
BRYANT

KENSINGTON PUBLISHING CORP.
www.kensingtonbooks.com

DAFINA BOOKS are published by

Kensington Publishing Corp.
119 West 40th Street
New York, NY 10018

All Kensington titles, imprints, and distributed lines are available at special quantity discounts for bulk purchases for sales promotion, premiums, fund-raising, and educational or institutional use.

Special book excerpts or customized printings can also be created to fit specific needs. For details, write or phone the office of the Kensington Special Sales Manager: Kensington Publishing Corp., 119 West 40th Street, New York, NY 10018. Attn. Special Sales Department. Phone: 1-800-221-2647.

Dafina and the Dafina logo Reg. U.S. Pat. & TM Off.

ISBN-13: 978-0-7582-6533-3
ISBN-10: 0-7582-6533-6
First Kensington Trade Paperback Printing: November 2014

eISBN-13: 978-1-61773-023-8
eISBN-10: 1-61773-023-8
First Kensington Electronic Edition: November 2014

10 9 8 7 6 5 4 3 2 1

Printed in the United States of America

Thank you, Lord, for blessing me with the gift of storytelling; for the wisdom to utilize that gift; and for the readers who seem to enjoy it.

The Prelude

WHAP!

"Wake your ass up, Pleasure."

The sting of the slap delivered to his cheek roused Graham "Pleasure" Walker to consciousness, but just barely. He moaned as he shook his head to clear it. His tongue felt heavy and dry in his mouth. He could barely lift his eyelids, and his eyes burned behind them. He tried to shift his body into a more comfortable position, but grunted in pain at the tight binds around his wrists and ankles.

He was tied but he felt like he was floating above the ground.

WHAP!

"Wake your fine motherfucking ass up. We got business to tend to, motherfucker."

He winced and tried to brace himself to hit the floor but then remembered he was bound to a chair. One of his leather dining room chairs.

Unable to hold his head up, he let his chin drop to his chest as he blinked and shook his head slowly, waiting for more clarity. When his vision focused a bit more, he was looking down at his limp dick lying across his right thigh.

I'm naked?

He looked up and shifted his eyes to look around as much as he could at the living room of his Jersey City penthouse apartment. The rich black and charcoal gray décor. The floor-to-ceiling windows that overlooked the Hudson River and displayed the New York skyline across the water. However, it felt almost surreal as he struggled to remember just how he came to be naked and tied to a chair.

Think, man, think.

His thoughts were clouded. He couldn't get a firm grasp on anything.

What's wrong with me?

His eyes drifted closed and his body slackened, but the ties at his wrists and ankles kept him in the chair.

"Do you remember me, Pleasure?"

A firm hand roughly grabbed his chin and jerked his face up. He opened his eyes to find a woman dressed in all black with her face covered by a black ski mask and her hands in leather gloves. He shook his head yet again to clear it.

WHAP!

He winced from the pain. She'd used the back of her hand that time and her knuckles dug into his cheek with the blow.

"Well, I remember you," she said snidely into his ear, from behind him now.

She lightly bit one of his broad shoulders. Slowly she deepened the bite.

"Shit," he swore sharply, his tall and muscled frame jerking.

She laughed and smacked the back of his head before coming around him with her hand trailing across his chest. "Not bad at all for a man-whore," she said, leaving him.

He eyed her as she moved about his living room and touched things that apparently caught her eye. Who is she? What does she want?

He closed his eyes as he let his head hang back, trying to match her frame or her voice or her movements to one of the many wealthy women who'd paid to be sexually pleasured by him. He'd put many miles on his dick screwing women and had charged well for his skill. Very well. Over the years, his clients numbered well into the hundreds. Some were regulars; others were one-night stands he'd easily forgotten as he transitioned from exotic dancer to dick-for-hire.

Woman after woman, trick after trick, he had asked them all the same thing as he would slay them with his dick game and get a rush from the looks on their faces as he looked down at them with each stroke.

"Who am I?"

"Pleasure."

"And what am I giving you?"

"Pleasure."

But none of them knew him. He was a stranger to them. And that was just the way he liked it.

"You haven't done badly for yourself over the years," she said from across the room.

He slowly turned his head to eye her standing before his fireplace. In between slow blinks, he saw her pick up a picture frame from his mantel.

He blinked again.

She looked at it and laughed bitterly.

He blinked again.

She took a small step back to hold it high in the air.

He blinked again.

She viciously flung it into the unlit fireplace. "Fuck you and her," she spat as she flew across the room like she was rabid, to snatch up his chin again.

He fought hard to snatch his face away from her pinching grip. He tried and failed. He had no strength.

She grabbed him by the neck, pressing her fingers deeply into him until he struggled to breathe. "Just as fine as ever," she whispered into his face, laughing maniacally before she pressed a kiss to his mouth and then released him with a rough jerk.

"Who are you?" he asked, his throat dry and pained.

That earned him a gut punch that made his body instinctively try to curl into a ball. The restraints kept him locked in place as a deep, throbbing ache in the firm muscle of his thigh finally caused him to wince. The pain brought back the memory of being struck from behind in the hall and painfully pierced with a needle as he unlocked and opened his apartment door.

"Damn," she swore, hating the thought of that. "How dare you forget me? After all these years? After everything I should have meant to you, motherfucker?" she stressed.

What?

The majority of the women in his thirty years of life were his clients—there were so few he would consider more to him than that.

He struggled to open his eyes as he felt her hands on his thighs and then wrapping around his dick. He couldn't lie about the fear that spread through him. What now?

"Don't," he said, his voice as weak as his body.

Moments later he felt her mouth surround his tip, licking it before she took his soft inches into her mouth. He took no pleasure in her work. His still-sluggish thoughts were busy trying to figure out who she was and how to get free.

"Don't worry, you're not going to die . . . yet," she said, her threat whispered against the damp flesh of his now-hard dick.

His head dropped back. The tips of his long and slender dreads scratched his back as he fought hard to figure out just who the hell she was . . .

Chapter 1

Essie

1998

"I'm sending you to live with your father."

Graham had on his headphones and the sounds of Aaliyah played but he heard his mother clearly. Not bothering to turn away from his computer to face her, he shrugged his shoulders and took another swig from his can of soda.

"Today," she said, firmly.

That made him stiffen a bit as he reached to set the can back on his desk. Nevertheless, he caught himself and relaxed his body as he pretended to be lost in the music. Pretended she didn't exist.

Pretended his heart wasn't pounding in his chest.

A firm hand rested on his slender shoulder. "Son," his father said. "You hear your mother talking to you?"

Graham couldn't hide his surprise as he turned in his swivel chair and looked up at his father. He nodded and removed his earphones. "Yes, sir," he said, standing up to face him. He was sixteen with a thin and athletic build, but his father still towered over his six-foot height by another four inches.

His entire life he'd grown up on the comparison of their looks.

"Tylar, that boy came out your guts!"

"Your daddy sure spit you out, Graham."

"Ain't no denying that one, Ty."

The broad face with high cheekbones, deep-set eyes, and slashing eyebrows but soft, full lips and long, thick lashes had drawn many a woman's eyes—and other body parts—to his father. Thus the end of his parents' marriage.

Tylar Walker smiled and wrapped an arm around Graham to hug him to his side. "Looks like I have a roommate," he said with a smile.

"I wouldn't exactly call it that," Cara Walker said from behind them, still positioned in the doorway.

He felt his father stiffen. "Cara," he said in warning.

She shook her head and stepped inside Graham's room, kicking sneakers and dirty clothes out of her path. "You act like it's a wonderful thing that he just got expelled from school for fighting every damn week like he has no sense," she said, her tone sharp and rising with every word.

Graham eyed her. "Ma, I didn't—"

"Didn't what, Graham?" she asked, tears brimming in her eyes. "Didn't want to get suspended three times before they finally expelled you? Didn't want to waste all of the money we already paid for you to go to private school? Didn't want to waste living in a good community with nothing but opportunity? Huh?"

"Cara," Tylar said again.

The sight of her crying softened some of Graham's anger toward her. "I'm sorry, Ma," he said.

She swiped at her tears as she turned to leave his bedroom. She paused and turned back. "Life doesn't owe you a damn thing, Graham," she told him fiercely, her finger pointed in his direction. "It's yours to either throw away or to thrive. You remember that if you don't remember shit else I *tried* to teach you."

And she was gone.

Tylar cupped the back of his head, patting it comfortingly. "Pack up your clothes. We'll get the rest of your stuff this weekend. Okay?" he said. "Let me talk to your mama for a little bit."

Graham nodded and turned to grab his oversized Polo duffel bag, which hung on the back of the leather chair sitting in front of his desk. As he removed his clothing from hangers in his walk-in closet, he caught sight of the five-by-seven picture frame on his nightstand. Dropping a pair of shorts atop the duffel, he leaned over to pick up the photo of him at just five years old, flanked by his parents. "Better days," he muttered, shaking his head before carelessly tossing it onto his unmade king-sized bed.

Any dreams he'd had years ago of them being one big unhappy family again were gone.

His parents had divorced more than three years ago, and everything about his life changed. His father eventually moved out of the home in the suburbs of Bedford, New York, and rented a one-bedroom unit in a duplex apartment building in Brooklyn. Graham was shuttled back and forth between them.

Well, I used to be.

He finished carelessly pushing his dry-cleaned clothes into his duffel bag. He dumped the books and notebooks from his book bag to shove his precious six pairs of Air Jordan sneakers inside that. For a second he contemplated a suit and dress shoes, but he shook that idea away. His father didn't go to church every Sunday like his mother.

For that he was more than glad.

Shaking the sudden tension from his already-broad shoulders, Graham heaved the strap of the duffel bag over his head so that it crossed the thin but still athletic build of his chest. With one last look at his room, and barely a moment of regret, he walked down the hall to the wrought-iron staircase.

"I just want to know why he's so angry."

"He's a boy," Tylar said. "It's probably just a phase... regardless, he know I don't play that shit he been pulling around here."

Graham paused at the top of the stairs at the sound of his parents' voices.

"So it's *my* fault?" his mother asked.

His father sighed heavily and Graham could picture him wiping his mouth with his hand. "Look, I'm not going to argue with you. I thought the divorce put an end to all of that."

"And did the divorce put an end to you slinging your dick into every piece of pus—"

Graham purposefully coughed and cleared his throat as he noisily came down the stairs and into the den. Thankfully, the rest of his parents' words evaporated. It was an old argument he was tired of witnessing. "I'm ready," he said.

They both looked at him.

"Tell your mama bye," Tylar said, shoving his hands into the front pockets of the green uniform pants he wore for his job as a sanitation worker for the city of New York.

Graham walked over to stand before her. At just sixteen, he towered over her by four inches already. "Don't cry, Ma," he said, reaching to hug her close with one arm.

"The weekends belong to me," Cara said, rising on the tips of her toes to press a kiss to his cheek. "And most holidays."

He nodded even as he stepped back from her and started toward the archway leading into the spacious foyer.

"And you call me every day, Graham," she called from behind him.

His mind was already focused on leaving that house and starting his new life with his dad. He paused on the brick wraparound porch just long enough to look around the cul-de-sac. He was happy to see the last of the tree-lined streets and quiet atmosphere. *To hell with this boring shit.*

He placed his bags on the rear passenger seat of his father's dark blue Ford Expedition before hopping into the front passenger seat. He instantly inserted his ear buds and let the sounds of Jay-Z's "Hard Knock Life" cause his head to bop.

"It's a hard knock life for us..."

His words stopped when the ear buds were pulled from his ears with twin pops as the suction was released. Graham looked over at his father. His eyes widened when he held out his hand and waved his fingers.

"Man, Dad," he moaned, removing the Discman and ear buds to hand over to him.

Tylar slid the CD player into the middle console. "This ride back to Brooklyn is plenty of time for you to tell me what's really been going on with you," he said, turning the key in the ignition and placing the SUV in drive.

Graham stayed quiet.

"You got kicked out of school so much for fighting that they held you back in the ninth grade, son," his father said, side-eyeing him as he drove. "Now you're expelled just a few weeks before the end of your sophomore year. You want to be twenty and still in high school?"

Graham slumped in his seat and looked out the passenger window. He wasn't in a talking mood, but he knew that didn't matter. He couldn't ignore his father the way he did his mother. Still, he had no plans on sharing anything he didn't want to share, and nobody could change that. Both his truth and his lies were his to tell.

★　★　★

Graham lay across the king-sized bed that dominated the one bedroom in his father's apartment. It was just the beginning of June, but during early evenings the heat was sweltering and the only air-conditioning unit was in the bedroom. While his father was at work during the day, Graham soaked the air up because at night that oscillating fan he used barely cooled him off as he slept on the sofa bed in the living room.

So far, his requests for an A/C unit had been met with "McDonald's is hiring twenty-four seven, son. Twenty-four. Seven."

The luxuries of a two-story home with an in-ground pool in the middle of suburban New York made his father's stylish but small apartment seem like the projects.

He looked around at the room. The walls were bare, there was a pile of dirty clothing growing out of the top of the hamper, and a thin layer of dust needed to be handled. The décor left a lot to be desired, but there weren't many men willing to go further than a comforter set and matching curtains, and Graham was 99 percent sure one of his father's women had picked that out.

And there were many.

Graham shook his head at the line of women—all pretty as hell with banging bodies—that his father paraded in and out of their small apartment. In just the two weeks since he'd moved in full-time he counted six. He heard the sex cries of each and every one through the thin wooden bedroom door as he dug his head under the pillows and tried to sleep.

Brrrnnnggg.

He dropped the remote onto the bed and picked up the cordless phone from the nightstand. "Hello," he said, his eyes still on a Jean-Claude Van Damme movie on the fifty-inch television.

"Hey, lover."

Graham pressed the phone closer to his ear at the sound of the soft, sexy, and feminine voice. His heart pounded.

"Excuse me?" he asked, grimacing at the way his voice cracked.

"Who is this?" she asked with wariness.

He pressed the back of his head onto the pillow and looked up at the white ceiling. "This is Graham...Tylar's son," he said, being sure to deepen his voice.

"Oh...oh shit. I'm sorry," she said. "I called your dad's cell, and when he didn't answer all morning I thought he was off from work."

And another one bites the dust.

"He's at work. You wanna leave a message?" Graham asked more out of politeness than anything. He already knew she was on the shut-out list—whether she knew it or not. He picked up the remote and started turning up the volume on his movie.

"Tell him Yvonne called."

Click.

He dropped the phone back on the bed and laughed. *Daddy running through 'em like tissue.*

As far as Graham could tell, all of the women were fine with being in rotation with one another because he had yet to see one just drop by and run into another. Everybody played her position. And well.

It was obvious the last thing his father wanted was to be remarried, and Graham couldn't blame him. The only female Graham came even close to banging was a white girl he went to school with who gave out blow jobs as if they were lollipops. Cheap lollipops.

Still, he hadn't given up his virgin card, and ear hustling his father straight slaying women left and right just a few feet from where he slept wasn't helping.

"Stop, Nikko. Stop!"

Graham rolled off the bed and looked out the window that overlooked the driveways of their apartment building and the one next door. A little brown boy of about ten was wetting a slender teenage girl with a hose. Graham's eyes widened at the sight of the bra covering her small but plump breasts being exposed by the moisture.

"Your ass is mine," she screamed before she fought through the stream of water to snatch the hose from him.

Graham looked on as she dropped the hose and chased the little boy inside the building. He felt disappointment when she was gone from his view. So did his dick. He looked down at it pressing against the front of his oversized basketball shorts.

Moving away from the window, he rubbed the length of his semi-hardness. "I need to jack this off," he muttered, pulling down on it.

Instead of heading for the shower to use the water and soap to help him nut off some of his horniness, Graham fell across the bed and resumed flipping through the cable channels for the next hour until his urges faded and he felt sleep claim him. He didn't fight it.

I always have somebody to fuck . . . in my dreams.

When Graham awakened with a stretch of his long limbs, the room was dark save for the light from the television. The room was cold from the air conditioner running on high even though the temperature had dropped outside with the disappearance of the sun. Shivering, he climbed off the bed and turned the window unit on low.

The cable box said it was after ten.

Daddy shoulda been home.

Graham frowned as he opened the bedroom door to check if his father was sleeping on the couch.

"You love this good pussy, don't you, Ty?"

Graham froze at the sound of the whispered words floating toward him from the living room. One of the lamps on an end table dimly lighted the room, just enough to cast a glow on the two bodies on the couch. One straddling the other. One curvier than the other. One moving against the other.

"Give me that good pussy," he heard his father whisper back.

Graham stood transfixed in the hall just inches from the entrance to the living room, looking on as some woman he couldn't place gripped the back of the couch as she glided her hips back and forth. She leaned back, and the move thrust her breasts up with her hard nipples almost pointed to the ceiling.

His dick hardened in a rush. He couldn't move. He couldn't look away.

He didn't want to.

His father moved his hands from where they gripped her buttocks to palm her breasts and then stroke her nipples with his thumbs.

She gasped hotly before she moaned.

"Damn, you can ride a dick," Tylar said, leaning over a bit to watch the back-and-forth motion of her hips.

She sat up straighter and then shifted her body easily to press her feet into the sofa as she squatted above him to slowly move her hips in a tight circle as she sat atop the tip.

"Mo-ther-*fuck*-er," Tylar groaned in sweet agony as his legs shot out straight with his uniform pants and boxers still gathered around the top of his boots.

She laughed and licked her lips as she rose onto her toes and began vibrating her ass up and down with the speed and intensity of a power driver.

Graham's eyes and mouth widened. *Look at that chick go.*

"That's the nut drainer," she said, looking down into Tylar's face before licking hotly at his open mouth.

Suddenly her eyes darted up and locked on Graham where he stood with his dick hard as jail time.

His body became tense with alarm as he stepped back,

expecting her to scream out in surprise or shock—or something.

But she didn't.

Her smile was devilish as she leaned forward and pressed a thick brown nipple into his father's mouth, keeping her eyes locked on Graham. "I love dick-dick-dick-dick-dick," she said huskily as she continued to ride his father and then lifted a finger to beckon Graham forward from the darkness.

But he didn't move. Excitement had his heart racing and his dick throbbing at a crazy pace as she caused the blood to rush through his body.

"Dick-dick-dick-dick-dick," she said, uncurling her tongue to wickedly flicker the tip of it as she continued to stare in Graham's direction.

He knew she could still see him and she wanted him to see her.

Graham swallowed over a lump in his throat, his hand going down to wrap around his aching erection. *Damn.*

"Your pussy getting hotter," Tylar moaned against her fleshy breast.

"I wonder why," she said, smiling at Graham over his father's shoulder as she pressed his face against her body.

Graham felt out of breath. Hot. Bothered. Horny. Needing to nut. Needing to nut so badly. He panted as he reached inside his shorts to free his dick as he watched her watching him as she rode his father harder.

Tylar broke his head free of her grip. "This dick gone cum," he said thickly.

"Cum for me," she ordered them both softly, her fingers digging deeply into the softness of the couch.

Graham locked his knees and bit his mouth to keep from crying out as he felt the first surge of cum fill the line. He jacked his dick harder and nearly broke the skin beneath his lip as he bit down to keep from hollering out at the exact moment that his father's cries of passion roughly filled the air.

Never once did she break her gaze on him even as she soon let out short, high-pitched shrieks as she found her own release.

"Shh," Tylar whispered. "You gone wake my son."

Too late.

She just smiled weakly and blew said son a kiss.

Graham's heart was pounding as he backed into the bedroom with his hand and dick wet and sticky with his release. He eased the door closed with his shoulder before he snatched his T-shirt off with his free hand and quickly cleaned himself with it.

He had barely dropped the shirt to the floor and lain on the bed before the door opened. Closing his eyes, he feigned sleep.

"Did we wake him?" she whispered.

"No," his father answered.

At the sound of her voice, Graham's gut clenched. He was glad when the door closed and he was alone. As he rolled over onto his stomach, the nervous anxiety clashed with his after-nut glow. He couldn't believe what he'd just experienced, and any shame he could possibly feel for being a peeping—and jacking off—Tom were barely noticeable.

Best nut ever.

Chapter 2

Essie

Two Weeks Later

Graham hitched the wide black straps of his Nike backpack higher on his shoulders as he strolled up the block toward their apartment building. It was late morning and everything was relatively quiet for a summer day. He figured the majority of their neighbors were working or sleeping—something he would've been doing if he hadn't hit the streets early to hunt for a job.

I'm sick of being broke.

He hoped the four applications he'd filled out and the one interview he'd had that day turned into something. His mama used to give him a weekly allowance. Unless it was a necessity, the only paper his father was giving out was the want ads.

Jogging up the brick steps of the duplex, he paused when the front door opened and Essie Nunez leaned her frame against the doorjamb. She didn't say a word even as she leveled her wide-set eyes on him and gave him a knowing smile. The same knowing smile she'd given him since the night he watched *her* sex his father and she watched *him* jack off.

Graham's gut instantly clenched as if in a reflex to an oncoming punch. He felt nervous in her presence. Nervous and out of sorts. He fought between a desire to rush past her so fast that he knocked her over, or to turn to run back down the stairs and up the street away from that smile.

Essie was well into her thirties—if not older—but had the type of body and wardrobe that made teenage girls seem boyish. From her messy topknot down to the crimson polish on her toes, everything spoke of being sexy and knowing it.

Unable to deny himself, he flicked his gaze over everything from her juicy gloss-covered lips to a red tube top that did nothing to hide hard nipples in the center of large, pendulous breasts. Her middle was a little soft from the three kids she'd borne, but even the slight muffin top over the top of her cut-off shorts looked inviting to him. And those shorts exposed her thick thighs, and her plump pussy pressed against the seat like a fist.

Essie was thick, maybe even thicker than a lot of men's taste, but Graham had seen firsthand that she knew how to move every bit of her pounds with ease. Lots and lots of ease. He licked his lips and glanced away at the hot memory of her shifting from a sitting to a squatting position.

When he looked back at her with his eyes squinted against the summer sun, she hadn't moved from her spot blocking the doorway. She gave him that knowing smile again as she reached inside her tube top to pull a soft pack of Newport cigarettes and a lighter from her cleavage. She pressed a cigarette between her glossy red lips.

I wish it was my dick in her mouth.

It jumped to life like it agreed.

"Excuse me," he mumbled, taking the last two steps up onto the wide porch to stand before her.

Essie took a deep inhale on the cigarette, causing her breasts to rise high. "I asked your daddy to help me move some boxes down to the basement and he said to ask you," she

said, turning to press her back against the doorjamb to allow
him to enter the apartment building. "You mind?"

Figures. He enjoys the pussy and I get the work.

Graham shrugged his broad shoulders.

"Good," she said, giving him a slow once-over before
pushing off the doorjamb and turning to enter the foyer.

Graham followed behind her, forcing his eyes not to dip
down to take in the motion of her hips and buttocks as she
made her way down the long hallway to her apartment. Essie
was the resident babysitter/bootleg daycare for the block, and
he could hear the noises of children grow louder as they
neared her place.

She opened the door and Graham's eyes widened at the
sight of kids of varying ages laid out on the floor staring at a
cartoon on the flat-screen television. Eight set of eyes—
including that of a one-year-old who was digging in his
nose—all locked on him.

" 'Sup?"

Graham's eyes shifted to a dark-skinned, round-faced boy
with eyes that were wide, serious, and as white as milk.
"Whassup, li'l man?" he said before turning to follow where
Essie disappeared through a door.

He stepped inside her bedroom. The scent of stale cigarettes
and her perfume surrounded him as he quickly took in the
unmade queen-sized bed, melted candles, and dozens of saucers
stationed about the room with dried coffee and cigarette ashes
in them.

It didn't feel right to be in her bedroom.

"In here," she called.

Not right at all.

He walked across the spacious room and came to a stop at
the door leading into her bathroom. She was sitting on the
edge of a claw-foot tub with her legs crossed as she lifted her
chin to push out a stream of silver smoke through her pursed
lips.

His eyes shifted about the small bathroom. "The boxes?" he reminded her gently when he didn't see any.

"Box," she emphasized.

Graham frowned. "Huh?"

She smirked as she took another drag from her cigarette before dropping it into the open commode and rising to her now-bare feet. The hiss of the ember put out by the water echoed as she snatched her tube top down around her waist, exposing her breasts to him.

Graham's mouth fell open. *Titties. Big-ass titties.*

She unbuttoned her shorts and eased them down over her hips to fall down around her ankles.

Graham nervously backed into the wall, knocking something off it and onto the floor.

BAM.

"Sorry," he mumbled, looking down at a broken picture frame on the floor by his foot. He tried to bend to pick it up.

Essie stepped close to him and pressed a hand to his stomach.

Graham tried again to step back from her, but the wall resisted him. "Ms. Nunez—"

She swallowed the rest of his protests when she kissed him.

His eyes widened at the feel of her tongue easing between his open lips. The first feel of it made his heart pound. The soft, quick flicker of the tip against his made his dick hard in a rush.

She chuckled softly against his mouth. "Dick-dick-dick-dick," she whispered, reaching quickly to stroke the length of him.

Graham gasped in shock and pleasure as he squeezed his eyes shut.

Oh shit. Oh shit. Oh shit.

"Dick-dick-dick-dick."

Graham felt like he wanted to run—needed to run—but he couldn't. This was a woman his father had slept with, but that didn't matter. Nothing did except the feel of her lips and hand. His heart pounded. His thighs trembled. He felt light-headed.

She stopped kissing him.

Graham cried out when he opened his eyes just as she squatted before him.

She's . . . she's . . .

He released a high-pitched squeal.

I'm gonna cum. Please don't cum. Don't cum. Don't—

The bathroom door leading from the hall squeaked as it opened.

Shock replaced the pleasure in Graham's eyes as he looked down at the solemn and wide eyes of one of the little boys Essie babysat.

"Go watch TV, Esai," she said gently to the boy over her shoulder, Graham's dick still in her hand.

Even as the boy turned and walked back out of the bathroom, politely closing the door behind himself, Graham tried to free his dick from Essie's grasp.

She looked up at him, her mouth still glistening wet from her neck game on him. "Don't worry about him. He mute. He couldn't tell nobody even if he wanted to."

"I'm good, Ms. Nunez," he said, forcing firmness to his voice as he pressed his palm to her forehead.

She licked her lips and looked at his dick—eye to eye—before shifting her gaze to look back up at him. "Oh, you're *real* good . . . and you'll be just as good as your daddy in a few more years. Keep drinking your milk," she said, finally freeing his privates as she stood up.

As Graham fought to shove his hard penis back inside his shorts and boxers, he admitted to himself the regret and relief he felt.

She sucked my—

Essie stepped inside the tub and then turned on the shower.

Graham stood there watching the soft sway of her body as she moved.

Nobody will believe this shit.

"I won't tell if you won't tell," she said, reaching her hand out to beckon him to join her.

I can't fuck my dad's—one of my dad's—girls.

His eyes locked on the way the water from the showerhead splashed off her body.

I can't . . .

That's what his head said.

I can't not fuck her.

That's what the harder head said.

"You know you want it," she taunted. "Come and get this pussy, boy."

He rushed out of his clothes feeling—and he was sure looking—awkward and lacking in experience.

All of that was about to change.

He reached behind him and turned the lock on the door leading into her bedroom.

Click.

Graham raised his fingers to his nose and inhaled the scent still clinging to his skin. He didn't want to ever wash his hand. The smell of Ms. Nunez was just too damn good to him. Everything about her was good to him.

Shaking his head in wonder, he couldn't wipe the smile from his face as he sat on the sofa not even paying attention to the television casting its lighting on his face.

"Why the hell you keep smiling like you crazy?"

Graham stopped grinning with a quickness as his father walked into the living room. "Something funny on TV," he mumbled, feeling guilty.

"*Law & Order?*" his father asked.

Graham's eyes focused on the bloody crime scene on the television. He hadn't noticed it. Shrugging, he looked over his thin shoulder at his dad. "You going out?" he asked.

"Nah. Got a friend coming over for a li'l bit," Tylar said, walking into the kitchen to pull a can of beer from the fridge.

"Who?" Graham asked, hating the thought of having to listen to his father sex Ms. Nunez again. *That would be awkward as hell.*

Tylar frowned. "Since when do you care?"

Graham just shrugged and picked up the remote to flip through the channels. "You want me to bounce?" he asked.

"Nah," Tylar said over his shoulder on his way back into his bedroom.

Graham dropped the remote not caring what show was on the television as he replayed in his mind finally losing his virginity. Again and again and again. A chill raced over his body as his cocky grin spread across his face again. *Way better than jacking off.*

He couldn't believe it.

Damn.

He was still lost in his memories of the feel, the smell, and the taste of pussy when the downstairs doorbell sounded. "I got it, Dad," he called out, pulling on his semi-hardness as he rolled off the sofa and made his way to the front door of their apartment.

The system to buzz the downstairs door open was broken. Graham jogged down the stairs in his sock-covered feet. He paused on the steps at the sight of Ms. Nunez opening the front door to let in his father's date for the night.

Oh shit.

"Thank you," the woman he didn't recognize said as she eased past Ms. Nunez's unmoving figure.

"Who you here to see?" Ms. Nunez asked, her Spanish accent heavy.

The woman, a tall and slender cutie with an ultra-short pixie cut, looked taken aback. "Ty—"

"Thanks for letting her in for me," Graham rushed to say, moving down the stairs quickly and drawing the eyes of both women. "Right up here."

Ms. Nunez arched her brow even as she smiled slowly at him. She mumbled something in Spanish as the woman moved up the stairs.

"You're Tylar's son?" she asked.

Graham didn't bother to answer as he led her up the stairs. He was too busy hoping Ms. Nunez didn't flip and start some trouble before he could get them safely inside the apartment.

"Gra-ham," she called up the stairs in a singsong fashion.

He kept it moving, pushing the door to the apartment open wide and stepping back to allow her in just as his father walked out of the bedroom.

"Hey, Missy," his father said warmly.

"Hey you," she said, biting her bottom lip as he pulled her close for a hug.

Graham rolled his eyes and closed the door. *Daddy keeps me in the middle of his drama.*

As they made their way into the bedroom, he dropped back down onto his spot on the sofa.

Brrrnnnggg.

"I got it," he called out even though there was no way in hell his father was answering the phone while he had company over.

Turning the volume on the television down, Graham snatched up the cordless phone. At the sight of his mother's info on the Caller ID, he started not to answer. It had been a few days since they spoke on the phone, and twice he'd missed his weekend to stay with her. "Hello," he said, already regretting his choice to talk to her.

"Well hello, stranger," she said.

He lowered his head until his chin almost touched his chest. He heard the sadness in her voice and he felt guilty. He loved his mother and he didn't want to hurt her. *She just don't understand.*

"So y'all phone *is* working?" Cara asked.

"Yes ma'am," he said, rubbing his large, slender hand over his head. "What you doing, Ma?"

"Missing my son," she answered smoothly, as if it had been sitting on the tip of her tongue just waiting to be used.

"I'm coming this weekend," he said. "I just been looking for a job."

"Well, that's good to know. Let me talk to your daddy."

He raised his head to look over at the closed bedroom door. With the volume so low on the TV, he could already hear the familiar squeaking of the bedsprings. If Missy was lucky, she'd get to stay the night. If she was like the rest, she would be tiptoeing past the couch and out the door in two hours, tops.

"He's not here," Graham lied, picking up the remote and raising the volume.

"You're home alone?" she shrieked in disbelief.

"He had to work late," he lied again, shaking his head.

"What garbage is he picking up at nine o'clock at night?"

"Ma, I'm a'ight."

"Probably laid up with some woman."

Buzzzzzz.

He frowned at the sound of the downstairs doorbell. Rising to his feet, he walked to the window to see if he recognized any cars parked down on the street. *If this another one of my daddy's—*

Buzzzzzz. Buzzzzzz. Buzzzzzzzzzzz.

"Ma, I was about to watch a movie and then go to sleep," he lied yet again, walking back across the floor and reaching behind him to pull up his sagging shorts.

"You do that," she said. "Love you."

"Love you too, Ma," he said, distracted, as he opened the door.

Buzzzzzzzzzzzzzzzzzzzzzzzzzzzzzzzzzzzzzzzzzzz.

He hung up the phone and turned to toss it back on the chair before he made his way back down the stairs. Graham paused at the sight of Ms. Nunez standing on the porch with her foot holding the front door open.

Buzzz—

At the sight of him, she lifted her finger from the doorbell and stepped inside the hall, closing the door. "Come here," she ordered him.

Graham shook his head. "My dad's busy. His insurance lady—"

"Don't lie to me, *joven amante*," she said in a soft voice that was just as chastising as a mother to her child. "Come here."

The head on Graham's shoulder said no, but the one below his belt wasn't in agreement.

Ms. Nunez climbed the stairs instead. The closer she got, the more he could smell the scent of her perfume. The same scent that clung to her skin that afternoon. He liked it best in the valley between her breasts.

"You think I care about your daddy?" she asked, stopping on the step just below the one where he stood. "You changed all that today, baby."

He licked his lips. "Ms. Nunez, we can't—"

"Essie," she insisted, reaching up to stroke him. "Like you did this afternoon."

He closed his eyes as he brushed her hand away.

"You think your daddy care?"

Her question brought forward the memory of that constant squeaking from his father's bedroom. The last thing on his daddy's mind right about then was Ms. Nunez. *Or me.*

And for the first time, Graham had a way better idea of just what his father was experiencing. He wanted to feel it again.

When she unzipped his pants, freed his hardness as she got down on her knees, and took him into her mouth, Graham didn't offer one single protest.

Chapter 3

Essie

One Week Later

Graham dived into the pool and swam the length of it with his arms slashing the water. He felt like he was in a cocoon and the silence was a blessing. At the wall, he turned and pressed his feet against it to launch himself forward for another lap. He had a lot on his mind, but beneath the water, nothing mattered at all.

The last place he wanted to be was back at his mother's, but he had to admit it was a relief not to play referee in his father's female drama. The weekend was almost over and he was headed back to dramaville, but he was ready to leave the 'burbs.

He allowed himself a few more laps before he finally pulled himself up out of the water and sat on the edge to wipe the chlorinated water from his eyes and nose.

"So you were too sick to go to church but you're swimming?"

Forget that church.

But he didn't say that out loud. Instead, he gave his mother his best smile and looked up at her as she stood over him in a pretty orange dress and matching wide-brimmed hat. "Dad doesn't have a pool. I just wanted to enjoy it before I go back home today," he said.

Her face saddened. "This is still your home too, Bear," she said, using her childhood pet name.

"I know, Ma," he said, sounding as aggravated as he felt.

"Come on, get dressed so I can take you home," she said, turning away from him.

"Daddy not coming for me?" he asked, rising to his feet and grabbing his towel from the lounge chair where he'd tossed it earlier.

"Nope."

Man, I hope Daddy ain't got one of his chicks there.

"I don't think he's home," Graham offered quickly, as he followed her up onto the deck and through the open French doors into the kitchen.

"Tylar sent me a text. His car is in the shop, but there's an afternoon program at the church, so I gotta take you back this morning . . . or you can catch the train," she offered, pulling on an apron over her church clothes and then oven mitts before opening the oven door.

"We leave right after we eat?" he asked over his shoulder as he headed up the stairs to his room to shower.

Cara laughed as she pulled a roaster from the oven. "I thought so," she teased.

Graham quickly showered off the chlorine and changed into a T-shirt and shorts before packing his bag. His stomach grumbled at the smell of food from the kitchen. His Mama could cook, and her food topped the takeout dinner they usually ate at his father's. Still, good food couldn't touch the goodies Ms. Nunez was giving him every chance she got, and he was ready for some more.

It was all he thought about as he finished packing his bag, ate dinner with his mother, and sat quietly in the passenger seat of her Mercedes SUV as she drove him back to Brooklyn. As soon as she double-parked on the street that was packed bumper-to-bumper with vehicles, he climbed out and moved to the rear of the gold vehicle.

"Hey, Graham."

He looked over his shoulder at the pretty shorty from next door, LeLe, waving to him from her front porch. He smiled and waved back but snatched up his duffel bag and kept it moving onto the sidewalk. Pre–Ms. Nunez, he would've been sweating the cutie. But after working up the nerve to chat it up with her, the whole innocent vibe made him want to protect her, not fuck her. Now they were in a nice friend zone.

He still liked her—but he liked sexing Ms. Nunez more.

She came down off the porch as he gave his mother one last wave over his shoulder. He eyed her. She was all caramel pretty with straight, thick hair that almost reached her waist. She was slender but there was promise of a curvier shape in her hips.

"I'm glad you're back," she said, walking up to stand before him.

Graham smiled at her, liking how she looked in her bright yellow sundress. "Missed me?" he asked.

"It's boring 'round here without you," LeLe said, reaching up to playfully swat his head.

"Let me put my stuff up and check in with my pops, and I'll be back down later, a'ight?"

LeLe nodded, her eyes all soft and flirty, as she reached up to tug at his collar. "I wanted to ask you something," she said.

Uh-oh. He laughed nervously as he backed away. "A'ight," he said, before turning to jog up the stairs.

His eyes went down the hall to Ms. Nunez's door, but he fought the urge to go to her and instead continued up the stairs, already reaching in his pocket for his house key. He paused, hoping like hell his father wasn't "entertaining" and he wasn't about to walk in on a live porno set. Being sure to rattle the doorknob as he unlocked the door, he finally entered.

Thankfully, the living room was empty.

"Pops," Graham hollered out, dropping his duffel bag by the closet where he had to stash most of his clothes and shoes.

The bathroom door opened and Tylar walked out wearing nothing but a towel and a smile on his face. "I thought I heard you. How was your weekend?" he asked, strolling into the kitchen and leaving damp footprints on the hardwood floor.

Graham shrugged, his eyes darting to the ajar bathroom door. "I can go downstairs, if you want," he offered. *Maybe I can go knock Ms. Nunez boots real quick . . .*

Tylar opened a bottle of water and shook his head before taking a deep swig. "Nah, I'm done," he said afterward.

"Hey, Graham."

His eyes widened as Ms. Nunez strolled out of the bathroom. She was dressed in a tank and sweatpants, but her hair was damp and it was clear she didn't have on a bra as her nipples nearly poked through the thin cotton material. His heartbeat quickened and his gut clenched in surprise. An image of her riding his father flashed and he swallowed over a lump in his throat. A lump symbolizing the guilt, anger, and jealousy he felt before he finally spoke. "Hi, Ms. Nunez," he said awkwardly, forcing his eyes away from her as she strolled over to his father.

"See you later, Ty?" she asked.

Graham scowled as he slumped down on the couch and turned on the television. He hated the thought of his father and Ms. Nunez. He thought they were done. *I thought I was enough for her.*

He glanced over his shoulder at them just as his father soundly slapped her ass and then gripped one fleshy cheek in his hand as he pressed a kiss to her mouth. "Let me spend some time with my boy, a'ight?"

Graham pressed his eyes shut and turned to face the TV when her hand eased down the front of the towel.

"Bye, Graham," she said as she passed him on her way out the front door.

He forced himself not to look her way.

"Graham, wake me up in an hour," Tylar said, headed toward his bedroom.

"You got plans?" he asked, even as his jealousy made his throat tight.

"Later. Yeah," his father answered over his shoulder. "You can tell me more about your weekend when I get up."

"Nothing to tell," Graham said, keeping his voice more calm than he felt. "What about yours?"

Tylar just chuckled deeply. "It was...quite a ride, son."

Graham forced a laugh.

"Glad you're home, son," Tylar said before entering his bedroom.

Graham said nothing. For the next hour his eyes were locked on the television; his thoughts were locked elsewhere. *Man, fuck her.*

He snatched up his keys and left the apartment. As soon as he reached the bottom step, he looked back at Ms. Nunez's door. It was closed. She usually left it open when she sat on the front porch.

He was glad because it wasn't her that he was looking for.

LeLe was sitting on her porch watching her younger brother play with his remote-controlled monster truck in the driveway. She looked up and smiled as soon as she spotted him.

Smiling back at her, he made his way down the steps and next door to look up at her as he braced himself against the wrought-iron banister. "So what you wanted to ask me?"

LeLe looked surprised as she pushed her hair behind her ears. "Who said I'm ready to ask?"

"A'ight. My bad," Graham said, his eyes on her slender, pretty face before he shifted them to look at her little brother instead.

"You got a girlfriend?"

The eyes went back to her face. A heated memory of Ms. Nunez undressing him flashed but he shook it away. *She probably did the same to my father today.* "No," he finally answered.

"Oh," LeLe said softly, her voice shy and soft as she looked down at her hands.

Graham glanced over at his apartment building just as Ms. Nunez stepped out onto the porch. She released a stream of cigarette smoke through pursed lips as she eyed them openly. He ignored her and looked back to LeLe. "You want to go to the movies?" he asked.

"LeLe! Nikko!"

They both looked to the front door of LeLe's home at a woman's shrill cry.

"My grandmother," LeLe explained. "Time to eat."

Nikko snatched up his toy and raced down the short distance of the sidewalk and up the stairs past them into the house.

"The movies?" he nudged.

"I want to," she said quickly, rising to her feet. "I just have to ask my dad."

"That's cool."

"I'll be back out after we eat," she assured him as she made her way across the porch to the open front door.

"A'ight."

He watched her until she gave him one last soft smile and disappeared inside the house. As he made his way back next door he felt Ms. Nunez's eyes on him, but he ignored her as he jogged up the stairs and walked past her. He thought she would have something slick to say to him and was surprised when she said nothing at all.

Man. FUCK. Her.

Eventually entering the house, he headed straight for the bedroom door and knocked twice on it with his knuckles.

"I'm up," Tylar called out to him.

Graham walked into the kitchen and opened the fridge. He was pulling a can of soda out when his father walked up to him. "Where you headed, Pops?" he asked, taking in the white linen suit he wore.

"An all-white boat party with a friend," Tylar said, snapping his fingers as he two-stepped and then spun.

Graham smiled and shook his head.

"I saw you talking to the little honey next door again," Tylar said. "You getting anywhere?"

"I asked her to the movies," he admitted.

"My boy," Tylar said proudly, holding out his fist.

Graham pounded the top of it lightly with his own. "Your *broke* boy," he stressed.

Tylar eyed him. "My *unemployed* boy," he returned even as he reached in his back pocket and pulled out his wallet. "But it's for a good cause, so..."

Graham smiled broadly as his father handed him a crisp fifty-dollar bill. "Thanks, Pop," he said.

"Wrap it up. No baby mamas." Tylar pushed a condom in his hand as well. "You need more?"

"Nooo...no. I'm good," he said, pushing the money and protection into his pocket.

"You ain't got no choice. Like father, like son," Tylar said, striking a pose before smoothing his hand over his mouth and chin.

Graham shifted uncomfortably at the thought of him and his father sexing Ms. Nunez. *Like father, like son.*

"A'ight. I'm out. Don't be out too late," Tylar said, pulling his son close for a quick hug and a brief kiss to his temple. "Love ya."

Graham knew that was true. Guilt reigned heavily. His father had plenty of women, and Ms. Nunez was just one of many, but she was still his father's friend, and no man liked another man pissing on his territory. "Me too," he answered.

As soon as the front door closed, Graham walked into the bedroom to enjoy the feel of the air-conditioning. He eyed the disheveled sheets on the bed and opted to sit in the club chair on the other side of the nightstand instead. *I'm not lying up in their dried-up sex juices.*

He checked out the window to see if LeLe was back outside before settling in to watch a *Martin* rerun.

Knock-knock-knock.

Frowning, he dropped the remote and left the bedroom headed to the front door. *Maybe it's LeLe or—*

"Ms. Nunez?" he asked even as he looked at her pushing past him to walk into the house smelling like cigarettes and something fruity. "My dad's not here."

"I saw him leave," she said, turning to face him as she pulled her T-shirt over her head. "I wanted you."

Afraid a neighbor would happen down the stairs and see her, he shut the door. "I don't want you," he told her, his hand still on the doorknob as he fought—and won—not to look at her breasts.

"Liar," she said, bending a little to push her pants over her hips and down her legs. "I missed you."

Naked, she came across the room and pressed his body against the door with hers. He closed his eyes as she pressed her lips to his neck.

"You don't want me?" she asked mockingly as she stroked his hardness and then freed it from his shorts.

Graham hissed at her touch.

"Come and get this pussy, little boy," she said, tugging on his dick to lead him behind her into his father's bedroom.

Graham followed her, not caring in that moment how she hurt him or that she was leading him to the same bed where she'd lain with his father.

★ ★ ★

"What the fuck is going on here?"

Graham sat up straight in the bed, his heart pounding from being startled from his sleep.

"Do you need it spelled out for you, Tylar?" Ms. Nunez asked, sounding smug.

Graham eyed his father standing to the foot of the bed. "Dad—"

"You mad?" she asked, rising from the bed naked.

"Two dicks in one day?" Tylar said coldly. "You sore?"

Graham struggled to rise from the bed, his legs tangled up in the sheets. "Dad—"

"With all the women you screw, is your dick sore?" Ms. Nunez asked, standing up in Tylar's face.

"So this is supposed to be payback?" he asked, waving his hand at the bed. "You picked the wrong one if you think I give a shit about a piece of pussy—a slack-ass piece at that."

WHAP.

Graham's mouth fell open when she slapped his father. He rushed forward, barely holding the sheet around his waist. He stepped between them.

"Dad—"

"Get your slack ass outta here," Tylar roared, his eyes blazing.

Barely a second ticked by before she jumped up and reached past Graham to flail her fists at Tylar as she cursed violently in Spanish.

Graham winced and hollered out as a few of the blows landed on his head and shoulders. He wasn't sure what happened next, but he felt their bodies sandwiching his as they tussled. He felt her climb up the front of him.

"Move, Graham," his father said in a hard voice.

He opened his eyes. Ms. Nunez's naked body was across his shoulder on her stomach with her legs thrashing about.

"Move the fuck out the way, Graham!"

He stepped out of the fray and his eyes widened to see his father had one arm wrapped around her head, covering her mouth, and the other binding her arms to her side like a wrestling move. *Damn...*

Graham followed them as Tylar carried her out of the room and across the living room, pressing her writhing body against the wall as he freed one hand to open the front door. Graham's heart was pounding like crazy at the scene unfolding around him. "Dad, don't!" he screamed as he watched him throw her out the door.

"You mad I had your son, you punk ass!" she screamed as she scrambled to her feet. "His dick bigger and better too."

"Stay the hell away from him, you crazy bitch," Tylar said, turning to brush past Graham to walk back into the apartment.

"I got what I wanted from him...plenty of times," she screamed, turning to storm down the stairs with the soft flesh of her body jiggling.

Graham looked down the steps behind her and spotted LeLe standing at the foot, looking shell-shocked. She eyed Ms. Nunez's naked body and then looked up at him standing there with a sheet barely wrapped around his nakedness. He saw the hurt in her eyes.

Tylar stepped back outside the apartment and tossed the pile of clothing he carried down the stairs behind Ms. Nunez.

"Dog," she spat.

"Slut," he countered without hesitation.

Ms. Nunez disappeared around the staircase and soon the sound of her door slamming echoed.

Tylar stormed back inside the apartment. That door slammed as well.

LeLe turned and flew out the door.

Graham knew he couldn't follow her without clothes, and he wasn't sure what he would say to her anyway. "Damn," he swore, lightly banging his head against the wall before he finally entered the apartment.

He was surprised to see his father picking up his keys and striding toward the door. "Dad, I'm sorry," he said.

Tylar looked surprised. "For what?"

Graham's face filled with confusion.

"Son, there are women you screw, and women you marry," he said. "Essie is a woman you screw and I got plenty of those. Now, if that was someone I was lining up to marry, then I'd woulda fucked you up—so don't make that mistake. But with a trick like Essie, you did what a man supposed to do when a ho backs him in a corner."

Graham was now unsure. *Is he hurt and hiding it?*

"Now, my date is waiting for me downstairs in her car," Tylar said. "I just came back for the tickets I left."

Tylar stepped around him and opened the door. He stopped and looked back at him. "Did you wrap it up?" he asked.

Graham nodded and clutched his sheet tighter in his fist. "Yes sir."

"Good."

And with that he was gone.

Interlude

Present Day

He *was too high to cum.*

"You think I got all night to give you head," she said in disgust, releasing his dick so forcefully that it vibrated back and forth like a diving board.

He was glad for that. He wasn't sure what this crazy bitch was going to do with it.

"Let's see what else your man-whore money bought you," she said, the heels of her booties tapping against the hardwood floors.

Having her roaming freely through his home—his domicile—felt just as violating as being trapped. No one came to his home uninvited. No one. None of his clients even knew where he lived. None were invited over. What he offered to them had nothing to do with that.

And it damn sure shouldn't be filled with someone crazy enough to drug him.

Who is she?

He was high and weak, but even in the haze he had long since pushed aside the idea of the woman who took his virginity being his captor. Ms. Nunez—Essie—would have to be in her early fifties. Although her obsession with his father led to her using him to pay

Tylar back for all the other women he slept with, she ended up harassing them so badly in the days after his father discovered them in bed that they eventually moved.

Crazy enough? Yes. Strong enough? Hell no.

Or was she?

"Nice kitchen, Pleasure. I could just see me in there making dinner for you," she said, her voice growing louder as she neared him. "Just slicing and dicing."

The hairs on the back of his neck tingled beneath the full curtain of his waist-length dreads as she came up to stand behind him.

"Really sharp knives."

The first feel of the cool steel pressed against the warm pulse of his throat jolted him from his stupor.

"Don't worry, this isn't a part of our unfinished business."

She removed the blade and turned swiftly to shove it into the back of his leather sofa. She slowly walked the length of it, cutting a jagged line in the material before plunging the knife into the plush cushion with a grunt.

He used every bit of the strength still in his body to drop his head back. "You sure it's not Tylar you want?" he asked.

"Tylar?" she said, the brown eyes peering through the slits in her mask filled with confusion and some other emotion that gave him trepidation.

"No, trust. It's you I want, and it's you I got," she said, coming over to straddle his hips and grip the sides of his face to jerk his head up until his eyes locked with hers. "Finally."

Chapter 4

Geneva

2002

"Running and boxing does your body *so* good."

Graham smiled as he pressed a kiss to the shoulder of... of...

He couldn't remember her name.

Pressing his face against her nape, he wrapped his arms around her slender frame and pulled her against him as they lay in bed.

"And that made you do my body so good," she purred, reaching behind herself to stroke his muscular thigh.

He'd met her just that afternoon at the barbecue his father and his girl, Kia, had at their new house. A little conversation and a few dances later they'd headed to an obscure motel. The entire night, including the cost of the moldy room, had been less than a hundred dollars. Well worth the blow job alone. He loved a swallower.

"Maybe we can go running together," she offered, turning over on her side to face him with a smile.

"Actually I don't live in Brooklyn anymore," he said, his

eyes searching her round face and wide eyes. "I was just in town for the barbecue."

She pouted and reached up to lightly pinch his chin.

"When my dad moved in with his girlfriend I headed back to my mom's in the 'burbs," Graham admitted, rolling over onto his back.

"You don't seem happy about it," she said, propping herself up on the pillow as she lowered the sheet and then traced the contours of his abdomen with her forefinger.

Graham just shrugged, but truthfully, he wasn't happy about it. The best thing that ever happened for him had been moving out of Bedford. Being there every day was a constant reminder of shit he wanted—needed—to forget. Now he was back after four years, and the memories were not as sharp and painful. *Shit seemed so far away.*

"I usually don't do one-night stands, you know," she said, pressing her cool lips to his muscled chest.

"I didn't think so," he lied, reaching down onto the floor to dig his cell phone out of the pocket of his jeans. "Put your number in my phone."

Just as he handed it to her it began to vibrate.

"This time of the night that can only be your boo," she said, handing him the phone back.

It was.

"Go ahead," she prompted, getting up from the bed to walk naked into the bathroom.

Waiting until she closed the door with a squeak, he answered. "Hey, Geneva," he said warmly.

"Hey, I thought maybe you was asleep," she said.

Graham reached up and twisted one of his short, spiky dreads between his fingers. "Nah, I was just about to call you," he lied, reaching for the remote and turning the television on.

"How was the cookout?"

"Cool," he said, his eyes darting to the bathroom door. "I wish you could have come with me."

"Grammy, you know I would've come if I didn't have the meeting for the church conference *plus* you stayed over," she said gently. "You know the Rev is not having it."

Geneva was a preacher's kid, and although she was nineteen and officially "grown," she still lived under his roof and abided by his rules. "I'll be home in the morning," he said, holding a finger to his mouth when the door opened and his one-nighter emerged.

"Let's have breakfast before church," she offered. "And then maybe you can come and get *you* some Jesus."

"Your church?" Graham asked, taking his eyes off his companion as his heart double-pumped.

"Yes," she stressed. "Where else, Grammy? My father's the minister. Your mother is on the usher board. You were baptized there. Remember?"

Remember? I wish I could forget.

"Look, G, I'm gonna holla at my dad for a sec and then turn in," he said, kicking the sheets from his body as he motioned toward his dick for NoName. "I'll call you when I get up."

"A'ight. Night-night."

Beep.

"Come suck my dick," he ordered her, picking it up with his hand and stroking it from the base to the tip.

"That big old dick?" she asked, coming over in all her dark-skinned fineness to take his inches into her hand.

"I'm blessed," he said, with a big smile.

"Damn right you are," she moaned before kneeling on the bed and dipping her head down to lick the tip with her tongue.

Graham dug his fingers into her curly weave and held her head locked in position as he began to grind his hips up off the bed, sending his dick a little deeper into her mouth.

Closing his eyes, he tried to focus on the feel of her tongue. Tried to forget everything that church meant to him.

"Shit," he swore as her teeth raked across his hardness.

"Soh-wee," she mumbled around his thickness filling her mouth.

He barely heard her. His thoughts were elsewhere, and as badly as he tried to beat them away, run from them, or free them from his head, there they remained.

It was so long ago, almost fourteen years, but when he allowed those thoughts to step forward, it *always* felt like just yesterday.

He cringed at the memory of the intruding hands and mouth of his eleven-year-old church buddy Lionel on his penis. Touching and tasting and violating him before he even knew that what they were doing in that closet in the basement of the church didn't just feel wrong, it *was* wrong.

Graham shook his head and thrust his hips up, sending his dick gliding across her tongue almost to her tonsils. She gagged.

He didn't care. The tears he'd cried that day all those years ago welled up in him and he wanted to forget. He wanted her to make him forget.

"Suck it nasty," he ordered her, feeling frantic, anxious, and angry. So very angry.

No-good molesting pervert. No-good violating pervert. I hate him. I hate what he did to me.

"Hey," NoName cried out, pushing his hands off the back of her head as she lifted it.

Graham eyed her, his chest heaving not from the pleasure she tried to give but the pain that felt fresh, exposed, and raw.

She wiped the slick wetness from her mouth and chin as she eyed him. "You every bit of a foot long," she said with a little animosity. "Your dick way too big to be ramming down somebody's throat like that. Damn."

Graham sat up in the bed, his hardness standing up to shadow the ridged lines of his stomach. "My bad," he said with honesty.

Her expression softened. "You just a freak, that's all," she said, reaching out to stroke his calf before pulling his foot into her lap.

Graham flopped back down on the bed, focusing his eyes on the television as the video for "Shake Ya Ass" played on *BET: Uncut.* He picked up the remote and raised the volume.

"Shake ya ass . . . Show me what you workin' with."

NoName jumped up to her feet on the bed and turned around to start twerking her ass like it was her 9-to-5. Graham couldn't deny that seeing the way her butt moved in a thousand different directions was giving new life to his hard-on.

"Them videos hoes ain't got shit on you," he told her, grasping the thick base of his dick in his hand.

NoName squatted and placed her hands on her thighs as she worked nothing but her ass while she looked over her shoulder at him. "Tell me something I don't know," she said, twerking her left cheek and then her right in a back-and-forth motion that was mesmerizing.

With his eyes locked on her, he reached out to grab one of the condoms strewn across the top of the battered nightstand. "Come sit on this and do that," he said thickly, wagging his condom-covered dick at her.

He pursed his lips as she twerked her way back down onto her knees and backed up until her pussy was in position right above the thick tip. He guided his inches inside her, enjoying the look of her pussy surrounding his hardness as she leaned forward, smoothing her hands down his legs to grasp his ankles as she twerked on.

"Dammit, girl," he said, slapping her round ass cheek before gripping her hips.

He just lay back and let her work, enjoying the feel of her pussy walls clutching him. He bit his tongue lightly as he felt his nut coming on quick. Probably too quick but he didn't have a care. *Fuck it.*

NoName sat up straight and started gliding back and forth on it like she knew he was going to come and wanted to milk it. He grunted and felt his body jerk as she did just that. *Shit.*

Just before he closed his eyes he was able to make out the name in the elaborate tattoo on her lower back.

Nora. That's her name.

Graham hitched his duffel bag up higher on his shoulder as he walked out of the Metro-North train station. He smiled when Geneva spotted him and instantly headed in his direction. She was already dressed for church in a lavender shift dress that looked good against her caramel-brown complexion and auburn shoulder-length curls.

My shorty.

He'd met her when his mother finally nagged him into going to church a few weeks ago. Cara brought him there for the Word but he left with Geneva's phone number. He had no complaints. *Well, just one...*

"Hey you," she said, her soft voice soothing him as she hugged him close and pressed a brief kiss to his chin.

He embraced her quickly and stepped back before his dick woke up. Even after a night of sex with... Nora and being far from new to sex in the first place, the fact that Geneva was a virgin made him want her even more. Even the most innocent of touches from her made his dick hard enough to cut a diamond like it was dust.

"Hungry?" she asked as they walked to her white convertible BMW.

"You know it," he said, opening the passenger door.

Geneva cleared her throat and remained standing by the driver-side door.

Shaking his head and wiping away the smile that spread across his chiseled, handsome face, Graham tossed his duffel onto the rear seat before coming around the car to open her door. "You're welcome," he said before she could even thank him.

Geneva winked at him before she grabbed the lapel of his lightweight khaki jacket and pulled him down from his six-foot-nine-inch height to lick his lips.

Shaking his head, he used the muscles of his arms to pick her up so that her body was against his and he was able to see the light spray of freckles across her nose. "You're too tall," she said, not sounding like she meant it as she moved her hands up to grip the sides of his face.

Graham captured her mouth with his and enjoyed the taste of her tongue and her lips. Her little moan of pleasure in the back of her throat pushed him to deepen the kiss until his tongue traced the length of hers before circling it slowly and then sucking deeply on the tip.

Geneva broke the kiss gently but kept her forehead against his and breathed hotly against his open mouth. "You make me want to do things, Graham Walker. Nasty, dirty, freaky things that"—she swallowed hard—"would send me *straight* to hell."

"For a taste of your goodies I would gladly go to hell," he told her, burying his face against her neck and deeply inhaling her sweet citrus perfume.

"Graham!" she exclaimed with wide eyes. "That's blasphemous."

He chuckled. "God knows what's on my heart...and on my brain, so no need to lie. He sees all and knows all."

"Preach, Brother Graham," she teased, lifting one hand up to wave it as if she was in church. "I think you like church more than you put on."

Graham's eyes searched hers and for one second—maybe even less—he considered telling her his truth. His secret. His shame.

But what to say: *It's not every church I hate, just your father's church, where I should have been safe and sheltered from one of the older boys molest—*

He shook his head, hating even to think the word.

Giving her one last kiss, he set her back down on her feet and moved away from her to climb into the car. Not since his high school days had his feelings about what happened affected him so much. Back then, it was the anger he clung to, and the anger that led to him fighting anybody who even tried to treat him as if he was weak.

"Hey, you okay?" she asked, reaching over to grasp his hand.

"I'm good," Graham said, shifting in his seat and nodding.

"Good enough to go to church with me?" she asked.

"I got something to do for my mom," he lied with ease. "I already promised her."

"Okay."

Graham peered out the window as she drove the streets of Bedford headed to their favorite diner on Bedford Road. He spotted a woman with a curvy shape and a form-fitting dress about to climb into a convertible Jag. To him the lines of her body were sleeker than the luxury vehicle.

Just like Nora.

Although it was early October, she'd done the kinds of tricks and treats on him that had nothing to do with Halloween. The type of things most women saved for men who made some sort of commitment. As good a time as he had, she had effectively freaked herself into the category of women to screw and never the type to marry.

Geneva slid her hand onto his thigh and squeezed it gently. He tried to smile away the guilt he felt. She offered him conversation, companionship, and comfort. All of his other tricks delivered the sex.

And Geneva was none the wiser.

As she sang along softly with some song on the radio, he

looked over at her profile. He knew she deserved more. Better. The best of him.

He just wasn't sure he could deliver.

The cab pulled to a stop in front of his mother's French Colonial–styled home and Graham hopped out, having already prepaid the cabbie back at the restaurant. He and Geneva had lingered so long over their breakfast that he convinced her to head straight to church and let him get home on his own. He paused on the sidewalk to look up at the house, still grappling with having to move back in two months ago. Living with his father while he was single was enough of an adventure. Dealing with his father living with another woman—especially when Graham knew firsthand that Tylar was anything but faithful—no haps. He wasn't trying to be around to witness the drama unfolding when his dad got caught.

Giving his short dreads a rub, Graham jogged up the steps and used his key to enter the house. He headed straight to his bedroom for a long and hot shower that gave him the energy he needed to go for a run. Removing the towel from around his waist, he stood in front of the full-length mirror on the back of his door and studied his reflection as he dried off.

During the year between being sixteen and seventeen, he'd had a four-inch growth spurt that sent him up to six foot five inches. Wanting to look less gangly and awkward, Graham had started boxing, running, and lifting weights a year ago and now had the muscle definition he wanted. Not big and bulky like he chewed on steroid pills and would burst with a pinch, but lean and chiseled like the basketball player everyone thought he was.

Getting pussy was his sport.

He smiled playfully as he popped his hips, causing his dick to rise and fall quickly, as if he was raising an arm. Even at rest he hung seven inches easily, and every woman he blessed with his magic stick let him know just how hung he was.

Graham pulled on boxers, basketball shorts, and a hoodie with the sleeves cut off before plopping down on his bed to pull on his sneakers. He paused when he spotted the college brochures on his pillows. He ignored them and jerked on his socks and Jordans.

Because of his expulsions, Graham had been held back twice during high school and attended an adult education program and earned his GED that June. Although his mother had secured him a job in the mailroom of the advertising firm where she was a head copywriter, she was hell-bent on him going to college and getting a degree.

It just wasn't a part of his plans. Not that he had any real plans. He just knew it didn't include more school, studying, and taking tests. Not yet, anyway. *Fuck that shit.*

He pulled his hood up over his head and walked to the door, only to turn around in the threshold. He retraced his steps and reached under his bed to reach inside an old sneaker box for a nickel bag of weed and a blunt before putting the box back.

Graham had just pushed it into the pocket of his hoodie when his bedroom door opened. His surprise read on his face at the sight of his mom still in her nightgown and house coat. "You didn't go to church?" he asked, coming over to kiss her cheek.

Cara shook her head and pulled a crumpled tissue from her pocket to swipe at her nose. "Came down with a head cold this weekend," she said, sounding nasal.

"Well, I'm about to head out for a run," he said, moving past her.

"Next Sunday you will be in church, Graham," she said with a sniffle. "No excuses."

He paused on the steps and grimaced. Hard. "Why—"

"No excuses," she repeated, her voice hard and unrelenting.

He frowned and kept moving down the stairs.

"And don't act like you didn't see those brochures on your pillow, either," she called behind him.

He held his baggie of weed tighter and left the house with a slam of the front door.

Chapter 5

Geneva

"Graham!"

He jumped a bit in his seat on the padded pew as his mother pressed her elbow into his side. "Huh?" he asked a little loudly, drawing the curious looks of nearby parishioners.

She gave him a hard and meaningful stare.

When he glanced over at Geneva sitting on the front pew beside her mother, her eyes were locked on her father as he delivered his sermon from the elaborate pulpit that seemed high enough above the parishioners to truly look down upon them. He tried to will her to look his way as he enjoyed her profile, but she didn't.

Shifting his eyes about, he froze when he spotted a honey eyeing him from across the large expanse of the church. He assessed her quickly but efficiently: light-skinned cutie with thick full lips, a cute pug nose, and long brown hair with natural blondish streaks. Early twenties. Stylish. Flirty. Doable.

He sat up a little straighter as she smiled at him and licked her bottom lip slowly with a hot little bite as she directed her eyes off him. Forcing his eyes away from her as well, he looked up at Reverend Garrett in the pulpit.

He was a tall and broad man with a bald head and a stern jaw. His purple robe with elaborate gold trim made his figure all the more imposing. Geneva hadn't introduced Graham to her father yet, and he didn't mind one bit. He could just imagine the questions with which the minister would drill him.

"Seek ye first the kingdom of God," Reverend Garrett roared into the microphone before taking a few steps back and wiping his forehead with a handkerchief.

Graham glanced at Geneva's profile again before darting back to his admirer. She boldly met his gaze before looking away with the hint of a smile at her lips.

He looked away as well and shifted in his seat as he rubbed his large hands on the pants of his khaki suit.

In the last week since he cheated on Geneva with Nora, he'd decided to try his best to be faithful. His *very* best. However, it was getting harder to resist all the temptation. Girls were throwing it at him left and right. Graham officially had the town of Bedford on lock. *These preppy good girls love my bad-boy flow.*

He glanced back again and bit back a smile when he saw her covertly waving at him, with her hand draped over the side of her lap. His eyes shifted up to her face and he was surprised to find her still looking forward with a look of pure innocence on her face.

A sneaky good girl. The best kind.

She coughed and cleared her throat.

He looked down at her hand again and saw she was making signs with her slender fingers. He frowned, burrowing his thick brows above deep-set brown eyes. *What is she doing? Sign language? Gang signs? Numbers? Oh yeah. Numbers.*

Graham counted each set of fingers she splayed.

5-5-5-2-0-0-1. 555-2001. Her phone number.

That girl wild.

"Call me," she mouthed, making a motion with her hand to imitate a telephone before a middle-aged man sitting next to her looked at her and she quickly slid her fingers into her shoulder-length hair to rake instead.

For the rest of the church service Graham tried to keep his attention focused anywhere else but on Miss Temptation. He studied the intricacies of the floor-to-ceiling stained-glass windows depicting biblical figures. *White Jesus, huh?* He eyed a toddler fastidiously extracting things from his nose and slipping them into his mouth. *Li'l nasty ass.* He spied one of the dozen or so church ushers leaning in the door frame with his head bobbing slowly as he went through a cycle of nodding off in and out of sleep. *A face-forward fall would make my motherfucking day. Fall! Fall! Fall!* Once another attendant came over to relieve the sleepy usher, Graham turned his wandering attention to the many hairstyles of the ladies—and some of the men—of the choir just as the organist began to play and they all rose to their feet. *Like a black woman can really grow bleached-blond hair.*

As the voices of the choir singing "Ain't No Need to Worry" filled the church up to the twenty-foot ceilings, Graham's eyes squinted as he sat up straight in his seat and eyed a skinny man with a goatee in the back row.

Lionel?

His stomach lurched and he frowned as his eyes stayed locked on the man. Then he relaxed because he knew it wasn't Lionel. It couldn't be. He hadn't been back to the church since his parents moved to New Jersey years ago. Not looking at him every week and avoiding ever being alone with him had relieved some of Graham's stress about attending that church, but he still had never felt comfortable since that day. And he never would again.

Naw, that ain't him, just another caramel-colored Negro.

Still . . .

Graham jumped up and walked down the deep purple

carpeted aisle, past the usher and out the double doors leading to the foyer of the church. *Man, hell with it.*

He fingered the pre-rolled blunt in the inside pocket of his blazer. He started to head downstairs to the bathroom but carried himself outside instead. Walking across the parking lot, which was large enough to hold two hundred cars or more, he pulled his blunt out and leaned against the hood of a Benz as he lit it.

Graham kept his eyes on the entrance into the parking lot, prepared to toss the blunt before someone got too near to him. Keeping the blunt pressed between his lips, he reached for his cell phone and checked the time. 11:45.

He snapped his flip phone closed and slid it back into his pocket. The blunt still pressed between his lips bobbed as he moved his mouth.

With a deep inhale, he closed his eyes and tilted his head back a little before finally releasing a thick silver stream of smoke. He opened his eyes to watch the smoke float up among the rust- and gold-colored leaves of a low-hanging branch.

Graham had nearly finished the blunt when the doors to the church opened and Reverend Garrett stepped out onto the wide porch with his wife and Geneva by his side. He had removed the elaborate robe covering his suit, but there was no mistaking that he was the head of the church just from his stance and demeanor.

Taking one last toke, Graham dropped the blunt to the ground and put out the embers with his shoe as he watched Geneva looking around. Looking for him.

Pushing up off the car, he slowly crossed the lot as worshippers began to make their way to their vehicles.

When she spotted him, Geneva left her parents' side and walked to meet him just as he reached the side entrance to the fence surrounding the lot. "Come on, I want to introduce you to my parents," she said.

Graham locked his feet. "Right now?" he asked.

"Yes," she stressed, grabbing his hand and tugging him forward behind her.

"I don't want—"

"Too late," she said, lifting her chin in her parents' direction.

He followed her gaze and saw her parents already looking toward them. Their mouths were moving and he knew they discussed him. Questioned him. Judged him.

Releasing a short breath, he hoped the smell of weed wasn't too strong on him as they made their way down the street and then up the stairs, going against the crowd leaving the church. Graham nervously twisted his short dreads when Geneva released his fingers as Reverend Garrett's eyes zoned in on them holding hands.

"Mommy...Daddy, this is Graham. He's Sister Walker's son," Geneva said.

The introductions were necessary. Geneva's father had only taken over the ministry of the church in the last year, and they had never met in the months since Graham moved back to Bedford. *My luck just ran way out.*

"Nice to meet you, Graham," Mrs. Garrett said, her head tilted to the side in the large-brimmed hat she wore over her sleek bob.

"*Very* nice," Reverend Garrett added, reaching out to take Graham's hand into his with a tight squeeze.

"Yes, sir," he said. "My mother's probably wondering where I am..."

"Let me walk you to her car," the Rev said with a smile that was tight and forced as he finally released Graham's hand.

"Dad—"

Mrs. Garrett reached out a soft but restraining hand on Geneva's elbow.

"Nice to meet you again, Mrs. Garrett," he said.

"I'm sure we'll see you next Sunday. Right, Graham?" she asked politely.

He opened his mouth but didn't form the lie that would appease her curiosity. Instead, he shrugged helplessly.

"Walk with me, son," Reverend Garrett said.

Although Graham towered over the minister by at least five inches, the man was still an imposing figure as they walked down the brick steps together. "Your mother is a good woman," Reverend Garrett said, lightly slapping Graham's broad shoulder. "And I know she wants nothing but the best for you, son, the same way I want nothing but the best for my daughter."

Graham tensed as they stepped off the steps and onto the sidewalk.

"I'm sure she wouldn't approve of you smoking weed any more than I would approve of a pothead for my daughter," he said, taking Graham's hand in his again to hold tightly.

"I don't smoke—"

"Liar," Reverend Garrett said shortly. "I smell it all over you. You think I don't know what weed smells like? You think ole Rev is a dummy, boy?"

Oh shit. "Nah. I mean no sir."

"Stay away from Geneva," he said with another tight smile before turning to walk back to the steps. He paused and turned. "And don't bring that mess back around here."

Graham looked past him and up the steps to Geneva standing there next to her mother. He gave her a smile and a wave before turning to walk back to the lot to where his mother had parked that morning. She was standing near the front of her Benz talking to some other Bible-toting prim-and-proper church ladies.

Afraid they would smell the weed on him as well, he removed his blazer and came up on the rear of the SUV to hop into the passenger seat. He smiled and gave a wave when his mother and the church ladies all looked through the windshield at him. Letting his head fall back against the headrest, he covered his eyes with his hand and let the effects of the weed really hit him.

★ ★ ★

Graham slowed from a full-on run to a fast walk as he came up on the pond in the center of the subdivision. Hopping up on one of the wrought-iron benches, he pulled his cell phone from his pocket. Ten missed calls from Geneva. He smiled a bit and slid the phone back in his pocket.

Everything was going just as he planned.

Graham had learned a lot from his father about getting what he wanted—how he wanted it—from a woman. Graham wanted Geneva and he wanted her to ask for it. The Rev's warning to stay away from her had just kicked the game plan up a few notches.

"He's a preacher but he know what weed smell like," Graham mumbled as darkness began to fall around him as he eyed the still pond. "Fuck outta here."

Bzzz . . . Bzzz . . . Bzzz . . .

Graham pulled out his phone with one hand and reached for the half a blunt he'd stashed inside the top of his sock. He didn't recognize the number sending a text. He never saved contacts in his phone—another bit of advice from his father on not being caught in the worst kind of three-way: a dude and the two chicks he's banging.

"You didn't call. Thought you needed a reminder that all this good, wet and deep pussy is ready for dick," he read aloud, squinting his eyes as he lit the blunt.

"Whoo-oooh-eee!" Graham exclaimed after he read the text.

Damn.

Geneva wanted him faithful . . . so Geneva had to give up them panties. That was his logic. Plain and simple. Pussy was getting thrown at him left and right from old and new members of his lineup. He really liked Geneva but his nuts were about to burst from overload.

Deleting the text after another quick read, Graham didn't bother to respond. He entered Geneva's number instead, but then he deleted it. He'd told her earlier that her father didn't want them together and he was respecting the man's wishes. After hanging up with a feigned sad good-bye, he had ignored all of her calls and texts for the rest of the day.

"Bring me that pussy," he said with a laugh as he released a stream that was a mix of weed smoke and cold air from the October night.

The trees of the park shadowed the sky and he knew that in the morning there would be frost. His stomach growled at the thought of the oxtail stew, brown rice, macaroni and cheese, and homemade cornbread his mother made for Sunday dinner.

Tossing the rest of the blunt away, he jumped off the bench and started the three miles back to the house at a full run. Bedford was a small, affluent community and Graham said a silent prayer there were no police patrolling. His head and face was deeply shielded by his hoodie as he did his nightly run.

He had just come through the unguarded gates of the subdivision, passing a couple walking their dog, when he spotted Geneva's BMW parked in the driveway behind his mother's vehicle.

"And the pussy is brought," Graham said with pure satisfaction as he made his way up the street and then up the front porch into the house.

He removed his hoodie and placed his cell phone on silent before following the voices echoing through the lower level of the house from the den. His mother and Geneva were sitting on the large wraparound sofa flipping through family photo albums.

"Baby Graham naked-in-the-tub pics time," he said jokingly as they both looked up when he sauntered into the room.

"Just one," Geneva said, her eyes showing her unease as she looked up at him.

Cara closed the large photo album and stood up to move across the room and place it back in the lower drawer of the armoire encasing the fifty-inch television. "I'll leave you two alone," she said with a meaningful stare at Graham behind Geneva's back before she left the room.

"What are you doing here, Geneva?" he asked, crossing his arms over his chest and pretending he didn't notice how cute she looked in her hot pink velour sweat suit.

"Come sit down, Grammy," she said, patting the brown suede sofa next to where she sat.

He shook his head and stepped back from her with a feigned sad expression. "Your dad said—"

"Forget what he said," Geneva said as she jumped up to her feet and crossed the short distance to stand before him. "I thought you liked me?"

Graham looked down at her. In heels, she reached his shoulder, but she was in sneakers. "I do, but I think it's important for your dad to like me too, so I think we should just leave things off. It's just too much drama, G."

Tears welled up in her eyes. "Graham, don't do this," she pleaded softly, reaching up to stroke his cheek.

Graham's eyes shifted to the swell of her breasts above the open zipper of her jacket. *Big ole titties just going to waste . . . right along with the pussy.* "I didn't answer your calls and texts because I knew it would be hard to walk away from you," he said, turning from her and dropping his tall frame down onto the couch. "Never hold you or kiss you again . . ."

Geneva dropped down to her knees before him and took his large hands into hers to hold tightly as she looked at him with her big, bright eyes filled with sadness and alarm. "Hold me now. Kiss me now," she said softly, pulling his arms around her as she moved in closer to him.

Graham pulled back and tried to free his hands from hers. "Geneva—"

She released his hands to wrap her arms around his neck and press her upper body to his.

He let his hands drop and leaned back even as he felt his dick harden at the soft feel of her body against his. "No, Geneva," he said sharply.

She released him and sat back on her heels, looking away from him as one solitary tear slid down her cheek.

Graham slid off the couch and down to his knees before her, lifting his hand to hold her cheek as he used a thumb to wipe away her tear. "Geneva," he whispered to her, bending to press a kiss to her brow as she dropped her head.

Her shoulders shook with her tears. It was like his show of emotion to her broke what little control she had over herself. He held her close. "Graham, I love you," she whispered into his neck before she pressed a kiss just behind his ear. "I love you so much."

His heart beat faster at her words. "I love you too, G."

And the kiss behind his ear was followed by a quick and hot lick of her tongue against the same spot. Goose bumps raced across his back and his arms as she leaned back just enough to kiss him.

Graham fought not to come on too hard as he kissed her back, drawing her tongue out to suck the tip gently as his hands shook in anticipation. Her moan of pleasure was his aphrodisiac. He gently pressed her downward until she lay beneath him.

He didn't care that he was salty and damp with sweat.

He didn't give one complete damn that they were on the floor of his mother's den.

And he definitely did not give two damns that her father didn't want him within two feet of her.

Graham pressed a trail of kisses along her jawbone. She tilted her head back for more, exposing the soft and intimate spot below her chin. He tasted it, causing a shiver to race across her body, before moving on to suck the hollow above her collarbone.

She gasped hotly and her hips jerked slightly upward off the floor.

I found her hot spot.

Alternating licks with kisses, he stayed there, enjoying her body's innate response to him. He eased his hand from her hip to the rim of her sweats, sliding beneath the elastic to shift the moist seat of her cotton panties to the side.

Geneva's fingers clasped the back of his head, weaving between his dreads. "Yes, Graham," she sighed.

The first stroke of his finger against her throbbing clit made them both tense. "Damn, it's wet," he moaned against her neck, closing his eyes with a wince that had nothing to do with pain.

Geneva bit her bottom lip and opened her eyes to look up at the ceiling in wonder as Graham pressed down on her clit before rubbing circles against it. She gasped again and spread her legs.

"Feel good?" he asked her, lifting up to look down into her face as she nodded earnestly, then looking down at her hard nipples pressed against the material and the sight of his hand in her pants.

Feeling bold from her glazed-over eyes, he ran his finger along the middle of her pussy lips before finding her opening and sliding the tip of his middle finger inside.

"No!" Geneva said in alarm, snapping her thighs closed and trapping his wrist and hand between them.

Shit.

He fought the urge to show his frustration on his face. "What's wrong?" he said, his eyes studying her face as he tried not to focus on how hard his dick was.

Her eyes shifted away from his as she licked her lips. "Will...will...putting your finger inside me...uh...will it—"

"Hurt?" Graham asked, ready to resume before he nutted himself.

She glanced up at him and looked away again. "I took a purity vow when I was thirteen," she said in a voice so low he couldn't even pronounce it a whisper.

Graham leaned in closer.

Geneva turned her head on the floor and pressed her face against his ear, hiding herself from him. "They have my doctor check me to make sure I don't break my vow," she said.

Graham felt his erection ease as he frowned deeply in disappointment. "I understand," he lied, pressing kisses into her hair as he felt his frustration damn near drive him crazy. It was hard to step back from the edge of being so close to sex.

If she was worrying about the harm his finger would do, then he knew there was no way he was slipping his dick in her.

Not tonight, anyway.

Chapter 6

Geneva

Graham stepped out of the shower, not bothering with a towel as he enjoyed the feel of the air against his damp skin. Leaving his en suite bathroom, he crossed his bedroom to stand before the full-length mirror on the back of his closet door. Because of his height he could only see from just below his shoulders to his feet. He stared at his reflection as he flexed and posed, enjoying the definition of his chest, arms, and abdomen. He was lean but still strong. "Just need to bulk up," he said, boxing the air with his fists.

He turned his body and eyed his upper arm. First the left. Then the right. "I need a tat," he said, slapping and rubbing his shoulder. "A panther or some shit."

Moving over to flop on his back on his made bed, he picked up his cell and dialed Marco, his friend from back in Brooklyn. "Whaddup, dude," he said as soon as he answered.

"What's up with you?"

"I need a tattoo. Who you recommend?" Graham asked.

"Nobody out there in White-ville," he said, sounding sarcastic.

"You funny."

Marco laughed. "There's this female that is bad ass. She did the tattoo on my neck."

"Your neck?" Graham balked, sitting up on the bed.

"That's right. Thug life. Pow-pow."

Graham just laughed. "Is this another thug-life fool or is she in a shop, 'cause I ain't about that disease life."

"In a shop," Marco said. "Bring your ass to Brooklyn. I'll take you to her...and introduce you to somebody that'll make you forget the church girl."

Graham's eyes shifted over to the picture of Geneva sitting on his nightstand table. She'd given it to him in a frame with love quotes inscribed on it. "I doubt that," he said.

"We'll see," Marco countered. "When you getting in the city?"

"Shit, I'm on the way," he said. "You home?"

"I will be."

"A'ight." Graham snapped the phone shut and dropped it on the bed, but then immediately picked it back up.

Smiling, he texted Geneva: *Touch your pussy.*

Graham lay there tapping the phone against his chest as he waited. It took all of a minute.

Bzzzzzz...

He flipped the phone open and accessed the incoming text.

I CANT. AT DINNER WITH THE PARENTS.

SOON AS I GET HOME. OK?

Graham tossed his phone aside and got up off the bed to enter his walk-in closet. "This shit getting old as fuck," he muttered.

Geneva was sweet-spirited. Loving. Kind.

Geneva was pretty, curvy, and sexy without even trying.

Geneva was someone he had truly come to love.

But Geneva's virginal ass was holding on to her purity.

In the two weeks since the night on the floor downstairs

in the den, Graham had slowly groomed her into more sexual adventures. Nipple sucking. Clit stroking. Blow jobs. Nevertheless, she was not having his dick anywhere near where it truly mattered.

He was thankful for the climaxes, but nothing compared to the feel of sexing a woman. Being inside her. Riding inside her. Feeling her cum against the dick as it was deep *inside* her.

Pussy made his world go 'round, and right now he was in one helluva a rut.

Graham's movements were nothing but angry jerks as he swiped on deodorant, sprayed Polo cologne over his body, and put on his clothes. "What type of crazy fool has his grown-ass daughter checked to make sure she ain't fucking?" he stooped to ask his reflection. "A sick, twisted fool. That's who."

Grabbing his keys and his cell phone, he didn't bother to grab a blunt because Marco would have plenty when he got to Brooklyn. Plenty of weed and available, non-checked, non-guarded, freaky-deaky pussy.

His dick throbbed with life at the thought of that.

"Another cherry popped."

Graham sat up on the bench and eyed the black panther on his forearm. He liked how it was shaded and looked more like a sketch with a charcoal pencil than just a solid black outline. "Thanks," he said, looking over his shoulder to smile at Lola.

She smiled and the small diamond piercings in her dimples deepened. "No problem," she said, her voice raspy and soft.

Graham eyed her as she came around the table to rub ointment on the tattoo. Her skin was the color of shortbread cookies and her waist-length dreadlocks were a dark blond that made her shaped dark brown brows and slanted greenish-brown eyes all the more present. Her makeup highlighted her high cheekbones and full lips. She was petite but her hips were wide enough to birth a nation with ease. The low-slung jeans and leather bustier she wore exposed the tattoo sleeve on her left arm, a tattoo of a scripture on her right rib cage, and a row of small black figures from her neck to the round of her shoulder.

She was pretty, edgy, and sexy as hell.

Lola bandaged the tattoo and taped the edges well to keep air out. "Remember everything I told you about taking care of it," she said, looking up at him as she rubbed the edge with her black fingernails.

He inhaled deeply of the scent of her perfume. Something warm and spicy but with a hint of sweetness. The kind of scent that made a man want to bury his face in places. The base of her neck. The warm space between her breasts. Her inner thighs.

She walked away from him as his eyes dipped to take the back-and-forth motion of her hips and buttocks in the stilettos she wore. Lola turned and caught his eyes just as he shifted them upward. She just shook her head and waved. "Have a good night," she said.

Graham smiled bashfully and pulled the white long-sleeved tee he wore back over his head.

"Hey, baby," Lola said.

Graham jerked the shirt down just as a brown-skinned cutie with a Caesar cut pulled Lola close to kiss her. He sat transfixed as he watched the women's passion. He could just see them in bed together. All soft and sensual and slow. He could see himself in the bed with them...receiving all that softness, sensuality, and slowness.

Geneva or no Geneva, they offer and I'm down!

He stood up and held his puffy red vest in front of his body to help block his hard dick from showing. By the time he made it to the waiting area, his erection had eased and he pulled on his vest as he reached Marco.

"I bet you they can teach classes on eating pussy," Marco

said, eyeing the two women as he raised his short and pudgy frame from the chair and dropped the copy of *Inked* magazine he had been flipping through.

Graham frowned as they walked out the shop. Night had fallen but the streets of New York were alive with people and noise. "Eat pussy?" he balked. "Naw, they bleed out that shit ev'ry month. I'm good."

Marco looked at him like he was crazy before he stepped to the edge of the street to flag a cab. "You missing out," he said. "Trust."

"Whatever," Graham said, zipping up his vest and taking out a matching skull cap to pull down over his dreads as a sharp and cold wind seemed to cut through him.

They both turned at the sound of the roll-down gate being lowered and locked. Graham's eyes zoned in on Lola and her stud as they shared another hot kiss as the other tattoo artists waved their good-byes and took off down the street. They both stared openly at him and shared a smile before The Stud slapped Lola's ass, then groped it and jerked her lower body closer to grind against her as Lola sucked her tongue.

Hey, dick. Rise and shine.

Graham knew they were getting off messing with him when they laughed and waved before walking arm in arm down the street. He didn't give a damn. He was just enjoying the show. He turned his head to watch them walk away until they disappeared from his sight as they descended the stairs to the entrance of the subway.

A yellow cab finally pulled to a stop beside them.

"Yo, Marco, I'm gonna head home," Graham said, already reaching in his wallet for his MetroCard.

Marco paused in his move to climb inside the rear of the taxi. "Word?"

"Yeah," he said over his shoulder, running the short distance to descend the stairs and pay his fare. He had just reached the platform when he spotted Lola and The Stud getting on the train headed for Grand Central Terminal. Not wanting to miss it, he jumped on another car and then made his way through the crowd to their car.

Lola spotted him first and nudged The Stud where they sat seated in the corner.

He saw them whispering to each other as they stared at him. He didn't stop until he was leaning his back against the pole in front of them.

"Yo, the show's over," The Stud said, her face almost as pretty as Lola's but her clothes, flat chest, and low fade those of a man.

"You sure?" Graham countered cockily. "I felt like I was part of the show for y'all and I didn't want to mess it up."

They drew the curious stares of several train riders.

The Stud moved to stand up but Lola placed her rose-tattooed hand against her thigh to stop her. "Trust me, we don't need anything you got to get off," Lola said, pulling a cell phone from inside her bustier and looking down at it as she quickly swiped it with her thumb.

"Don't knock it 'til you try it," he said.

Lola licked her lips and cut her slanted eyes up at him. With her height, she barely reached his chest. She turned her phone and lifted it up to his face. "If you can't compete with that, then step off," she said.

In the picture The Stud was wearing a strap-on that looked as big and brown as a small tree trunk.

"Don't mess with that, brah," some man said from behind him before the people around them started to laugh.

Graham knew he had a big dick, but this was offensive in its size. Offensive and unreal.

"The only thing I got for you is some bad-ass tats," Lola said in her husky voice. "We good?"

Graham shrugged and smiled. "We good," he asserted.

Lola reclaimed her seat and The Stud lifted her leg to cross it over Lola's.

Graham lifted his hand and scratched his scalp through his skully. It was dry, and that reminded him of how Geneva would sit him on the floor between her legs to grease and massage his scalp with coconut oil. That was the kind of girl she was, and he couldn't deny that he really cared about her.

He dug his cell phone out of his pocket and was disappointed that Geneva hadn't called or texted him back. He started to call her but snapped the phone shut as the train came to a stop. He figured a night without speaking to him should rattle her.

Lola and her girl stood up.

"Holla at me about getting them dreads together," said The Stud, passing him a business card before she followed Lola off the train.

Graham dropped down into one of their vacated seats and eyed the card. The Stud's name was Kezia, and she was a beautician specializing in natural hair. Shrugging, he slid the card into the pocket of his vest and eyed his phone again as the train pulled to a stop in Grand Central Terminal.

He jumped a little in surprise as the phone suddenly vibrated in his hand. Geneva's phone number appeared on the screen. He sent it to voice mail. Geneva was drawing him in when there was no hope for them. He thought by now he would've had her in love with his dick, but her fear of her father outweighed her love for him.

Bzzzz . . .

A voice mail.

He opened it and smirked at her detailing how she was touching herself and thinking of him. He envisioned her using her fingers to spread the lips the way he taught her so that he could see the real goodness on the inside and not just her 'fro.

He texted her: *Don't tease me with what I can't have.*
Bzzz.

"You know I can't," he read the incoming text to himself.

Reversing his decision not to call her, Graham dialed her number, his hand tightly clutching the phone as he pressed it to his ear. "G," he said when she answered.

"Hey, baby, where—"

"We need to talk," he said.

"What's wrong?"

"Look, some things between us gotta change one way or the other—"

"What? What's wrong?" she wailed.

Graham shook off the pang of pain he felt at the hurt in her voice. Frowning, he moved on, taking the familiar path through the crowded station to the platform for the train to Bedford. "Meet me at the station in forty-five minutes."

She released a heavy breath filled with her reluctance. "My father won't—"

"Geneva, when the hell you gonna grow up?" he snapped in frustration. With her. With her father. With their pseudo sex life.

With his love for her.

"Are you gonna meet me or not?" Graham said, leaning against the wall as he awaited the train with less than a dozen other people.

The line was quiet—or at least he thought so until her soft whimpering came through. Graham wiped his mouth with his hand. "Just meet me at the station in forty-five minutes. Okay?" he asked, deliberately softening his tone.

He ended the call without waiting for a response. She didn't call back.

A few minutes later he boarded the train and took the seat farthest away from anyone. For the duration of the ride he enjoyed the solitude and the sound of the train against the track. His thoughts were varied but clear. He didn't even want a blunt to cloud his thoughts.

As the train pulled to a stop, Graham was the only one on his car to step out onto the platform. The October night air was chilly and raced through his clothing like it was nothing. He made his way inside the terminal and then crossed it to leave the building. He didn't spot her car in the near-empty parking lot.

She didn't come.

He was disappointed but not surprised. It wasn't just her hymen her father kept an eye on. Pushing his hands into the pockets of his jeans, Graham made his way to the taxi stand and felt lucky that a town car sat there.

Lights suddenly reflected against the windshield. He glanced back over his shoulder and slowed his steps at the sight of Geneva's BMW pulling to a stop behind him. He turned in the gap between her car and the taxi as she climbed out.

Graham's pulse quickened at the sight of her, and he took a deep breath as he walked over to where she stood by the door to her car. "You came?"

Geneva smiled and reached up to pluck something from his dreads. "You didn't give me much of a choice," she said lightly, smoothing her hands over the jeans she wore with a form-fitting cream turtleneck.

"Things got to change, G," he said in a rush, admitting to himself that he pushed the words out before he lost his will to have the conversation.

"What things?" she asked.

"Yo . . . I want to have sex but you not giving it up until you get married . . . and your father hate me so you'll never marry me . . . and I'm nowhere near ready to be married," he said, moving to sit on the back of a bench on the sidewalk. "I feel like I'm putting in a bunch of time for a relationship that may be going nowhere."

Geneva slid her hands into the back pockets of her jeans as she walked over to stand between his knees. "So I'm a waste of time?" she asked.

Graham balled his hands into fists and lightly pounded them on his knees. "I'm used to having sex—"

"But I suck *it*," she said, her eyes darting down to his crotch meaningfully before they widened.

"I like pussy," he snapped, splaying his fingers as he raised his hands. "I like being in pussy. I like stroking in pussy. I like feeling pussy when I make it cum. I like when the pussy makes my dick wet. I like to nut up a pussy. I'm about pussy, pussy, pussy, pussy."

Geneva's eyes continued to widen with each declaration until she looked frightened for her life. "Graham."

"Nah, G, don't Graham me," he said, waving his hand dismissively as he looked away from her.

"Graham," she repeated, sounding reproachful.

His frustration with her made him feel like fleas were nipping at his neck. He looked up to the night sky as he stomped his booted feet on the seat of the bench. "Look, Geneva, I want to be with you," he said, shifting his head to look at her. "You not feeling me like that?"

Geneva stepped up and held his face with her hands. "You know I am...but you know I can't," she stressed. "Hell, my annual is coming up in a few weeks."

Graham tensed. "So you just gone let your daddy pussy test you 'til your ass forty?" he snapped.

"What makes you think I won't get married until I'm forty?" she exclaimed.

He looked incredulous. "*That's* what you pulled out of what I just said?" he said sardonically.

She eyed him as if she was confused.

For the first time Graham wondered just how deep Geneva's naïveté ran and how weak her spine was. *Innocence is one thing. Stupidity is something else.*

"I know something we can do," she said, leaning in to wrap her arms around his neck. "And I *know* you want to."

Graham lowered his head to her shoulder as she slid her hand beneath his vest and rubbed his back above his shirt. "Does it involve pussy?" he said, his eyes focused on his boots.

"Close," she said, rubbing her face against the tips of his dreads.

Graham stiffened. His eyes shifted from left to right as his brain raced a mile a minute. "Close?" he asked, recalling her words before that.

And I know *you want to.*

"Real close," she stressed, stepping back to turn around and give her full bottom a wiggle in front of him before looking over her shoulder with a flirty wink.

And I know *you want to.*

Graham's brows lowered so severely over his deep-set eyes that the color of his irises was indistinguishable. "I look gay to you?" he asked, his voice low and ominous.

She turned. "Huh?"

"What do you mean you *know* I want to," he asked, rising up to stand on the seat of the bench before stepping down off it to stand in her face.

She stepped back from him. "Why are you so mad? What did I say?" she asked, pressing her hand to her chest.

"I ain't fucking gay!" he roared, spittle flying from his mouth.

"Graham—"

"I. AIN'T. GAY!"

Geneva kept stepping back from him until she stumbled against the hood of her car. Her fear was clear. Her lips moved like she was trying to form words but nothing came out.

And I know *you want to.*

Had someone in the church known and spread the word of what Lionel had done? Graham wiped his eyes as an image of Lionel touching him flashed. Stepping forward, he grabbed her, his fingers digging into the flesh of her upper arms.

Geneva cried out before she wrenched her body free from his grasp and slapped him.

WHAP!

Graham reached out to grip her wrist.

"Hey! Let her go."

Graham looked over his shoulder. The driver from the taxi had hollered out his window at them.

"Let me go, Graham," Geneva whined.

He looked back to her and she grimaced with the pain he was causing her. He let her go. "G, I'm—"

She turned and quickly climbed behind the wheel of her car.

He stepped up to grab the handle of the driver-side door. She had already locked the doors. "I didn't mean to hurt you."

She said nothing as she glared at him and started her car.

"G, don't leave like this," he said, feeling panicked.

She shifted the car into reverse. "My father was right about you," she said coldly through a crack in the window just as the faint sound of police sirens echoed in the air.

Her words stung harder than her slap. His jaw tightened in anger as he released her door and stepped back from it with his hands high. "To hell with you and your daddy. Maybe *he* want the pussy and scared somebody else gone get it," he said, lashing out at her. Angry. Hurt. Wanting to hurt.

Through the windshield, he saw Geneva's pain-filled eyes and a tear racing down her cheek as she reversed away from him and exited the parking lot.

All his anger instantly disappeared as regret consumed him. But the sounds of approaching sirens forced him to push everything aside, flee the parking lot, and run through the darkened streets of Bedford to reach home.

Interlude

*T*he feel of ice-cold water splashing against his naked skin caused him to release an abject cry as he was jarred from sleep. The bonds on his wrists and ankles snapped into his skin as he instinctively tried to extend his limbs.

He didn't even realize he had dozed off. He had no clue if just minutes or hours had passed. He licked his parched lips and felt a deep thirst for water.

"No time for sleeping, slut," she said into his ear with a lick against his lobe that repulsed him. She moved past him with her gloved hand trailing down his tattooed arm and then his thigh before she reached over and lightly smacked his dick sending it from his right thigh to his left before rebounding back.

"Who knew selling dick for a living paid so well?" she mocked, turning to toss the glass she held into the fireplace.

He felt tiny shards of glass fly out and pierce the skin on random spots of his body. He winced as her fiery anger flipped to her weeping, with her gloved hands covering her masked face as her shoulders shook with her tears. Just moments after that she flung her head back, spread her arms wide, and laughed as she turned in circles.

This bitch crazy.

She came to a stop and locked her eyes on him. "Do you know how long I have waited to have you, Pleasure?" she asked him in a low voice.

Even crazier than I thought.

He took her in. She was of average height and build. Nothing spectacular or memorable. The length and hue of her hair was hidden beneath the hood she wore. Every inch of her body shielded by dark clothing. She didn't mean to be revealed until she was ready. That was clear.

Who is she?

His eyes, though heavy and weary, leveled on her. Studying her.

Geneva had loved him. That he knew. But was this her? Physically it could be. He hadn't seen her in years but it was possible. But the Geneva he knew? The Geneva he loved? He doubted very seriously that this could be her.

Their story had come to him in those moments just before he passed out again but he couldn't imagine such a crazy act from the woman he'd known all those years ago. He had so much regret in the days after he blew up at her at the train station. The side of him he'd revealed was enough for her to end things, and he had felt the loss of her in his life for a long time after that.

"I've waited a long time for this . . . pleasure," the masked woman said, before turning to walk across the room and out of his line of vision.

Raising his head, he eyed his captor as she stood by the windows of his living room looking out at the bright lights of New York across the Hudson.

He wondered about her thoughts, her plans . . . for him.

Who is she?

"I can't believe this shit," he mumbled with a grunt of pain as he took a deep breath before focusing his eyes on her again.

She twisted her gloved hands together and shifted slightly back and forth on her feet before leaning her shoulder against the glass.

Her gaze still locked on some undeterminable spot out the window. He wondered if her thoughts were as erratic as her behavior.

"It's not too late to let me go," he called, wanting his voice to carry across the distance.

She turned and shook her head. "Wrong again," she snapped before crossing the room to stand before him.

"Man, who are *you?" he asked, his anger and annoyance rising.*

She lifted her right hand so high in the air that her upper arm covered her face before she brought it down and slapped him across the face with such force that the chair he was tied to rocked before tipping over with a loud thud.

"Ah!" he cried out as the side of his head hit the floor forcefully and the ties cut deeper into his flesh.

She stretched out on the floor, moving quickly and crazily, with her face close enough to his for him to detect the smell of cigarettes and liquor on her breath and to see the craziness in her eyes as she laughed maniacally.

Chapter 7

Joy

2004

"Don't scratch my car."

Graham first spotted a pair of black high heels and shapely legs in black opaque stockings before he allowed his eyes to travel upward to a leather skirt cut high on her thighs and a sheer white blouse. Standing up to his full height, he eyed the tall beauty standing before him as he wrung out excess water from the shammy he was using to wipe down the blood-red Chrysler.

Damn, she fine, he thought, tilting his head to the side as he eyed the mixed Asian and African American beauty with shocking honey-blond hair that somehow worked with her olive complexion and the golden tones of her makeup. She had small breasts, but her ample thighs and hips more than made up for it. Even from a distance, he could smell her perfume and it made him want to get closer to her. Every movement of her body seemed to convey or convince that she was pure sex appeal.

She was dope and she knew it.

"I got you," Graham said, looking away from her as he

finished drying the hood of her vehicle with large sweeping circles that caused the muscles of his arm to flex and relax beneath the smooth brown of his skin.

"Humph."

He glanced up and caught her eyeing him as she lit a cigarette. His eyes dipped to take in the pucker of her glossy lips as she inhaled from the cigarette and soon exhaled a stream of smoke. Deciding to ignore her, Graham kept at his job of drying the left side of her car as one of his coworkers at the detail shop tackled the right.

"She could love on this dick long time," Pogo said, in a horrible imitation of a Vietnamese accent from the memorable scene in *Full Metal Jacket.*

Graham looked over at the short, thin man who was every bit of sixty or seventy years of age and looked dwarfed by his navy blue uniform. Following Pogo's line of vision, he watched the sway of her skirt against her shapely thighs as she slowly paced and talked on her cell phone.

Graham was not short on women by any means, but this thoroughbred pacing before him was nothing like any of the other girls on his roster. Her style and demeanor made that clear. He doubted she even shopped in a Walmart, much less worked the register like Monique. She'd probably never even been in a run-down motel like the one where Jacia worked as a housekeeper. And for sure she wasn't busting suds in a diner like Yvetta.

He eyed her as she tapped her gold cigarette lighter against her palm as she continued pacing. Everything about her said she was a career chick. Teacher. Nurse. Secretary. A nine-to-five, weekdays-only, indoors-always type of career. Something like that.

Something out of my league.

Looking away from her, he stretched his tall frame before stooping down to wipe large circles to dry the door. His parents stayed on his back—and his nerves—reminding him of the straight-A student he used to be. They kept reminding him of the potential he was wasting.

"If you put as much time into working your brain as you did working on your body, you'd be hell," his mother always said.

He knew they were right but he was enjoying life. He worked, made money, kept women eager to please him, brought fly gears and kicks, smoked weed, and partied. Life was real good.

Rising to his full height, he eyed his work as he stepped back from the vehicle. He could easily see her cruising down a highway in the bright red car with her golden hair blowing in the wind. "I'm done, Pogo," he said, his voice as deep as the trouble his parents constantly warned him about.

He removed the cotton band holding his chin-length ebony dreads off his square, handsome face and looked up at the August summer sun causing sweat to soak his blue uniform. The sky wouldn't even begin to tint with darkness until eight or nine, and his boss always took full advantage with extended hours until the start of fall.

There were already four other cars washed and awaiting detailing. *Shit.* Scratching his scalp, Graham doubled the band and tied it around the ends of his thin dreads as he walked inside the building to the employee break room. Like the rest of the odd mix of old furniture, the refrigerator had long since seen its better days, but Graham was happy it worked just fine to keep an icy chill on the bottled water inside it.

Bzzzzzz.

With his head still tilted back to empty the bottle, he reached for his cell phone from his back pocket and flipped it open before looking down at the picture of Lola and Kezia kissing. The tattoo artist and hairdresser still liked messing with him because they knew he wanted a threesome with them bad. They wouldn't give in no matter how many times he asked them for a fair shot to fuck them and make them love dick again or even flashed his big dick at them. Nothing.

Lola did his tattoos and Kezia made sure his dreads were always fresh.

"You still coming through tomorrow?" he read the text aloud as he walked out of the break room.

Using his thumbs, he replied. *NAH. NO ENDS THIS WEEK. NEXT FRIDAY?*

Graham had just stepped back out into the sun and the heat immediately pressed against his body. He was surprised to see the red convertible still there with Ms. Everything patiently sitting in the driver's seat.

"She's waiting on you."

Looking away from the car, he glanced over his broad shoulder at Pogo vacuuming floor mats atop the large table in the corner. His heart swelled with surprise as he licked his bottom lip and made his way over to stand by her car. She glanced up at him from behind oversized shades and then held up a finger instructing him to wait, with annoyance lining her pretty face.

Graham frowned in displeasure. *The hell . . . ?*

Blowing dismissive air between his teeth, Graham turned and headed toward the white Range Rover Pogo was already working on.

"Hey!"

Graham heard her call out to him but he kept it moving. He figured the most she could have for him was a tip and he'd live without it.

"Six footer," she called out.

Her voice sounded closer and he looked back just as she pulled her car up beside him. Coming to a stop with a heavy breath, Graham looked down at her. "That's six foot nine," he told her, crossing his sculptured arms over his chest and causing his tattoos to stretch across his muscles.

She leaned back in the leather passenger seat as she eyed him from behind her shades. "Come ride with me," she ordered him, her voice soft but cocky. Sure. Demanding.

"What?" Graham asked, making a face.

She leaned forward. "Get in."

Graham looked left and then right. Everywhere but at her.

"I don't have all day, Six Foot Nine," she said.

His eyes shifted. He quietly assessed her. "For what?"

She smirked. "You scared?" she asked.

"Oh, I ain't never scared," he assured her with a boldness he felt building. In his eyes, their levels were equalizing. *She* stepped to *him*.

With one eyebrow arched, she reached to hit the power button to unlock the passenger door. A dare.

Graham felt a thrill of excitement from his mundane life. He walked around the front of her car and opened the passenger door. "Yo, Pogo," he called over to his elderly coworker. "Tell the boss man I went home sick."

Pogo smiled broadly, displaying every tooth of his ill-fitting dentures. "You a baaaaaad boy," he joked.

Graham winked at him before he bent his tall frame to slide onto the smooth leather passenger seat.

"You ready?" she asked as she shifted the car into drive.

Leaning back against the door, he locked his eyes with hers. "Are you?" he countered.

She laughed as she accelerated across the expanse of the parking lot.

"Graham . . . Graham . . . wake up. Wake. Up."

He stirred at the feel of warm, petite hands pressed against the muscles of his chest. With each slow blink of his eyes, the sight of the all-white bedroom became clearer until he was looking through the sheer curtains surrounding the four-poster bed to the bright sun glaring through the bay windows of her bedroom.

It's morning.

That's all he knew for sure.

Graham turned his head on the pillow as he felt her straddle his hips. He smiled at the sight of her tousled blond hair barely covering the heart-shaped tattoos on the tips of her breasts and the weed she was placing inside a split blunt.

"I have to go to work today," she said, reaching down to pick up something on the bed beside him.

He frowned in disappointment. "I thought you were on vacation?" he asked, suddenly aware of his mouth and tongue tasting like a horrible mix of bad breath, old food, and stale cigarettes.

Joy set the open blunt on his chest and then opened the tiny glass vial she held. "It's Monday. Vacation over," she said, glancing up at him briefly with her slanted eyes as she sprinkled the weed with coke.

Seven days had passed.

Damn.

Graham could hardly piece together anything more than snippets of wild sex, getting high, and occasional breaks for food—all while in the bedroom of her Harlem apartment. It was the best seven days of his life. *Two thumbs in a bucket, fuck it.*

Pressing his hands to her hips, he felt his dick stir from both the feel of her moist pussy snuggled against it and the anticipation of the weed-and-coke blend. He'd never laced his blunts before, but after some gentle urging from her his mind was blown and he wanted more. More of her. More of the powder. More of the rush.

"Don't go," he said, easing his hand around her wide hips to grip her buttocks and then continue down to slide one long finger inside her from behind.

Joy carelessly tossed the now-empty vial onto the hard-wood floor before rolling the blunt as she wet it with the tip of her tongue. "I have to. We're prepping for a big murder case coming up in two weeks," she said with the blunt now pressed between her lips as she lit it. "If I want the lead paralegal spot for Mr. Warren, then I have to be on my A game. So my vacay is so over...and yours as well."

Graham pulled her up onto her knees and used his hand to guide his hardness inside her. She held the blunt with her lips as she leaned back and placed her arms behind herself to grip his legs as she enjoyed the roll of his hips and the thrust of his dick. "You sure?" he asked her, enjoying the sight of her clean-shaven mound as his dick slid between her lips.

She sat back up straight to blow a stream of smoke directly down into his face as she took over the ride and worked her hips in fast and furious pumps that quickly drove him to an explosive nut that made him holler from his gut. "I'm very sure," she said, standing up on the bed and leaving his dick blowing in the wind before she hopped down off the bed with the blunt still in her hand.

"Shit," Graham swore, closing his eyes as the last of his nut left him in a jolt that was draining.

"I cannot have too much of this," she said, leaving the lit blunt in the ashtray atop her ornate wooden nightstand before turning to walk away.

Moments later, he heard the shower in her adjoining bathroom start with an echoing blast. Just the thought of the water hitting against her body almost—*almost*—made his desire for her kick into second gear. Sitting up, he pushed a few of the many pillows on the bed behind his head and shoulders as he reached for the remote and the blunt. Bending one leg and pressing his size thirteen foot into the plush pillow-top of the bed, he smoked the blunt and flipped through the channels of the plasma television on the opposite wall.

As he watched a rerun of *Sanford and Son*, he blazed through half of the blunt easily, glad that the laced weed didn't affect him the way it had when Joy introduced it to him a week ago. His tongue and his extremities had gone numb and the back of his head tingled as his heart pounded like crazy.

He chuckled at how the high coupled with the fear nearly blew his mind.

Graham was carefully putting out the embers of the tip of the blunt when Joy strolled back into the bedroom with a plush pink towel wrapped around her honey-toned body with her blond hair up in a loose topknot. She stopped and looked at him in amazement.

"What's your plans for the day besides *thinking* you gone lay in my bed all day?" she asked, releasing the towel from her glorious body and quickly patting away the dampness from her skin.

Graham's focus was on the slight jiggle of her breasts and thighs as she moved. "So you kicking me out?" he asked. "Shee-it, I was 'bout to make me a sandwich."

Joy balled up the massive towel and fired it at him.

Graham caught it easily in one large hand.

"Listen, there are many things I'm open to doing, but taking care of a grown man is not one of them," she said, as she removed a pale peach bra-and-thong set from one of the drawers of her dresser.

"I took care of you all week, though," he said, briefly flipping back the sheet and looking pointedly down at his now lifeless and spent dick.

Joy quickly pulled on the lingerie and walked into her closet. "Sex don't pay the bills, Six-Nine," she called out.

Bills? She charging me for the drugs and sex now? The hell . . . ?

Frowning, Graham simultaneously wiped his face with his hands and elongated his frame, causing his feet to dangle off the edge of the queen-sized bed.

"Go to work," Joy said, leaving the closet and hanging the outfit she held on the ladies' valet by the framed full-length mirror leaning against the wall.

Using the well-developed muscles of his stomach, he sat up in the middle of the bed as he raked his fingers through his slender dreads. His broad shoulders were already feeling the fatigue of the weed and the nut...until the coke would kick in and give him new life. "Work ain't a part of my plan right about now," he admitted.

Joy paused in spraying her pulse points with the perfume he had come to love to smell on her skin. "I hope laying up in my apartment isn't either," she said before disappearing into the bathroom again.

"Fuck it, then." Graham kicked away the crisp cotton sheets entangled in his legs before shifting to sit on the edge. "It was fun while it lasted."

His dreads lightly swung back and forth across his chiseled cheeks as he stood and made his way across the hardwood floors to the bathroom. Her shower still had the room hot and steamy. It immediately clung to his nakedness and filled his nostrils. Joy was standing before the mirror above the pedestal sink, applying makeup she didn't need in a circled area she'd cleared on the mirror. She barely spared him a glance with eyes even more hooded by the effects of the weed.

"I got time to shower before you boot me out this bitch?" he asked, already walking past her in the spacious and stylish bathroom to turn on the jet spray.

She paused in lining her lid with a brown eye shadow to look at his reflection. "Are you mad about having to go to work?" she asked, her voice condescending.

Graham paused in his move to step inside the shower stall. "My ass was working when *you* scooped *me* up," he said. "Don't forget that."

"So what's all the drama about going back to that shit?" she asked with a rare use of profanity as she pressed one hand against the edge of the sink and the other against her hip as she faced him.

He ignored her and stepped under the spray, avoiding wetting his dreads as he soaped the contours of his body so vigorously that his elbow kept jabbing into the slate-tiled wall. He ignored that as well.

His anger at feeling discarded like food that had spoiled rose in him with more heat and intensity than the spray of water against his form. *Man, to hell with this.*

He leaned his upper body out to eye her. "Look Miss High and Mighty, you should've let me know you just rent a dick for a week," he said, hating that even in the midst of his anger, he felt drawn in by her exotic beauty. He wanted nothing more than to grab her face and kiss every bit of the gloss from her plump, heart-shaped mouth.

"Renting?" she said snidely, closing her makeup bag sharply and not sparing him a glance. "Humph. I'm not even renting this apartment. I don't rent, I own."

Fueled by the weed, the coke, and his fiery emotions, Graham stepped out of the shower. He had to correct his large body as he slipped and slid across the floor until he stood towering over her petite frame by nearly two entire feet. He grabbed her wrist to stop her retreat.

Joy looked down at his hand and then up to lock her glazed-over eyes on him. "Release me, Six-Nine," she ordered in a quiet voice that contradicted the strength underlying it. "Release me. Wash your ass. Go to work. I will see you when I get home."

Both his stance and his grip on her wrist relaxed. "Home?" he asked, his eyes filled with perplexity.

She freed herself from his loosened grasp before she left the bathroom. She returned almost as quickly holding a key and another glass vial in her hand. Joy handed him the key and opened the vial just long enough to tap a small amount of the powder on the back of her hand to snort before capping it.

His brows dipped in surprise. He knew she laced her weed with it. He didn't know she snorted.

"Fabulous pick-me-up," she said, pressing it into his hand as well before licking any residue from the back of her hand. "It'll get you through the day."

As she walked back out of the bathroom, Graham looked

down at the key and cocaine—both were new additions to his life. He closed the lid of the commode and sat both things atop it before climbing back in the shower. Even as he washed, and through the steam swirling around him, his eyes kept shifting to the top of the commode. He slowly began to recognize a desire for both. A want. A hunger.

Rinsing away the suds, he turned off the shower and didn't even bother with a towel as he stepped out, nude and wet, onto the heated tile floor to pick up the vial. *Smoking it. Snorting it. What's the difference?*

Mimicking what he'd seen Joy do, Graham took his first sniff of cocaine.

Chapter 8

Joy

Six Months Later

"You a'ight, dude?"

Graham looked up over his shoulder. Pogo stood beside where he sat on one of the battered sofas of their break room. He saw the older man's face fill with concern.

He dropped his head and looked away. "I'm a'ight. Just got a cold," he lied as he felt his nose run. He sniffed and swiped at it with the back of his hand.

When the older man didn't move, Graham looked up at him in question.

Pogo walked over to the door but he did not walk through it. Instead, he closed it and came over to sit down on the sofa next to Graham. "Let me talk to you, son," he said, reaching over to pat his fist against Graham's knee.

Graham laughed. "Yo, Pogo. I don't get down like that," he joked, hoping to lighten the mood because he could already see the serious light in the other man's eyes.

"I've seen and done a lot in my sixty-five years," he said with a sad smile. "A lot of shit I wish hindsight could change."

Graham sniffed again and swallowed, fighting the urge to

wipe his runny nose again. Fighting even harder to fight his crave to sniff the bag of powder hidden in his sock...again.

"I can already see that it's getting to you, boy," Pogo said. "I can see it all in your eyes and in the way you act 'round here. That shit ain't nothing to play with. Trust me. If you need help, I know a place. I'm *still* tryin' to recover from twenty years of chasing that shit."

Graham rose to his feet. "What shit?" he asked, playing crazy but far from it.

Pogo rose to his feet with effort and walked past Graham to the door. He opened it but paused in the doorway. "Get off that shit, boy," he said, locking eyes that were graying with age on him.

Laughing nervously, Graham walked over to the door leading into the bathroom that was nothing more than dingy walls with an even dingier toilet and sink. "Nah, you better get off that shit, Pogo, if you think I'm messing with drugs," he said, his heart already pounding in anticipation at the thought of getting to the package in his sock.

He closed the door and the stench of urine flooded his nostrils. Graham didn't care. Relieving his bladder was the furthest thing from his mind. Bending down he used his forefinger to pull the small baggie up the length of his ankle and free from his sock beneath his blue uniform pants. He barely took the time to stand up fully before he dug his pinkie nail inside the bag of coke and sniffed it with one nostril and then the other.

The bathroom door jerked open and Graham whirled to find Pogo standing in the doorway. "Damn. What the fuck is wrong with you?" he snapped, turning his back on his coworker and coming face-to-face with his reflection in the fading mirror. In one millisecond, he took in his red and tired eyes and the cocaine residue still around his nostrils.

His shame and anger came in a rush. Turning from the sink, he crossed the dingy floor in three long strides and grabbed the front of Pogo's uniform, lifting his slight figure into the air with ease until their eyes were leveled.

The fear Graham thought he would see in the old man's depths was not there, but sadness reigned. Sadness and pity.

The rage lining Graham's face softened as Pogo reached up to pat him as if he were a child. "This ain't even the worst of it," he said in a knowing voice. "That white bitch ain't nothing to love, boy."

Graham shook. He did love it. He loved it hard and fast. He'd gone from taking a hit once or twice a week to every day in just weeks, and in just a few more weeks he was snorting small amounts damn near all day.

Oh, he loved that white bitch so much. Moreover, he hated that Pogo had picked up on it. He hated that Pogo was minding his business and he hated that Pogo thought he wasn't in control.

His grip on Pogo's shirt tightened and he shook the man a little in frustration.

"What's going on here?"

Graham released Pogo to turn away from the sight of their boss, DiMarco, standing behind them. He swiped at the coke on his nose and heard Pogo fall to the floor and stumble against the door as he rose to his feet.

"Just a little misunderstanding, boss man," Pogo said. "We good."

Graham nodded and wiped at his nose again for good measure before turning to face them. "We was just playing around," he said, leveling his eyes on the silver-haired short and rotund man eyeing them through the smoke rising from the fiery tip of the cigar clenched between his yellow teeth.

DiMarco's eyes shifted to the floor and widened, and his unkempt, bushy brows plunged downward as he frowned. "I know you mofos not in here fighting over drugs," he roared, his Italian by way of Brooklyn accent thick and his voice booming as he pointed his cigar toward the floor.

Damn.

Graham knew without looking that he had dropped his bag when Pogo startled him.

"Both of you get your asses outta here," DiMarco said, pushing past both of them to scoop the bag up and then slam-dunked it into the commode with a splash. "And don't come back."

"Boss man, it's not even like that," Pogo tried to explain.

Graham looked on as DiMarco flushed the toilet. *All the powder gone to waste.*

"This my last time telling you two to get outta here," he said over his shoulder as he barreled through them again as he left the bathroom.

"Graham!" Pogo said sharply.

He looked away from the commode and swallowed down the panic he felt at the fifty dollars headed down to the sewer system. He forced himself to focus. "What?" he asked, his annoyance clear.

"What?" Pogo snapped in shock, his eyes fiery with his own emotions. "He just fired *us* over *your* shit."

Fired? The cocaine was starting to take effect and Graham wanted nothing more than to sit down and let it wash over him for the few moments before his adrenaline would shift and send him into overdrive.

"DiMarco," Graham called out before easing past Pogo to leave the bathroom and cross the break room to the short hall.

"DiMarco, let me holler at you," he said, stepping into an office dominated by a large-screen television and an even bigger desk that succeeded in making the portly man appear smaller in comparison.

"There ain't shit to talk about."

Graham didn't want to lose his job. He didn't know how he was going to explain it to Joy or his parents, who stayed riding his back anyway about his career choices. However, he knew he couldn't let Pogo go down with him.

"That was my shit and I yoked Pogo up for minding my business about it," he admitted, pushing his hands into his pockets as he looked down at his ex-boss.

DiMarco barely glanced up from the paperwork he was shuffling. "Then *you* get the fuck out," he said without hesitation. "I don't do druggies. You won't steal nothing around here to support your habit."

"You know I don't steal," Graham said.

DiMarco finally locked his coal-black eyes on him. "And I thought I knew you didn't do drugs," he said. "So don't show your face around here again."

Graham opened his mouth ready to release a dozen different comebacks:

"Man, go to hell with your onion-smelling ass . . ."

"Yo, DiMarco, who cares about this barely better than minimum-wage-paying job anyway . . ."

"Make me get out if you so damn tough . . ."

"Yo, your brother screwing the hell out of your no-good wife, probably right now . . ."

And many more, but he didn't say them. He swallowed back the retorts and just shrugged his broad shoulders as he walked out of the office. He took the opposite direction in the hall leading out of the building and into the crisp and chilly February air. He zipped up the winter coat he wore over his uniform and pulled out his skully to tug over his dreads as he moved wordlessly past the cars and his coworkers. He crossed the lot and kept on walking up the street even as he heard his name called. He never looked back. He never stopped.

Graham stood on the sidewalk outside his mother's house for twenty minutes. *What am I doing here?*

He licked his lips, feeling the coolness of them against the warmth of his tongue, dug his hands deep into the pockets of his black puffy jacket, and released a breath that was visible in the coldness. And still he found no comfort.

Graham had been out of work for a week, pretending to Joy that he was at work when, instead, he spent most of his days looking for a new job, at the gym, hanging out with his friends, or sneaking back into the apartment and leaving again before she usually got home from work. That had been his life for the last seven days, but this day—this Friday—the games and lies had come to a head. It was payday, and his routine of cashing his weekly paycheck and handing Joy the majority of it toward bills was undoable.

A cold wind whipped through the cul-de-sac and Graham shivered as it seemed to touch his bones. Still, it was nothing close to the freeze on Joy's shoulders when nothing went her way. Graham wanted nothing more than to avoid that. Not because he loved her—he cared for her, but not deeply. And not because he was afraid of her—she was half his size and her bark was far worse than her bite. Moreover, not because he was worried about not playing his role as the man of the house—he was only twenty-two.

Living with Joy was nothing but fun times. Plenty of sex. Plenty of coke. And plenty of freedom. They never argued. She was laid back and chill about everything. Her favorite answer to almost any question was "Whatever."

Who would want to ruin that?

All she asked for was help on the bills because she refused to take care of a grown man.

And that brought him to this moment standing outside his mother's house. *Shit.* Another woman he didn't want to disappoint.

Too late for that.

Graham stiffened his spine and took off up the steps before he lost his nerve and walked back to the train station. He was just about to ring the bell when the door opened and his mother filled the doorway dressed in a shirt and slacks and a sweater that was two times too big for her.

"I wondered how long you were going to stand out there," she said, all of her usual warmth missing as she turned to walk into the den.

As Graham shut the front door, he could smell the scent of his mother's perfume made stronger by the heating system warming the house. He paused and allowed the feeling of sadness that filled him. He hadn't seen his mother since he told her he was moving in with Joy. Not even for Thanksgiving or Christmas. Joy had surprised him with trips to the Poconos where they snorted enough coke to equal the snow outside their cabin.

"I'm waiting, Graham," his mother called out to him.

Shaking his head, he fought the urge to take a bump of the coke snuggled in his wallet and forged ahead into the den to find his mother sitting on the sofa with both her legs and her arms crossed.

Not a good sign.

"How you been, Ma?" he asked, taking off his coat and dropping down onto the sofa beside her. He leaned in to hug her and she leaned back to continue to eye him.

"What do you want, Graham?" she asked again, her voice stiff, her eyes shifting to take in every aspect of his face.

He fought the urge to wipe his nose or sniff as she continued to assess him like only a mother could. When she began to shake her head slowly and released a heavy breath, he felt his nerves go on alert. *What she see?*

"I wondered if you could let me hold something, Ma?" he asked, biting the bullet because he'd rather face a lengthy speech from his mother than go back to Joy's empty-handed.

"Where is *my* Graham?" she asked in a soft voice filled with an emotion that could be anger or pain.

He frowned in confusion and nervously laughed. "I'm right here, Ma. *You* a'ight?" he asked.

"I see you but I don't see my son...just whoever it is you have become," she said. "Because see, my son would never go weeks without calling and months without seeing me. Barely taking a moment out of your life—and not a second more— to call me on the holidays. Really, Graham?"

"Ma, I was out of town—"

"No, you out your ass *and* your damn mind," Cara snapped. "That's what the hell you're out of, son, especially if you're strolling in here treating me like a bank."

Graham shifted his tall frame to sit on the edge of the sofa as he dropped his face into his hands. "Ma—"

"Let me hold something?" she said in a mocking voice.

Damn. Graham flopped back against the sofa.

"I'll let you *hold* a belt before I take it back and whup your big grown ass," she snapped. "I'll let you *hold* the Bible before I pray you find your mind that you lost."

He bit the inside of his mouth to keep from responding as he looked at his mother. *Just sit, take it, and get the money when she done.* He knew his mother would not turn him down. He *knew* that.

"I called your father while you were out there trying to work up the nerve to come in. He's on the way," she said, rising to her sock-covered feet and pacing back and forth before the lit fireplace.

Aw man. Shit just got drawn-out. His parents hadn't joined together against him since he went to live with his father.

"Ma, I just lost my job and wanted to hold something 'til I get back on my feet," he admitted.

"And how many jobs have you lost over the years, Graham?" she asked, pausing in her pacing. "Correction: how many jobs have you taken to avoid using the smarts you have?"

Graham remained silent and stood up to walk into the kitchen to open the refrigerator. He sniffed and cleared his throat as he pulled a bottle of juice from the shelf.

"Why'd you lose this one?" she asked from behind him, sounding tired.

He closed his eyes as he drank the juice in large gulps. "The cold weather slowed up business," he lied, turning to face her and avoiding her eyes.

Ding-dong.

Cara pushed up off the door frame where she had been leaning to walk down the hall.

Graham grabbed a piece of paper towel to blow his nose. He scowled at the blood soaking the material. *The fuck?*

At the sound of his father's voice, Graham quickly jerked more paper towel from the roll by the sink and swiped at his nose as his heart pounded and raced erratically.

"We'll get to the bottom of it," he heard his father say just outside the kitchen entrance.

Graham turned and ran water on the paper towel and quickly wiped his nose again just before they entered the kitchen. Pushing the damp paper towel into his pocket, he turned to face them. "Hey, Pops," he said, taking in the small flecks of gray now lightening his father's closely shaven head.

Tylar sat a plastic Walgreens bag on the island. "Hey, stranger," he said, removing the navy trench he wore over a sweater and jeans.

His father had become a supervisor at the sanitation department, and his days of wearing uniforms and picking up trash on one of the trucks had been over for the last year. Tylar hadn't put as much effort into the success of his relationships. He was just shy of a year of his second divorce...and living with the woman that helped ruin his marriage.

Graham leaned back against the sink and crossed his arms over his chest as his father took his turn assessing him.

"What are you on?" Tylar asked, his face grim.

Graham's face filled with surprise for a few seconds before he forced himself to look unmoved.

"What are you on?" his father asked again.

"Man, Dad, what are you talking about?" Graham said.

"Your mother cleaned out your old room a few weeks ago and found weed hidden in one of your shoes," Tylar said, reaching in the bag to remove a box. "Since you weren't answering either of our calls, we're both glad you showed up."

Graham felt relief until he spotted that it was an at-home drug test. His heart set off faster than a greyhound let loose on a racetrack. *Boom-boom-boom-boom-boom-boom-boom-boom.*

Tylar pushed the box across the smooth top of the island toward his son. "What are you on?" he asked again with concentrated eyes.

"Y'all not piss-testing me," Graham said in reply, afraid that their search for weed would expose that his habits had advanced. "I just wanted to borrow money, not get treated like I'm on parole or some shit."

Tylar pointed his finger at his son. "Watch your mouth."

"It's bad enough you threw away your private school education and never went to college," Cara said softly. "But we never raised you to smoke weed. Is that why your motivation to do better—be better—is shot to hell?"

He looked from his mother to his father. Her eyes filled with sadness and his with anger. *They tripping off weed? Humph. They don't know the half.*

"I gotta go," Graham said, pushing off the counter and circling the island to walk past them out of the kitchen.

He heard their footsteps as they followed him.

"Don't call me until you're willing to prove to me you ain't some pothead, boy," his father said sternly.

Graham snatched up his jacket, just wanting to be free.

"Me either, Graham," his mother added.

He paused before the door to look at them over his shoulder.

"We love you and we're here for you," Cara said in the moment just before he walked out the door and closed it firmly.

Chapter 9

Joy

Three Months Later

As the water pulsed against the defined contours of his body, Graham stretched his arms above his head and deeply inhaled the steam rising out of the shower. Sometimes it felt like the only peace he got inside their apartment was his moments in the shower. It was inside the 36 inch by 42 inch tiled stall that Graham didn't have to deal...

With Joy's slick backhanded comments or stony silence.

With his parents' disappearance from his life...after his disappearance from theirs.

With having no job and no ends to tide him over until he found a job.

Graham rotated his head and squeezed his washcloth to free it of the water. He'd washed every possible spot on his body. Nevertheless, when he thought of Joy awaiting him outside the door, he grabbed the soap and started his shower over. He smoothed the soap over the thin and soft hairs covering his muscled chest and then his arms before he glided down to do the same to the deep grooves of his abdomen...the tight ebony curls surrounding the base of his thick and long dark chocolate shaft...and to his muscled thighs and square buttocks as well.

A draft suddenly blew across his nude suds-covered body and he whipped his head to find the bathroom door open and Joy's friend, Inzia, standing in the doorway boldly eyeing him.

Graham paused and made a face. "Excuse me?" he said with attitude.

Inzia eyed his dick with a bit of a smile curving one corner of her mouth before she glanced over her shoulder. "You're right, girl. He is hung like a horse," she said, giving him one last look before she backed out of the frame and closed the door.

Graham was still standing there with his eyes on the door that caused another rush of goose bumps across his body. *What the hell was that all about?*

Still covered with soap, he stepped out of the shower. He paused and puckered his brows at the sound of feminine laughter reaching him through the door.

"He's not bringing any cash to the table, the least he could do is fuck me well," Joy said.

"I know that's right," another woman said.

"So it's good?" another asked.

He didn't hear Joy's words but the giggles and laughter sounded off again and the echoing of slaps had to be high fives. Graham felt his entire body flush with embarrassment. Not only was Joy discussing his sex with her friends outside the bathroom where he showered, she belittled his worth to their household and sat by while her friend checked out his body.

He was a man, and most men would be flattered, but he felt small and unnecessary to her life. A sorry-ass burden.

It didn't help that he knew he made it his business to sex the hell out of Joy because he knew that was all he had to offer her at the moment and he wasn't ready to give up everything she provided him, including a ready and steady supply of cocaine.

Crossing the floor to step back into the shower, he finished rinsing off before stepping out. Still wet, still naked, and not caring, he opened the bathroom door and took a bold step into the bedroom. Joy and her friends were lounging on the bed with one of her antique mirrors in the center of them with cocaine already cut up and arranged into neat lines, waiting to be snorted with a rolled hundred-dollar bill.

Joy's eyes got wide while her two friends' mouths got even wider as he strolled right up to them with his dick swinging back and forth across the tops of his thighs. He bent over and picked up the rolled money to snort two lines—one for each nostril.

"Damn," one of them whispered under her breath.

Graham gave Joy a hard stare as he rose to his full height and then stroked the length of his dick. He smirked when her lids lowered over her eyes a bit and she licked her bottom lip.

"Y'all travel home safely now, ya hear," Joy said, rising to her knees on the bed as she began to pull the V-neck cashmere sweater over her head.

The friend Graham didn't know chuckled a bit as she rose to her feet and strolled out of the room without looking back. Inzia licked her finger and then dipped it into the coke before she rubbed it around the inside of her mouth and on her gums. "One for the road for those bad-ass kids I teach working my nerves *all* day today," she said, smacking her lips.

Joy stood up on the bed and walked to the edge in her stiletto heels to press her hands against Graham's shoulders as she leaned in to suck his lips into her mouth with a moan.

Graham jerked his head back even though his dick was already hard in his hand. Doing coke made Joy horny, and everything was doable for her—and to her. It was during one of their coke binges that Joy sweetly convinced him of the thrills of anal sex. Lionel and his violation had never come to mind as he enjoyed one of his best nuts ever. In the hot moment as he fell back on the bed with his dick slipping out of Joy's ass, he wished he'd taken Geneva up on her offer years before instead of beasting out on her.

"I hate to miss the show," Inzia said, picking up the tailored blazer of her pantsuit to slip on before she too left the room.

Joy flipped her waist-length blond tresses back from her face as she undid the front clasp of her bra and shimmied her pencil shirt and thong panties down over her hips. She lifted her arms high above her head and tilted her head back as she laughed softly. "So you don't want me," she said, her words slurring.

Graham continued to massage the thick tip of his dick as he took in her bald pussy and the matching heart-shaped tattoo covering each nipple. *Sexy as shit.*

Joy stumbled in her heels on the bed, her steps unsteady. "Whoops," she said, laughing as her ankle gave way beneath her and she fell down, her ass landing on the center of the coke-covered mirror. She flung her head back and laughed.

"You cut yourself?" he asked, releasing his dick long enough to reach out for her.

"It didn't break. See," she said, spreading her legs wide and leaning back to lift them up into the air. Cocaine clung to the backs of her thighs and her buttocks.

Graham dropped to his knees at the foot of the bed and pulled the mirror—with Joy's naked body still atop it—to the edge. "So you don't give a fuck about this dick, huh?" he asked her, tapping it against her inner thighs and then her clit.

"I'm just proud," she said, arching her back as she brought her legs up to place her ankles on his shoulders with the grace and strength of a well-trained ballerina.

He brought his hands up to grasp her legs.

"Keep your horny-ass friends from ogling my dick," Graham told her, his dreads now free of the band he had loosely placed around the ends before his shower. "I'm not a fucking stripper or some shit."

"You could be," she said, sitting up and reaching beyond her legs to wrap her slender fingers around his dick to stroke.

"Man, whatever, Joy, you heard me," Graham said, his words coming slower as the effects of the drug hit him as well. The cocaine made the sting of his earlier humiliation dull. In that moment he didn't care about too much of anything, and that's why Graham *loved* that white bitch. She made him feel good. She made him forget.

He turned his face to kiss each of her ankles before flinging her legs open with a jerk and grabbing a handful of her dyed hair to pull her head down until her heart-shaped lips hovered just above the tip of his dick. He didn't have to ask. Just a moment later Joy's tongue was flickering against the tip, causing his thighs to quiver and his ass to clench as he winced in pleasure. Hoover vacuums had nothing on her sucking velocity.

Fuck her.

It was obvious fucking her was all they really had.

"Oh shit, excuse us, y'all."

Graham's head jerked around so hard his dreads swung around his face like a cape. He frowned at the sight of both Inzia and the friend he didn't know standing in the doorway. "What the..."

Joy stopped sucking to lean to the left of his body to eye them. She giggled. "What, y'all?" she said without a care in the world with her hand still wrapped around his dick.

The friend he did not know whispered something to Inzia before she spoke, her eyes locked on Graham's body even as she addressed Joy. "We wanted to talk about that... proposition you made us earlier," she said, with a smile as she traced one finger down the length of her neck and to the top of her cleavage exposed by her prim-and-proper shirt.

"Right now?"

The quiet one nodded her head.

Joy gave his stomach a lick and his dick one final suck and

blow of air. "Let me see what they want," she whispered up to him before climbing off the bed.

Graham watched her walk over to them and his eyes took in the sight of the cocaine still on her ass and thighs. He shrugged and gently stroked his own dick to keep it hard. *Them chicks is wild.*

Cocaine was still on the mirror and he used his free hand to pick up the rolled bill and snort it up from wherever he saw on the mirror until nothing but residue of its former glory remained. Flinging his head back, he moaned in the back of his throat and sniffed as he pinched his nose and closed his eyes.

"Shit," he swore, using one strong arm to knock the mirror off the bed before he rose just enough to let his body drop onto the middle of it.

Lying on his back, he placed his forearm over his eyes.

"Shit, shit, shit," he said, smiling broadly before he chuckled. He loved it.

Graham heard the bedroom door open and close. "Come get this dick, Joy," he said. "Get. This. Dick."

The bed dipped under her slight weight as she climbed onto it between his sprawled legs. Her hand stroked him before she guided his hardness into a standing position. Graham's eyes jerked open and he lifted his forearm at the feel of a condom rolled down the length of his dick. His eyes widened at the sight of Inzia and the friend he didn't know both naked and sitting on the bed sandwiching his legs.

He couldn't lie—the sight of their nudity both shocked and pleased him, especially when the quiet one moved behind Inzia to fondle her nipples and ease her hand down her stomach to play in the hairs of her pussy before she slipped one finger inside.

In a drug daze now heightened by the sight of his biggest sexual fantasy becoming a reality, Graham looked past them, half-expecting to see Joy join the mix. "Joy," he called out.

The two women laughed.

"Trust me, she's good," one of them said.

They laughed some more.

The bedroom door opened and Joy poked her head in, her hair now up in a messy topknot. "Give 'em what they want because they are paying very well," she said, holding up an eight ball of cocaine. "No more lying around here for free."

Graham lifted his head from the bed and opened his mouth to curse her, but she solidly closed the door before he could. *Ain't this a bitch?*

His anger and indignation dissipated when Inzia straddled his legs as she stroked him. "I just had to test this dick out, Six-Nine," she told him, using Joy's nickname for him. "I *had* to."

"You did?" he asked thickly, bucking his hips as he brought his hands up to massage her full breasts and rub her hard nipples with his thumbs as she squatted and then eased down onto his hardness until she surrounded him tightly.

She hissed in pleasure.

The other woman knocked his hands away.

"I got that," she said, climbing onto the bed to straddle his thighs behind Inzia.

"Oh shit," he moaned, looking on as she wrapped her arms around Inzia from behind and hotly licked the length of her neck. She used one brown hand to massage her nipple while the other eased down her body to play with her clit as Inzia rode him like she was on the back of a mechanical bull.

Graham stuffed a pillow behind his head and sat back to enjoy both the ride and the show.

He and Joy had become strangers who lived in the same apartment. In the last few weeks, they hadn't even had sex. He didn't care if she was getting dicked down by someone else, and it was clear she didn't care since she sent a steady stream of her friends to the guest bedroom she'd moved him into. His days were a mix of sex, coke, and sleep, with barely time to eat or sometimes even wash in between.

Sitting up in the bed, he felt his head spin and he pressed his hand to it as he gingerly opened his eyes to keep the morning sun glaring through the windows from jarring him. But there was no sun. He pulled his legs up and propped his arms on his knees as he took in the darkness of night outside his window.

How many hours had passed?

Graham shook his head to clear it, but his orientation was screwed, especially when he finally noticed a curvy body in the bed beside him. He raised the sheet. She was white and as naked as he was. He looked down at her profile. He had no clue who she was or what exactly went down between them.

He looked around the room as he flung back the covers and climbed from the bed. A filled condom still clung around his limp dick and there was one more on the floor, obviously discarded.

The door opened and Joy walked in still dressed in her usual work garb, this time a fitted bright red dress that matched her lipstick and her nails. She slapped the wall to turn on the overhead light. Graham eyed her as she wordlessly strolled past him and began snatching up the woman's clothing.

He frowned. *So she cares now?*

Joy held the clothes in a ball under one arm and used her free hand to yank the pillow from under the sleeping woman's head roughly before lifting it and bringing it down onto her head sharply. "You paid for two hours, not the all-day special. Don't play with me, Chelsea," she snapped.

Graham chuckled sarcastically. *Oh. Now* that *sounds about right.*

As Chelsea turned over and sat up in bed, exposing her rosy pink nipples and small breasts, he opened the box on his dresser and used the small spoon inside to scoop and then sniff four hits of cocaine.

"Sorry, Joy, I just got caught up," Chelsea said, sounding like a Los Angeles valley girl.

He leaned against the dresser and watched in amusement as Joy jerked the woman out of the bed by her arm and shoved her clothes at her. He pinched his nose and sniffed as Chelsea surreptitiously glanced at his naked body while she was hustled out the door.

"Can I call you?" she mouthed.

Joy paused and whipped her around. "No, you call me. Clear?" she asked, before turning her back around and guiding her out the door.

Still shaking his head, Graham turned and eyed his reflection in the mirror over the eight-drawer dresser. His normally high cheekbones were more pronounced and his reddened eyes sunken. His caramel complexion had a shine to it and his teeth felt gritty from not being brushed that day. His two- to three-day coke binges and sexing Joy's tricks was catching up with him.

At the sound of her heels against the floor, he looked over his shoulder just as she stepped back into the room. "You need to air this room out, Pleasure," she snapped, crossing the room to fling the windows open wide.

His eyes cut her. "Don't call me that," he said in a cold, hard voice that only hinted at his anger at her...and himself.

Joy turned on her stiletto heels. "Why?" she asked, her eyes clear and sharp. She wasn't high at all. He knew the signs of her inebriety.

"That's the name you whore me out with," he said in clipped tones. "That's for the clients, not my pimp."

Joy pouted mockingly. "Awww, is Graham's feelings hurt?" she asked in a baby tone as she walked over to him slowly.

He hated that he missed her sex. He wanted her. He was addicted to her. And she denied him. She denied them both.

She reached in her bra and pulled out folded cash. "Here's your cut...so get over it, Plea-sure," she said derisively, pressing the cash against his chest.

Graham grabbed her upper arms and jerked her body up against his as he lifted her from her heels easily. "So you don't want this dick?" he asked her, shifting one hand down to stroke her ass in her skirt.

Joy smirked. "I used to...but not anymore," she told him.

"So I'm just your whore?" he asked her.

"We both get what we want...right?" she asked, deliberately looking down at his open box.

Graham picked her up a bit higher and then easily tossed her onto the middle of the bed.

Ding-dong.

She took her time getting up off the bed. "That's your next trick," she said, smoothing her skirt. "You *might* want to flush that condom and wash first."

And with that she left the room.

Graham grabbed a T-shirt and pulled it down the length of his dick to remove the condom and clean his seed from his tool. He turned and lifted his spoon to hit the powder twice more just as Inzia strolled into the room wearing just a short pink raincoat. "Where's Yani?" he asked, speaking of Inzia's lover.

Usually it was the two of them who required his services.

Inzia tilted her head to the side and undid the belt before shrugging the coat from her body. "We don't need her," she said, before walking up to him in gold heels. "Hell, you can suck my titties, right?"

Graham shrugged. He didn't care. His feelings still stung from Joy's treatment of him. Squinting his deep-set eyes as he looked at Joy's friend, he decided to give her what he didn't give any other of his tricks. Somewhere in his brain the coke made him think Joy would care. He watched as she pulled a thin vial of coke from the side of her shoe and then moved across the cluttered room to lie back on the bed. His eyes took in the softness of her curves and he felt his dick stir.

Inzia unscrewed the cap and tapped out a thin line of coke

from the mound of her pussy and all the way up to the valley of her breasts, then she sucked her finger with a hot lick of her lips. Graham eyed her spreading her lips and patting her clit as he came across the room while unrolling a condom on his dick. He bent over to alternate with licks and sniffs until the line of coke was gone.

Throwing his head back, he roared a little and grunted before pinching his nose and shaking his head at the rush of adrenaline. "Shit," he swore, stumbling back a few steps as his body rocked back and forth.

Inzia flipped over on the bed, getting on her knees and reaching behind her to guide his dick into her as she backed up until he was deep inside her. She dropped her head and patted her hand against the bed as she adjusted to the feel of him pressing against her walls.

Graham looked down at her ass splayed before him as she worked her hips to pull downward on his stiffness with the quickness of a jackhammer. "Damn, Inzia," he said, laughing as he continued to rub his nose and struggle to remain on his feet.

He felt a dizzy brain freeze. He felt his nose run. He swiped at it; his eyes widened at the sight of blood. His heart pounded furiously and he felt flushed with heat.

"Yo, Inzia," he said, stumbling back and causing his dick to leave her with a loud suctioning noise. Graham's heart was pounding so loudly he couldn't hear anything else. His pulse was racing, and a tightening in his chest was increasing in intensity.

"Graham . . . Graham . . . you all right?" Inzia asked, coming over to him. "Joy! Joy. Come here. Hurry!"

That was the last thing he heard before he stumbled back against the dresser and then fell face forward onto the floor just before everything went black.

Interlude

Present Day

How long has it been?

He wondered that for the hundredth time as he lay on his side on the floor, his body still strapped to the chair and the cold floor chilling his naked body. Minutes? Hours?

He didn't know.

Click-click-click-click-click-click.

His eyes shifted everywhere they could at the sound of her heels against the floor.

Earlier she had pressed a kiss to his forehead in a decidedly reverse move from her antagonism when she'd first knocked him to the floor. After that she had wandered off somewhere in his apartment, leaving him in a silence that was both chilling and welcoming. Still, he knew she had not gone very far. He knew she was anything but done with him.

Click-click-click-click-click-click.

Could his tormenter be Joy, the woman he found the strength to leave after his overdose that night? After waking up in a hospital and being warned that he had a mild stroke from the accidental overdose, he called Pogo to help get him into a ninety-day rehabilitation program. Graham had never returned to Joy.

Was she back in his life and out for revenge for something she considered unfinished?

The not knowing was the worst, because at least if he knew the face behind the ski mask, he could get a good grasp on just what she was or was not capable of.

Click...click...click...

Black booties with at least a three-inch heel appeared in his line of vision. He steadied his body, readying himself for whatever. He was surprised when she disappeared around his back and he felt her struggling to turn the chair upright with his body still weighing it down. "If you loosen my ties I can get up by myself," he said, his body jerking with every one of her unsuccessful tries to lift him.

She said nothing to him and instead grunted as she hoisted the chair up by its back and then stepped on the side of it to push it up slowly until it rocked back and forth.

He winced as the ties cut against his already sore flesh.

She laughed mockingly. "You thought I was dumb enough to fall for that, Pleasure?" she asked, playfully nudging his head to the side before she came back around him and straddled his legs.

He winced as she pressed her buttocks against the still-tender spot on his thigh. She leaned forward, wrapped her arms around his neck, and pressed her upper body against his chest with a long, languid moan. "Don't I smell divine?" she whispered against his ear before grabbing a handful of his dreads and roughly turning his head to press his face against her neck.

He quickly contemplated biting her but she moved from his lap just as swiftly leaving behind nothing but her scent. He inhaled deeply. It was familiar. Very familiar. It filled him with wanting.

"I found it in your bedroom," his captor said, leaning against the back of the gutted couch as she eyed him. "I guess it belongs to the bitch in all the pictures around here," she said, her voice chilling over with every word. "Having her mug on your nightstand is very cute. I guess she's special, huh?"

Very, he thought.

"Well, fuck her. She don't have shit on me," she said.

"I can't tell," he said, working his head back and forth to relieve the tension in his neck. "Show me your face."

"Shut up," she snapped. "Trust me, when the time comes you will know exactly who I am and you will never forget it."

Chapter 10

Quinn

2005

One hundred and eighty days clean.

He felt good. Damn good.

Graham pulled his charcoal sketching pencil from behind his ear and drew a circle around the date on the calendar hanging on the door of his double-sided fridge. Sticking the pencil back behind his ear, he turned and eyed his studio apartment. Fully furnished. The smell of paint and newness still clung to the air. His first place to call all his own. *Not bad for twenty-three.*

A new start. A do-over.

I needed a do-over.

He was far from perfect, but he was ready and willing to do better.

Graham had his parents to thank for the apartment but he gave credit to no one but himself—not even Pogo—for his freedom from the devil he knew to be cocaine. During his relationship with Joy, he had cultivated an addiction far larger than some people took years to habituate. It would take many years for the urges to get high to leave him, but his will to stay sober was now much stronger.

He was one hundred and eighty days clean, and ninety days free from his in-patient rehab program. The withdrawals had not been easy physically or psychologically, but he'd made it through to the other side and was proud of the scars he wore during the battle.

The truth was things could have gotten worse, even more so than death. There was hardly anything worse to him than an existence fueled by drugs. Nothing.

Bare-chested with only black track pants on, Graham crossed the short distance to the weight bench and weight stand in the corner. He grabbed two of the twenty-pound free weights before sitting on the bench and doing arm lifts upward and then outward. Each movement caused his well-defined muscles to flex and soon a fine sheet of sweat coated his upper body. With a grunt he leaned forward and switched to triceps curls.

In rehab—and off his diet of cocaine —Graham's frame had bulked up twenty-five pounds. He had worked hard to lift weights and run to make sure it all went to the right places—which was anyplace but his rock-hard stomach. The weight suited him well and now he looked more like a professional basketball star than a tall, awkward, and gangly child.

Finishing his arm and chest work, he placed the weights on the stand and stretched his arms, causing the muscles of the wide breadth of his shoulders to tense. He crossed the hardwood floor again as he removed the band holding his dreads back from his face. They now swung below his shoulders. The feel of the tips grazing against his skin caused a rush of goose bumps and it almost reminded him of the touch of a woman—something he hadn't felt in weeks.

He wasn't interested in the hassles of a relationship—his

track record wasn't the best—and his sobriety outweighed pussy any day. Still, it didn't stop his dick from getting hard anytime the wind caressed it.

Graham stood beside his easel set up in the corner of the living room/sleeping space. Its position by one of the many windows lining the third-floor apartment gave him plenty of light and a good view of the park across the street. He took his seat and reached for his pencil again as he opened his sketchbook and eyed his rendition of the park's trees surrounding the tennis court and an ornate water fountain.

In rehab, he had rediscovered his love of drawing from when he was a child. At first it had been a good way to pass the hours, but soon he realized that he loved the challenge of taking something real and recreating its image on paper. Seeing his artwork form at his fingertips gave him an entirely new type of high. That he wanted. Needed.

Sliding his earphones over his bulky dreads, Graham filled his ears with Usher's "Burn" as he sat on his chair and got lost in his art, only sparing moments to glance out the window at his subject. There he remained sketching, correcting, and sketching again until he checked the clock on his cable box. Allowing himself a few more strokes of the charcoal to try to replicate the shadow created on the ground by the overhead leaves, Graham finally sat back and flexed his shoulders as he opened and closed his hand to ease the cramping from his grip on the pencil.

Closing the sketch pad and sliding it into his black leather carrying case, he rose. The case had been a gift from his mother, and the sight of his full name engraved upon it always made him smile. He could not ask for any more support and love from his parents as he tackled his sobriety.

Setting the case by the door, he picked up his Nike duffel bag from the sofa and jerked on his sleeveless black tank tee that showed off the new African warrior tattoo Lola did. The circular ink took up every inch of his broad shoulder, and it was Graham's personal declaration of his strength in fighting off his addictions—to drugs and to Joy.

Hitching the strap of the duffel bag over his head and across his body, Graham lifted his thin dreads. He grabbed his keys, cell phone, and carrying case before leaving his apartment and opting to take the stairs down the three levels to the ground floor.

As he stepped out in the well-manicured parking lot and surrounding grounds, Graham paused long enough to take in the silence. He was grateful for the quiet and the peace of Tarrytown, New York. It was just seventeen miles from his mother in Bedford Hills and twenty-five miles from his father's new digs in Manhattan—a happy medium between the two who were understandably concerned ever since he had called them from rehab and invited them up for a family day visit. They were paying his rent until he found a job. Tarrytown was a compromise among the three of them.

After everything he'd put them through, where he lived was the least of his concessions. Finding a job to pay his rent was another. They'd given him ninety days, and it was almost up. But he had a plan.

"Okay, let's see what you got, kid."

Graham stood, his hands on his hips, at center stage of the dimly lit club in nothing but a white pair of bikinis that barely kept his dick covered properly. He looked on as she motioned her finger in the air. Soon the sound of Maxwell's falsetto singing "This Woman's Work" filled the air.

Graham frowned. "Can I get something by a woman? I can't see grinding while some dude's singing," he balked, reaching up to lift his dreads from his neck as he eyed Vera, the thin, elderly black woman the bouncer told him was the owner of Club Trick.

She motioned with her spindly finger again and the music faded away. "Listen, the dancer's main motivation is to entertain women," she began, lighting a cigarette that was almost as long and thin as one of her fingers.

Graham shifted back and forth in his spot on the stage.

"If the combination of Maxwell hitting a high note singing the praises of women while you sling that twelve-inch dick around gets the money made...then you get the money made," she said, her raspy voice indicating her lungs were probably as dark as her lips from the cigarettes she had been chain-smoking since he first arrived.

She could have easily been Joy forty years ago.

He felt some unease that he was essentially selling his body again, but he pushed it aside because he planned to dance for the dollars and nothing else. Women were drawn to him, that he knew. It seemed like the perfect job to make good money and still have time to pursue his other interests.

When Graham offered no further resistance, Vera raised her hand again and the music returned. She rose from one of the swivel seats at the base of the platform and circled the stage to eye him closely as he performed.

Graham danced to the music, being sure to do plenty of snakelike motions that ended with him thrusting his hips forward to make his dick rise and fall. He stumbled once as he grabbed the chair and stood behind it while he imitated making love to a woman and he bit his bottom lip.

The music faded away again and he opened his eyes to find Ms. Vera's thin figure back in her seat, legs crossed with her foot swinging as if she was bored and would rather be anywhere else.

"You got the looks and the body to be a real moneymaker—believe me, I know," she said, flicking her cigarettes repeatedly in her hand.

Graham smiled.

"But your performance and those crazy expressions

you're making will dry up the juices of any twat you get wet with your looks," she told him, shaking her head as if he was just pitiful.

Graham's smile faltered.

·   "What's your stage name?" she asked, still eyeing him like a stud up for auction.

"Pleasure," he said instantly.

Vera nodded in approval. "You're certainly equipped for it," she said before releasing a round of laughter that was a mix of throaty cackles and dry wheezes.

Graham had no qualms about using the same name Joy used for him when he whored. His dick carried the miles, and it was up to him if he wanted to reclaim the name. He did. Joy took enough away from him, and the rest he gave to her with too much ease—the name he was keeping for himself.

"Work on your show and come back in a week at noon," Vera said, standing and picking up her lighter with the same hand in which she held her beloved cigarettes. "You're working the early-afternoon shift until you get your shit together."

Graham nodded as he jumped down off the stage and snatched up his clothes to dress before easing the strap of his duffel back over his head and then across his chest. With one last look at the three connecting circular stages, he moved past the zigzag arrangement of the seats and table to walk by the security booth, through the rear metal door, and out of the nondescript building.

"So let me get this straight."

Graham scratched his smooth caramel cheek as he eyed both Lola and Kezia sitting on his pull-out couch and trying hard not to laugh as they watched him. He focused his eyes on Kezia, her hair still in a near-bald Caesar cut, with large hoop earrings and no makeup to distract from her features. "So old Ms. Vera told you that your performance was bad enough to dry up a wet pussy?" she asked, her voice incredulous.

Graham rubbed his neck. "I called you two to help me out," he reminded them.

"Sounds like you need it," Lola said, her hand caressing the back of her lover's head as they continued to eye him.

"Why us?" Kezia asked.

"I can't fuck y'all," Graham said bluntly with a one-shoulder shrug. "Y'all made that clear—"

"Good," Lola said encouragingly.

"Trust me, I had my dream *ménage à trois*, I'm good," he said.

They both looked at each other in surprise before looking back at him seconds before the questions flew like gunfire.

"You did?"

"With who?"

"When?"

"How was it?"

"Did you finally learn to eat pussy?"

Graham made a face. "Y'all bugging," he said, walking into the kitchen area to grab a bottle of water from the fridge. He rolled his chair from over by the easel to in front of the sofa. "And I'm never ever eating out a chick."

"Your loss," Kezia said, her eyes dipping down to Lola's crotch in the low-slung jeans she wore with neon green heels.

"Right," Lola agreed in her husky voice as she continued to stroke the back of Kezia's head.

"Yo, I'm willing to watch if you want to teach me," he said, feeling left out as they continued to stare at each other.

Kezia unrolled her tongue and moved the tip quicker than that of a snake as she continued to eye her girl.

"Damn!" Graham exclaimed as his gut felt like it took a gut punch. *That would be hell on a dick too.*

Lola leaned forward and touched the tip of her tongue to Kezia's with a soft moan.

"Man, don't start that shit," he said, feeling his dick stir. "Last time my dick got wet and I wasn't in the shower was when the water in the toilet splashed up."

Lola and Kezia laughed.

"So y'all gone help me or not?" he asked. "Because I don't care how whack I look to y'all since there is no potential of pussy."

"None," Kezia stressed.

Lola cleared her throat lightly and gave Kezia a meaningful look with a pat of her thigh. Kezia stood up in her Polo tee and jeans to cross the floor into the kitchen.

Graham scowled a little.

"I have a question," Lola said, sitting with her face in her hand as she settled her serious green eyes on him in concern. "You sure a strip club is the best place for you to be and you trying to stay clean?"

He rolled forward in the chair to reach out and playfully pat her chin with a dimpled smile. "I'm good," he assured her, ever amazed that his infatuation with her and Kezia had gone from wanting to join them in a threesome to the two women becoming his closest friends.

"I saw you while you were on that shit, Graham," she said, stroking one of her waist-length blond-tinted dreads. "I don't want to see you back there."

Graham glanced away, embarrassed by his addiction, but he looked back at her, proud of his recovery. "I'm clean," he insisted.

She nodded. "I know," she assured him. "And I want you *stay* clean."

"I do too. Trust me."

"You went so hard, so fast," Lola said. "I tried to outrace my past by popping pills but...all I did was make everything worse."

Graham's gut clenched and he eyed her with a hard stare. "I didn't know that."

"Not a lot of people do," she admitted. "I've seen and been through a lot. I wanted to hurt motherfuckers that hurt me, but I just ended up hurting myself."

Her eyes saddened as she released a heavy breath. He looked past her for a second to see Kezia looking over at her in concern.

"The only advice I can give you is to not let anything—in the past, present, or future—push you where you're looking for some kind of alternate-reality-type shit again, you know?"

Lionel. Graham knew he was still running from that experience.

Lola was not much older than him, but sometimes she dropped little tidbits of knowledge as if she had lived for a hundred years. He remembered he'd asked her once why she seemed to know so much. Her answer came back to him clearly. Graham had never forgotten it. "Troubled times always have a way of aging a soul," he said.

Her green eyes opened a bit in surprise. "Right," she said in agreement.

Kezia came back over to them and stooped down to her backpack to pull out DVD cases. "You ever been to a male strip show?" she asked.

"Hell no," Graham balked with a deep glower.

"I think the first thing you gotta do is look at the competition," she said. "I brought a couple DVDs from shows I went to."

Lola rolled her eyes at his expression. "You want our help or nah?"

Graham eyed them and then the television. "A'ight," he said begrudgingly.

Kezia loaded the first disc into the DVD player and used the remote to turn it on. Graham's eyes widened at the sight of a male stripper upside down on a chair as he worked his entire body in a slow-motion body roll that was a smooth, seamless move.

Lola sucked air between her teeth and stood up to easily flip her body until she stood on her head with her feet pressed to the wall by the door to replicate the same move before she paused mid–body roll and looked at him. "Trust me, we got you," she assured him.

He believed it.

Graham sat on the bench outside the community college and kept checking the time on his cell phone. He had just a few more minutes before class started, and he didn't want to be late. Leaning forward a bit, he looked up and down the street to see if she—Quinn—was approaching. He felt disappointed that she wasn't.

Wanting to perfect his sketching abilities, Graham had signed up for a month-long free art class offered at the college. Just a few days later, a brown-skinned cutie joined the class as well. She had the looks and body that would normally set the dog in him on the loose, but what drew him was her smile as she slid into the seat before the easel next to his. All during class, she had asked for his help with her sketching and leaned over to squeeze or pat his hand whenever they shared a joke. After class, she introduced herself, and he felt himself drawn to her warmth and affability. He liked that they shared a love of art—although she wasn't very good at it yet.

It had become their habit to meet outside the campus and walk together to the building for their three-times-a-week class.

Graham didn't quite realize how much he looked forward to the one-minute stroll until that night. Taking one last look, he finally rose and walked through the gate alone with his carrying case lightly bumping against his leg. He was surprised at his desire to look back to see if maybe she was running to catch up with him. He was disappointed that she was not.

In the days after getting out of rehab, Graham had pushed so many people from his past out of his life. He missed Marco and all of his crazy Brooklyn tales, but Graham understood that he had to get himself together and focus on that. Most days he was either with his parents or alone in his apartment working out or sketching. He only saw Kezia and Lola on rare occasions, and he hated playing third wheel to their love. He was not looking for another relationship, and most women eyed him with hunger, so he dreaded any conversation.

Entering the building and jogging up the stairs with ease, Graham tried to push away his disappointment that Quinn was missing class. He turned the corner and entered the small room through the open door. His large steps faltered at the sight of her already positioned at her easel.

Theirs was a class of about twelve with an eccentric male art teacher who always wore brightly colored caftans that made his bald head all the more shiny, but Graham's eyes zoomed in on Quinn just as she looked over her shoulder at him. He loved that her heart-shaped face lit up at the sight of him as she raised her hand and waved.

Quinn was pretty. She had a head full of reddish-brown curls and a smooth caramel complexion. Her brows were perfectly shaped and her face was always done with makeup.

Graham walked over to his easel. "I was waiting for you outside," he said as he unzipped his case and removed his supplies.

"I was early and thought I missed you, and once I got to class I was too lazy to walk back," she said in a whisper as their professor began the class.

Graham glanced over at her sketch of what was supposed to be the beginning strokes of a dog's head. He frowned. *What the hell is that?*

He bit back a smile.

She leaned in toward him. "You want to get something to eat after class?" she asked, glancing over at him.

Graham felt uneasy. "Quinn, I'm not in the market for a girlfriend or nothing like that," he said.

Quinn paused in sharpening her pencil before she looked over at him with an arched brow. "Big ego, huh?" she asked, her voice teasing. "I just wanted a burger, not your heart... *or* your dick."

He didn't even know his body was tensed until he felt himself relax. "My bad," he said with a smile.

As she turned her face to look toward the front of the class, he studied her pretty profile. He couldn't tell if she was in her twenties like him or her early thirties but he liked her high cheekbones, her small pug nose, and the smile always in her bright eyes. She reminded him of a more dressed-up version of Geneva—especially her disposition.

She shrugged. "The burger? Or nah?"

"Cool," he said, trying to find comfort on the small seat for his large frame.

It felt good to have a friend.

Chapter 11

Quinn

Three Months Later

"You're a stripper?"

Graham looked up from the female form he was sketching on his pad as he sat on his couch to find Quinn staring down at his box of business cards sitting on the countertop. She held one in her hand.

"Huh?" he asked, dropping his head and sketching away.

"Really, Graham?" she asked, her husky voice tinged with annoyance. "Plea-*sure*?"

He looked up just as she came to stand behind his brown suede sofa. "What?" he asked innocently.

"Pleasure Principles," she read with her eyebrow arched. "For all your erotic needs."

He just smiled.

She squinted her bright, wide-set eyes as she tapped the card against her dimpled chin. "All on or all off?" she asked.

Graham laughed and shook his head as he shrugged.

"Bad boy," she teased as she dropped the card atop his sketch.

"Working boy," he emphasized, looking down at the

photo of himself greased up and in nothing but a strappy leather contraption that showed off his long dick as he advertised his contact info for private parties.

"Mmm-hmm," she said in sarcastic disbelief.

In the last three months his popularity at the club had surged as his performances improved. Vera had a few of her "superstar" dancers do revues through the state, and she had recently asked him to join the show. When the ladies inquired about him performing at bachelorette parties like other dancers, Graham had followed the lead of his counterparts and had business cards, flyers, and a website done. Pleasure the stripper, built to please, was in business.

Quinn sat on the back of the sofa and turned to slide down onto the seat in her jeans and turtleneck. "Don't fall in love with all your tricks," she said, picking up her own sketchbook.

Graham dropped his pencil to open and close his hand a few times to work out the kinks. "It's me they better not fall in love with," he said confidently.

"Don't let a big head"—she eyed his crotch—"make your other head big," she finished, looking pointedly at his face.

"How you know if it's big?" he asked.

"It's pretty hard to miss in them pants you love so much," Quinn said, pointing her pencil toward the outline of his dick.

Graham looked down at it and then raised off the sofa long enough to readjust himself. "Better?" he asked in his deep voice.

"Um, have you paid attention to your business cards? Your schlong is looking like a long exclamation point," she said.

Graham tapped his pencil against the sketch. "Schlong?"

Quinn laughed. "Schlemiel. Schlimazel? Hell, I don't know," she said, her husky voice filled with exasperated humor.

"How old are you?" he asked.

Quinn looked offended as she reached over to remove the clip holding her eraser to the sketchpad. "Nosy much?"

"Yes," he admitted.

"I'm not twenty-five...but not quite thirty," she admitted. "And I look good."

"You straight," he admitted, rising from the sofa to set his pad on the easel. "As a matter of fact, I'm going to hook you up with somebody."

"Right now, you're rolling with strippers, so I'll pass," she said, rising a bit to slide her feet beneath her rounded bottom. "I'm not into body oils *or* body rolls."

And that's why Graham adored Quinn. All of his gut instincts about her being the close friend he needed were on point. She was funny, smart, and a great listener. After the art class ended, they'd stayed in touch and even attended art shows together at local galleries.

"See, ask and you shall receive—"

"Knock and the doors shall be open unto you," she said, finishing the Bible verse with ease.

"Church girl, huh?" he asked.

"I used to be," she said, tapping her pencil against her sketchpad as she stretched out her feet and crossed her ankles in the leather booties she wore. "I need to go back. I have nothing but good memories. Matter of fact, we should go togeth—"

"I'll pass," he said, rising to his feet.

"Why?"

Graham felt that familiar sense of annoyance whenever anyone pressed about attending church. "Be right back," he said, standing up to pull his cell phone from his pocket before he stepped over her legs and left the apartment, pretending to dial a number.

As soon as the door closed behind him, Graham slid his phone back into his pocket and walked down the length of the hall to a window overlooking the parking lot. He didn't have a call to make, he just wanted to break Quinn's train of thought to completely avoid the church discussion. More advice from his father on how to sidetrack a woman.

He looked over his shoulder as the door to the stairwell opened. One of his neighbors stepped in the hall and gave him a long look before she waved and turned to walk down to her apartment.

His eyes dipped to take in the back-and-forth movement of her hips and the jiggle of her ass in the leggings she wore with heels and fitted long-sleeved tee. She gave him another long look before she unlocked her door and entered. His dick stirred to life as he pictured following her inside and pulling her leggings down as he bent her over the back of her couch.

"Shit," he swore, jumping up and down in place to fight back his urge.

Sexing a woman who lived so close was not a good idea when all he was looking for was one-night stands and sex with no ties.

Anxious to get back to his sketching to occupy his mind, Graham headed back to his apartment. As he stepped inside, he spotted Quinn slip a pill in her mouth before washing it down with a glass of water.

"Cramps," she explained with a rub of her flat stomach when she noticed his eyes on her.

Graham frowned deeply and he joined her in the kitchenette as she quickly washed and rinsed her glass before setting it in the dish rack. "TMI," he advised her.

"Deal with it," she said, playfully nudging his side with her shoulder.

"How's everything going?"

Graham turned from looking at his calendar on the door of the fridge. Quinn was looking up at him in concern. He nodded. "Real good," he said truthfully, knowing she spoke of his addiction.

She lifted one of his strong arms to wrap around her shoulders as she held him around his waist and hugged him close. "Here's to three hundred and sixty days," she said..

Graham nodded. "Three hundred and sixty days," he repeated, swallowing back his emotions. "No relapses."

"Of course not," she said with confidence in him.

Graham smiled a little as he hugged her close and bent down to press a kiss to the top of her head.

"Ladies, give it up for the one...and the only...Plea-suuuuuure."

He hit play on the CD player and opened the bathroom door of the hotel room wide before stepping inside the doorway with his hands on his narrow hips just as "So Anxious" by Ginuwine began to play.

The twenty or so college girls gathered in the junior suite all broke out in oohs and aahs as they took in his body in the pair of shiny skintight breakaway pants of gold that clung to the length of his semi-hard dick. The scented oil he wore emphasized the hard-earned definition of his muscles and made his tattoos gleam against his caramel skin.

He stepped out of the bathroom and worked his entire body in a series of sensual body rolls with each step that brought him deep into the middle of their circle of chairs. He kept his handsome face stern and serious as he locked eyes with each woman. He drew life from the desire, amazement, and heat he found in their depths. He could almost feel the heat he stoked in each one, and that made him just as hot.

"Good Lord," someone hollered out dramatically when he kicked his leg up high in the air and then brought his foot down on the back of the chair of the bachelorette. He leaned in until his dick pressed against her cheek and then pumped his hips in a slow back-and-forth motion that he knew made them all envision him thrusting away between their thighs in much the same fashion.

She blushed and fanned herself as she leaned back from his inches.

"Girl, could you quit this stallin'? You know I'm a sexaholic," Pleasure mouthed along with the music as he moved back into their circle and extended his strong arms forward as he worked his hips and buttocks in tiny clockwork motions that sent his dick flying up against his pants. Again. And again. And again.

He smiled as cuss words and dollar bills were flung at him. *"So anxious..."*

He rolled his body, being sure to work the muscles of his abs as he lowered his body backward with each refrain. Making his body deathly still for a few moments, he felt their gasps of pleasure and appreciation shoot through him like pure adrenaline. Smiling again, he reached to lightly slap his dick back and forth before rolling his upper body upward until he stood before them with his muscles tensed like a warrior about to go to war.

The music faded to silence.

He dramatically spun around.

"What's my name?" he asked the conservative cutie in jeans and a cardigan with pearls sitting before him with her mouth slightly ajar.

Her lips moved but no words came out.

He dropped to a squat before her and opened his arms wide as he mimicked fucking a woman from behind.

"Say it," he ordered her.

"Pleasure," she mouthed before she took a hard audible swallow.

He did a controlled back flip and lay on his stomach on the floor just as "We're Not Making Love No More" by Dru Hill played. He did several slow push-ups before swiftly flipping over onto his back and easing his hand down into his pants to stroke his dick.

"Damn it, Pleasure," one of the women said as the rest applauded or whistled.

Money rained down on him as it grew longer and harder in his hand.

He flipped back over and did a blend of one-arm push-ups and body rolls before jumping up to his feet and whipping off his pants with one hard snatch. He tossed them over their heads to float down onto the floor outside their circle, knowing he looked as good as they wanted him to in his black leather thong with a fringed sleeve and leather straps running around his muscled thighs.

He slowly walked around the inner circle and held his hand out to the bachelorette, pulling her to her feet when she slid her hand into his. He took her chair and easily lifted it high above his head as he continued to tease and tantalize them with his decidedly sexy gyrations. Carefully dropping the chair to its feet on the floor, he twirled her until she stood before it.

He nudged her until the backs of her legs hit the chair and she sat.

He straddled her lap and grabbed the back of the chair as he worked his hips to send that long, leather fringe-covered dick lightly against her cheeks and then her chin. He looked up and his eyes rested on the conservative chick again. The sight of her literally clutching her pearls as she bit her bottom lip actually caused a true stir of his dick. He had to force himself to look away from her, and so he turned and did a headstand while still circling and grinding his hips.

The women roared and he closed his eyes as he let the sound of that surround him along with their heat in that circle. It made his heart pump wildly. It stroked his ego. It fed him.

Graham was no more. Pleasure reigned.

He had found a brand-new high.

★ ★ ★

Pleasure finished packing the last of his equipment into his Nike duffel bag and left the bathroom. The suite was empty save for the bachelorette, Nina, and her friend Drea, who had hired him for the party. Even though he was fully dressed with his dreads pulled back from his face, they eyed him closely.

"Y'all have a good night," he said, heading for the door to the suite.

"Excuse me, Pleasure."

He paused and turned to find Drea picking up her purse and walking out of the room ahead of him. Nina smiled nervously as she walked up to him. Pleasure took her in: her tall, thick, and shapely frame with a short do that emphasized her high cheekbones and full, plump lips.

She smiled again uncertainly as she twisted her engagement ring around her finger. "I've been with my fiancé since we were in kindergarten," she began, stopping before him. "Our mothers are best friends. So we've been tied at the hip forever. Same schools since kindergarten...and...and we even made sure to get into the same college."

Pleasure fought the urge to frown as he wondered why she was bothering to fill him in on her relationship.

"I love him," she said with soft eyes. "I really love him, and in the morning I will gladly walk down that aisle and promise to love and to obey and to cherish him for the rest of my life."

Now he did frown.

"But tonight...if your...uh...*services* are available, I would like to...to...um..."

"To what?" he asked.

She shifted her eyes everywhere about the room but at him as she continued to work that ring.

"What services are you talking about?" Pleasure asked.

Nina looked up to the ceiling and then down at his dick print.

Pleasure's eyes widened. "You want me to fuck you?" he asked, his words rushed together by surprise.

She nodded. "I'll pay...if you do that sort of thing?" she asked, ending on a note of hope that was clear in her voice.

"But you love old boy, right?" he asked.

She looked slightly offended. "I do love him. I love him so much that I have resolved myself to dealing with the fact that he is not that great in bed and not working with much in the first place."

Damn.

"And so for the rest of my life I will be faithful to my good man, but tonight I want to know what good sex feels like before I settle," Nina said. "Just once."

Pleasure leaned back against the door and crossed his arms over his chest. He couldn't deny she was attractive, and he liked the thickness of her frame with her hourglass shape. And these days one-night stands or drive-bys was all he was open to for sex because he still was shying away from a relationship.

So should I fuck and make some cash in the process?

"I'm just a dancer," Pleasure admitted. He took in the curve of her breasts and the deep vee of her long-sleeved fitted sweater. Her nipples were already hard from the show or her anticipation.

"Oh," she said in disappointment.

He pictured her breasts to have dark brown full areolas against her shortbread complexion, maybe even with the same light spray of freckles he saw across her nose and cheeks.

"Fifty...for a half hour," he said, reaching out to press his knuckles up against her chin to lift her head.

Nina nodded slowly.

"Get naked," he ordered her as he lifted the strap to his bag over his head and sat it on the floor.

Pleasure looked on as Nina reached past him to turn off the lights.

He shook his head before she could. "Lights on."

"On?" she asked, sounding unsure.

"Most *definitely* on," he assured her as he pulled the sweatshirt he wore with his track pants over his head.

She kicked off her heels before removing first her sweater and then her jeans to stand before him in a matching black lace set. She splayed her fingers over her small belly as if to hide it.

Pleasure walked over to her and easily picked her up by her waist as she wrapped her arms and legs around his body. Nuzzling his face against her neck, he pressed a kiss to her pounding pulse as he felt his dick harden.

Nina shivered. "I need this," she whispered as she pressed fervent kisses along his shoulder. "You don't know how much I *need* this."

Pleasure pressed her body down onto the bed and stood up to step out of his pants and boxers. He stroked the length of his dick as he freed a condom from his wallet and covered his inches. "Let me see your body," he urged her, wrapping his hand around his thickness as he flung his dreads back from his face.

Nina sat up on her knees and reached behind her back to unlatch her bra to free her full heavy breasts. "I've never cheated on Carl before," she said, nervously licking her lips as she eyed everything about his sculptured body and throbbing dick.

"Carl?"

"My fiancé," she explained as she worked her hips back and forth to remove her panties.

Fuck him.

Pleasure lay on the bed and pulled her down beside him. Her body was warm and soft wherever they made contact. He enjoyed the smooth feel of her skin as he massaged her breasts and lightly teased her thick hard nipples with his fingertips. Holding them higher, Pleasure circled her nipples with his tongue and then sucked them into his hot mouth with a moan.

"Yes," she sighed, twisting his long dreads around her fingers as she pressed his head to her body and rubbed her thigh against his dick.

Pleasure gave her other taut nipple the same attention as he roughly jerked her legs open and dragged his thick middle finger between her pussy lips to the hot wetness inside. His dick got harder as he eased one finger and then another deep inside her to massage her rigid walls.

"Touch my dick," he moaned against her soft cleavage.

She did with long, smooth movements.

Pleasure's heart thundered as he worked his hips.

"Damn, you got a big dick," she whispered to him hotly as she arched her back and teased his tip with her thumb.

"Can you handle it?" Graham teased her swollen clit with his thumb as he continued to stroke his fingers deep inside her.

She nodded and spread her legs wider.

Pleasure eased his body between her legs and sat up on his haunches. Reaching behind each of her knees, he pulled her lower body up onto the top of his thighs and moved his hands down the length of her legs to spread them wide. Her pussy opened up before him and he bit his bottom lip as he pushed his thumb against her clit and guided his hard, thick inches inside her.

Her eyes widened. She cried out and arched her back as he filled her.

"You feel it?" he asked her, his face intense and his eyes locked on the sweet torture of her face as her walls clung to him tightly.

"Oh God yes," she whimpered, reaching her arms out to clutch desperately at the covers.

He knew she had not lied about her fiancé's size because

he felt her body's resistance to his width, and so he knew he couldn't dare give her any more than half of him. He hoped the man didn't fall in it tomorrow night when he made love to his wife on their honeymoon.

Not my fucking problem.

He worked his hips in a wicked clockwise motion that made his dick circle her pussy, and when the virtual clock struck twelve he rolled his eight-pack abdomen and his hips to thrust inside her.

"Yes," she cried out even as she reached forward to press her fingertips against the tight hairs surrounding his dick as if to stop him from going too deep.

Massaging the softness of her breasts and gently rolling her nipples between his fingers, Pleasure let his head fall back until his dreads touched his lower back as he continued to stroke inside her with a strong back-and-forth motion. He felt the muscles of her pussy contract and her inner heat intensified. *She's about to cum.*

Pleasure looked down at her and her face filled with anticipation and a bit of surprise. "You ever cum before?" he asked thickly as he quickened the pace of his strokes.

She met his stare and shook her head just before she cried out and her eyes became glazed over. "Make me cum," she begged.

He rode her harder and faster until he felt his own nut building as he stared down into her rapture-filled face. Her pussy opened up for him and he gave her a few more inches as he continued to pump away until his body became coated with a fine sheen of sweat and his heart was racing harder than horses' hooves on cement.

"I neeeeeeded thisssssssssssssss," she wailed. "Yes. Yes. Yes. Yesssssss."

Pleasure closed his eyes and his body tensed in the hot second just before his cum filled her. "Ah," he cried out, fighting through the pleasure and the sensitivity of his tip to keep fucking her until he was drained and she was spent.

He let his body drop down on hers and he pressed a kiss to her shoulder as he waited to regain control over his body.

"Thank you," she whispered, sucking his shoulder as she stroked his dreads and massaged his hard buttocks with her calf. "Thank you."

Pleasure forced himself to roll off her and lay on his side beside her. He barely found the energy to say, "You're welcome."

Bzzzzzzz . . . bzzzzzz . . . bzzzzzz . . .

Pleasure lifted his head from the pillow as the constant vibrating of his phone echoed in his ear. Using one strong arm, he flung away the pillows and patted his hand against the bed until he felt the cool metal of his cell. Turning over onto his back, he flipped the phone open and pressed it to his ear with his eyes still closed.

"Yeah."

He frowned at the silence.

"Yeah," he repeated with a snap to his voice.

Sitting up in bed, he snapped the phone closed and fought the urge to throw it across the room as he looked around, trying to recall just where the hell he was. For a few panicked seconds he wondered if he'd relapsed and lost himself during a cocaine binge.

Then he remembered he was still in the junior suite used for the bachelorette party. After a long, snore-filled nap Nina had dressed and left him there in the bed around three in the morning. He'd decided to wait until morning to make the hour-long drive back to his apartment.

With a yawn he leaned over to turn on the light over the bed. Flipping his phone open, he saw that the incessant buzzing was incoming texts and not incoming calls. Bending his legs, he rested his arms on his knees as he checked them.

"Put your schlong back in the sock and call me when you release your horny victims from the...Pleasuredome," he read aloud.

Quinn.

He skipped over the next few from her, knowing each one contained a wiseass comment more hilarious than the last.

"Heard you were worth every cent," Pleasure read slowly. "Interested in the same deal. Call me."

Pleasure frowned. *The hell?*

The only person he knew with a 973 area code was the girl who'd hired him for the bachelorette party. "Dina... Deborah...Drea...Drea."

Pleasure thought of the dark-skinned, petite woman. *Not very cute in the face but she got an ass a donkey would die for.*

He hadn't meant to lay The Dick down on Nina so well that she became his walking and talking advertisement. Now her best friend wanted a taste of the magic stick as well.

Pleasure smiled cockily.

The Dick had them up on the phone at four in the morning chitchatting about it.

I did fuck the shit out of her.

He'd sold his dick before, but then he had no say over to whom or when. And although his dick wore the miles, he'd had to split the money and lose his pride through her harsh treatment. *My pimpstress or some shit.*

This time he'd have all the control, and getting to bang beauties like Nina—or just decent chicks like Drea—with no strings attached wasn't a bad side hustle.

He texted her back: *I'LL CALL U L8TER.*

Flipping the phone closed again, Pleasure cut out the lights and flopped back on the bed to finish his sleep.

Chapter 12

Quinn

Four Months Later

"Two thousand two hundred and fifty," Pleasure counted aloud before wrapping a thin rubber band around the wad of mainly singles and five-dollar bills. Dropping that back into the small fireproof safe he kept in his apartment, he then opened his new laptop and logged onto his bank's website to check the balance in his savings and checking accounts. They totaled over six grand.

He kept his tips from dancing in the safe and the money from his whoring in the bank. Business was good and plenty. Pleasure hadn't had so much sex ever—and to be paid for it was just icing on the cake.

Pleasure climbed off the bed and crossed the floor with bare feet to look out the window and down into the parking lot where his new cherry-red two-door sports car sat. It was far from new and had well over a hundred thousand miles, but it was all his.

It felt good to give his father back his old Expedition he'd borrowed to drive, pay all his own bills, and have plenty to spoil his parents every now and then. Of course he had them thinking he worked in telemarketing, but other than that they were happy about his new life. They were just glad he visited them often, didn't ask for money, and was still clean and sober.

Looking over his broad shoulder, he eyed his sobriety calendar. He looked pensive. He hadn't marked the calendar in months. He was so busy between performing nightly at Club Trick, doing private shows, and tricking that he didn't have much time for anything. He turned his head and looked over his other broad shoulder at his easel. A fine layer of dust covered it as it sat neglected and discarded in the corner.

Knock-knock-knock.

Pleasure turned and eyed his front door before making his way across the room to bend his body to be able to look through the peephole. He smiled at the sight of Quinn on the other side. Stepping back, Pleasure opened the door wide, but his smile faded at her heartrending expression. "What's wrong?" he asked, as she walked in wearing a beautiful bright turquoise jacket under a matching cropped silk shirt. As always, her makeup was perfectly set.

"I miss my friend," she said, as she dropped her clutch on his unmade bed and turned on wedge heels to face him.

Pleasure shut the door and ran his strong fingers through his long, slender dreads as he leaned back against the wall. "I miss you too," he said, only half honestly. "I've been so busy working—"

She arched a brow. "Stripping," she inserted dryly.

"Working," he countered.

She shrugged and walked around his apartment.

"I know it's been a few weeks since we last hung out or caught up," Pleasure said, his deep voice seeming to echo inside the small apartment. "How's everything?"

She shrugged as she lifted the cover of his sketchbook and then shook her head at the empty pages. "Ryan and I broke up, and it would've been nice to have my friend beat him up or something," she said.

"Ryan? Broke up? Beat him up?" he asked, repeating the key points. "I *have* been busy. Shit, I haven't even had time to meet him yet and it's over already?"

She gave him a pointed look that said "Exactly" before she turned and walked over to his calendar on the fridge. She tapped it with her finger before turning away with another judging shake of her head.

"I got a new car," Pleasure said into the silence that felt condemning.

Quinn nodded in approval. "That's good, Graham. I'm proud of you," she said.

"It's the Corvette."

Quinn dropped her head before she looked at him with an incredulous expression. "Graham, you're six foot nine," she began. "Just how easy is it for you to climb your big butt in and out of a Corvette?"

He laughed and shrugged. "It's not that bad."

She held up both her hands palm forward and leaned back.

"So tell me about Ryan," he offered even as he glanced at the time on the cable box beneath his new seventy-inch flat screen on the wall. He had to meet up with one of his clients at four and then head to Club Trick. It was a little after two.

"How's everything going?" she asked, coming to stand behind the back of the couch to eye him.

"Can't complain," he said with a huge grin. "Can't complain at all."

Quinn released a heavy breath and rolled her eyes upward before she looked at him again. "That's not what I'm talking about."

Pleasure's smile dimmed a bit as he was filled with understanding. He nodded and licked his lips. "I'm good. No relapses. Much less cravings. I'm good," he repeated.

"Good," she said, reaching down to pick up her clutch and tuck it under her arm. "I'm happy to know what your empty sobriety calendar and empty sketchbook isn't telling about you not staying clean."

"I been real busy," Pleasure said again.

"Too busy to stay focused on staying clean. Too busy to sketch." Quinn walked past him to the door. "At one time you needed them both very much."

True. Both had been such big parts of his staying clean. "Maybe I don't need them anymore," he said, looking down at her.

"You're also too busy for me," Quinn gently reminded him with the hint of a sad smile at her lips as she pulled the front door open. "I guess you don't need me anymore either."

"Don't say that," Pleasure said, reaching out to grip the edge of the door and block her exit.

His "Boombastic" ringtone suddenly filled the air. *Mr. Lover Lover . . ."*

"Don't go," he said to her, already moving across the room to pick up one of his two phones. The one ringing was the prepaid phone he used exclusively for his clients.

He didn't answer it but he recognized the number of Alicia Larrington, a wealthy pediatrician he'd met at one of their revues. He had already serviced her twice in two weeks. *Looks like she needs it once a week.*

He set the phone back down and turned to find Quinn still by the door. "Listen, I got a little time before work," he said. "Let me hop in the shower and we can go get something to eat real quick. Cool?"

She looked reluctant but finally nodded in agreement.

Pleasure walked into his small bathroom and ran the water steaming hot before stripping off the shorts he wore. He relieved his bladder, brushed his teeth, and pulled his dreads back with a band before finally stepping under the spray of water with only a slight jolt at the feel of its heat. As he soaped down his body, with barely enough room for his large frame to fit, he thought of his next appointment. June was a pre-law student who could cum easier than any woman he ever bedded. Just sucking her nipples would push her over the edge until she was shivering and crying out with a dozen tiny explosions.

She made for a good hour.

Finishing up, he wrapped a thick black towel around his waist before stepping out of the shower. "Damn," he swore into the swirling steam, wishing he had gotten his underwear and clothes before he came into the bathroom.

Opening the door, Graham felt the coolness of the central air hit against every spot on his body. "It's cold as a bitch in here," he said.

Quinn turned from his windowsill with his cell phones in her hand and tears streaming down her face. "Really, Graham, you selling dick now?" she asked, her voice a mixture of disappointment and annoyance.

"What are you doing with my phones?" he snapped, walking across the room to snatch them from her.

"What are you doing being a whore?" she countered, reaching out to snatch his towel away and leave him standing there nude and wet.

Graham rushed to cover as much of his dick as he could with his hands. "What the fuck are you doing?"

"I wanted to see for myself what was on the market," she said snidely, turning to stalk across the room and snatch up her clutch again. "If that's all you think of yourself, then that's your business."

"You're right, it is my business...just like my phones," he said.

Quinn opened the door wide but paused to look back at him. "One of your balls is out," she said.

He freed his dick and bent down to scoop up his towel.

"Oh my."

Graham looked past her to see his forty-something neighbor Ms. Wilcox standing in the hall and looking directly into his apartment at his nakedness. He wrapped his towel around his waist.

"If you like what you see, it's for sale," Quinn snapped before she walked out of the apartment.

Just before the door closed behind her, Ms. Wilcox smiled and winked at him with a little wave of her fingers.

Pleasure tried for what seemed the hundredth time to call Quinn's number. It went straight to voice mail. He didn't understand her anger and hated to see how what he did with his time and his dick could end their friendship. What was her anger all about? Was their friendship the cliché of a boy who likes a girl who loves the boy secretly?

"Pleasure...you're up next."

He dropped his cell back into his duffel bag inside his locker and grabbed his bottle of oil to lather over his body. He wore a black thong with his dick encased in a satin sleeve. He pulled on the satin robe and his fringed boots, then released the band loosely holding his dreads. They fell down past his shoulders.

He crossed the small and cramped locker room of the club's basement.

"Get 'em warmed up for the headliner."

Pleasure paused and looked back to find Gary "The Finisher" Palms just zipping up his red patent leather thigh-high boots. The Finisher was a five-year veteran of the club, and his position as the last to perform had been locked in for years. He definitely brought in the women and thus the most revenue. He'd even flown overseas to perform and often bragged about the celebrities who requested his presence at their private events. The light-skinned brother with the slick curly hair and goatee loved himself almost as much as his legion of fans loved him.

Still, Pleasure was well aware that he saw him as a threat. He had come up the ranks quickly at the club. "Whatever, man," he said, before turning to take the stairs two at a time.

Pleasure was more than four inches taller than he was and probably twice as strong. *As long as he don't touch me, I won't whup his little emotional yellow ass.*

He stepped through the thick black velvet curtains that smelled of mildew just as the colorful lights surrounding the stage began to flicker in unison with his heavy bass-driven music.

"Welcome to the stage for your ultimate fantasy…Plea-sure!"

As soon as Unique, their in-house DJ, finished his intro, the stage went black. Quickly he moved to sit on the edge of the stage under the cloak of darkness. The stage lit up with the spotlight on him.

As his music played loudly he gripped the edge of the stage and spread his legs wide before bringing his feet down on either side of a slender white woman sitting before him. He rolled his body slowly before using his arm strength to elevate his legs above her head, then before doing a back flip and ending in the center of the stage with strength and force.

He spun, causing his robe to fly up around him before he eased out of it and flung it back. He turned to show off his hard buttocks and square back as he grinded to the music. When he spun back around the light coming through the open door caught his eye and moments later, *she* stepped out of the darkness of the back of the room and into the dim light around the stage.

Since the night of that bachelorette party, Ms. Prim and Proper Pearls had come to Club Trick for its ladies' night performances. He recognized her easily. She stood out with her pearls and pumps and country-club attire. She would nervously sit on the edge of her seat and watch his performance like a hawk. Whenever he approached her for a private dance she would timidly reach out to slide a fifty-dollar bill inside the rim of his thong as he gyrated his dick before her.

He smiled at her as he cockily walked forward and stroked the length of his dick inside his sleeve. She crossed her legs in the jean trousers she wore with a navy and red sheer polka-dot blouse.

She always came just in time for his solo performance and never stayed any later. In her everyday life he could tell she lived within the confines of rules and regulations with a great sense of right versus wrong. She was giving in to a temptation—a dirty secret—and it thrilled her. He thrilled her. She was there just for him and he knew it. He liked it.

The next day Pleasure parked his Corvette outside the quaint small house Quinn rented in Chappaqua, a city just ten miles from his apartment in Tarrytown. He spotted her Honda Accord in the driveway as he climbed from the deep bucket seat. He smiled a bit when he remembered her joking about getting in and out of the low-slung sports car. *She was right.*

He stepped up on the curb and walked the brick path leading to her front door. It opened before he could even knock and Quinn stood in the doorway with her face free of her usual makeup and dressed in a tank top and wide-legged sweatpants.

"So you remember where I live?" she asked, stepping back to let him enter.

Pleasure didn't miss that her eyes were puffy and slightly red. That made him frown in confusion, but he cleared his throat before turning to face her as she shut the door. "I thought we needed to talk," he said, pushing his hands into the pockets of his lightweight linen sports coat.

"About what?" she asked, moving to fold herself onto the suede sectional before her cold fireplace.

Pleasure removed his jacket and draped it over the back of the couch, leaving his white V-neck shirt exposed as he pulled up the linen slacks before sitting down on the sofa across from her. "I'm not saying my side hustle is something for me to get up in church and testify about, but it is *my* life and *my* decision," he stressed, crossing his fingers in the air between his knees.

Quinn sat cross-legged and rested her forearms atop her knees. "Look...I apologize for going in your phone. That was wrong—I was wrong."

"True," Pleasure interjected and then held up his hands when she gave him an irate stare.

"I just think you're so much better than that, Graham," she said as she lifted her shoulder-length curls from her neck.

"You know me, Quinn, but there's a lot you don't know," he admitted. "This world does not owe me any more pussy. I'm young. I'm having fun. I'm good. Trust me. Sex and money are not the two worst things I've loved in my life."

"Don't you want more?" she asked.

Oh shit. Pleasure sat back a bit as he saw a light in Quinn's brown eyes that made things so much clearer to him. "Um, no, I don't. Having to be accountable to someone else is more than I'm willing to deal with right now. I still have urges to get high. When I hit a mental wall, especially when I'm angry, I have to catch myself from thinking, 'Man, hell with it. Let me go get fucked up and forget all this bullshit,' " he said, hoping he clearly conveyed why a girlfriend was the very last thing he wanted or needed.

Quinn leaned back and propped her elbow on the back of the chair as she eyed him. She opened and closed her mouth a dozen times, showing she was struggling to say something.

No, Quinn. Don't.

"Look, are we good?" he asked, rising to his feet and picking up his jacket.

She nodded. "We're good," she said, rising to walk him to the door.

Pleasure felt if he could just reach the door and made it to the other side than Quinn would not dare ask him—

"So you've never thought of *us* together."

Pleasure closed his eyes and dropped his head so low to his chest that his chin almost rested on the top of a bicep. They'd just officially slid into the cliché zone. *Shit. Damn. Why, Quinn, why?*

"Graham," she said again.

He turned as he slid his jacket on and looked down at her. "No," he admitted, shaking his head regretfully. "I never did because I wouldn't want to lose you as a friend."

She was in love with him. He'd let his needs for a non-sexual outlet lead to him overlooking the affection she had for him. Feelings he didn't share.

Quinn crossed her arms over her chest. "Thinking about it and acting toward it is two different things. So you never looked at me in that way?" she asked, her big brown eyes disbelieving.

It was his turn to open and close his mouth as he struggled for words.

"Not once?" she asked with attitude as she arched a brow.

"Quinn—"

"So you blind or just dumb?" she asked, waving her hand up and down the length of her body. "Because all of this was hard-earned. Trust and believe that."

"Quinn—"

She held up her hands. "No, I'm cool. I'm good. I'm chill. I'm straight," she said with a smile too big to be authentic.

"You sure?" Pleasure asked, his voice filled with the disbelief he felt.

She nodded.

He reached out and lightly caressed her cheek. "I'll call you later," he said.

She nodded again.

He opened the front door.

"What's your rate?" she asked in a rush.

Pleasure heard her but he left the house like he didn't. He pulled the door closed but she was on the other side fighting to open it. He released it and moments later he could hear her stumbling backward and crashing into something.

Pleasure stood on the porch deciding whether to go check on her or not. *Damn.* Just as he turned, the door opened and Quinn stepped out onto the porch to stand beside him.

"So the strangers are okay," she said, her voice weepy. "Just not me, right?"

Everything between them became different.

Pleasure felt guilt and irritation nipping at him. "I'm sorry, Quinn," he said honestly. "But this is too much for me."

He turned and walked down the path to the sidewalk.

"Graham," she called behind him.

"I'll call you," he called over his shoulder.

"Graham."

"I'll call you," he repeated the lie.

He climbed in his car and cranked the car speeding off before she could reach the curb.

Interlude

Present Day

*H*e was ashamed of the way he'd treated Quinn all those years ago. Back then he considered it holding on to his sobriety when he eventually stopped answering her calls and then moved to a larger apartment complex without giving her the new address. Today, he knew he had just taken the easy way out and his actions had hurt her. He could only assure himself that removing himself from the picture had left her open to fall for someone else.

But had his rejection of her love—and in time, her friendship— warranted such drastic actions?

"Don't do this, Quinn," he said, his eyes locked on where she was flipping through the photo album his mother gave him for Christmas. She didn't flinch or look up.

"Yet another nice try, Pleasure," she said, before flipping a page.

A nice try was right. He didn't seriously consider his captor to be Quinn but he wasn't willing to at least make sure. He let his head fall back as he looked at his pristine white tray ceiling. He opened his mouth and took a deep breath before he roared so loudly in frustration that his throat hurt when he was done. He allowed his body to go slack in the chair as his chest heaved from the exertion.

WHAP!

He jerked his head up to see the large family album on the floor. She eyed him as she kicked it viciously, sending it sliding across the floor like a tornado on a treacherous path.

He was sick of her shit. He was beyond sick of all the bullshit.

"What do I have to do to get the fuck out of here?" he yelled, the veins of his neck protruding.

"Be rolled out in a body bag," she answered calmly as she reached over the back of the sofa and lifted a small black book bag.

"This is crazy," he told her.

"Crazy?" she snapped, her eyes wide inside the holes of the mask. "I'm not crazy, you slack-ass slut."

"You beyond fucking crazy," he shot back.

"FUCK YOU," she shouted, striding across the room and swinging the bag to slam it across the side of his face.

He bit the inside of his cheek to keep from hollering out even as pain radiated across his face, the back of his head, and his upper shoulder.

"You think I care if y'all say I'm crazy," she said in a hoarse whisper as she nudged his forehead with her finger. "Huh? Fuck all y'all, Pleasure."

Y'all? Huh?

He ignored the radiating pain and eyed her as he continued to try to work his wrists to loosen the ties. They hadn't given an inch.

"You ain't even begun to see crazy, smart-ass."

She squatted down to drop the bag on the floor and jerked it open as she continued to mumble rapidly under her breath. She extracted a syringe and removed the cap. "Time to dope you up again, Mr. Hercules, before you get all strong and break those ties," she said, slowly standing over him.

"What is that?" he asked, hating the thought of the needle and its ingredients.

"Just enough Oxycontin to keep your ass in check."

Pleasure flashed back to his days strung out on coke. He didn't want to be forced back into addiction. "Don't do this."

"And don't you waste your breath..."

Chapter 13

Assefa

2008

I cannot believe this. I still cannot believe this and I probably will never believe this.

Pleasure clasped his hands behind his back as he stood to the right of the groom in his custom-tailored tuxedo. Kezia had taken the time to connect and twist his dreads backward and then secure the ends with a black leather strap. He looked good. He even felt good.

Still...

He looked over at his mother and couldn't believe that she was so beautiful in her off-white lace-covered gown. She smiled at him from beneath her sheer veil, and he forced himself to smile back at her. He knew she had to have the same doubts and questions that he did. She *had* to.

But she was grown and she'd made the choice to wed. He could do nothing but respect that. Honor it. Back it up.

She was his mother and he loved her. He would fight for her even though there was a time he'd felt so much anger at her that he used to fight others to keep from lashing out. The feelings of anger had dulled, and he had a better understanding for the cause of that anger, and they were better. Much better.

At twenty-six, he had the best relationship with his mother since before the days of "the divorce," and now she was getting married again. He just wished he could have come to be at peace with her decision. That he was still working on.

He glanced back at the people crowding the church and did a double take at the sight of Geneva sitting in one of the rear pews. He hadn't seen her since that night at the train station, and the unexpected sight of her made his pulse race. She looked just a little older, but with a maturity and an awareness of self. His heart tugged and he knew that was a little of the love he would always carry for her.

He forced himself to look forward as her father officiated over the wedding ceremony, but twice more he glanced back at her. *Is she married? Still a virgin? Excited to see me?*

"What therefore God hath joined together, let not man put asunder," Reverend Garrett read from his leather-bound Bible. "Well...again."

The wedding attendees laughed lightly.

Pleasure forced a smile, looking on as the minister pronounced them man and wife. "You may kiss the bride," he said.

He looked on as his father and mother turned to face each other. Tylar raised Cara's veil and then pressed his hands against her jawline as she tilted her face upward for his kiss, which deepened as he wrapped his arms around her.

His parents had wed again.

After years of warring and fighting and accusing and avoiding, they had somehow rediscovered love a year ago and decided to do it all over again.

If this ain't the craziest shit—sorry, God.

This used to be the dream of his teenage years, and now as a grown man who had personally seen his father dog more women than any one man should be allowed, he didn't want him to pull his stunts with his mother...again. He loved them both and he didn't want to choose sides. The reverend cleared his throat and lightly patted his father's lower back. As his parents finally pulled apart to the applause of everyone looking on, Pleasure looked down and saw the reverend had extended his hand to him.

He looked down into the man's eyes and wanted so badly to say, "I'm not the skinny kid you thought wasn't good enough for your daughter, am I?" But he didn't.

Pleasure wanted to brush past him. But he didn't.

He slid his hand into Reverend Garrett's and tightly squeezed it just having to have that moment of dominance over the man before he turned to follow his parents down the aisle. His eyes immediately went to the spot where Geneva had been sitting, but she wasn't there any longer.

He felt relief.

The truth was that although he was the one selling his wares to women, in his eyes his father was the true whore. He didn't want to treat any woman he was in a relationship with the way his father had. Therefore, for now, until he was ready, he slept with attractive women and made money doing so, but all rules were laid out beforehand. All cards were on the table, and there was no chance of anyone being fooled or hurt or cheated.

Sliding his hands into the pockets of his slacks, Pleasure looked on as everyone left the church and surrounded his parents to offer hugs, kisses, and well wishes. They waved him over as the photographer worked his way through the crowd to them. Pleasure followed his parents' lead, not at all missing the appreciative stares of many of the women—young and old. As he moved through the crowd, he towered over the women and many of the men. He was a hard figure to ignore.

Bzzz...

He pulled his trick phone from the inner pocket of his

tuxedo blazer. It was a cheap throwaway prepaid phone. He didn't recognize the number and he had no one scheduled for the day.

"Graham," his mother complained at the sight of him flipping the phone open.

"It's work," he lied. "I'll be right back."

Walking away before she could insist he didn't, he moved to an empty section of the parking lot. "Pleasure," he said, his voice deep.

"Well, hello, Pleasure," a sultry voice said. "I understand you're the man to call about some...*work* I need done."

He chuckled. "I'm definitely the man," he said confidently.

"Time will tell that," she countered smoothly.

Graham could tell from her confidence that she was a woman in her thirties or early forties. Turning to look behind him to make sure he was still alone, he pressed his phone close to his ear to ensure she wasn't picking up too much of his background noise.

Early on he had learned to talk very little when he was with one of his clients. He revealed nothing about himself and asked only enough of them if he felt they needed to be warmed up a bit before he laid it down. He didn't care if they were married or not, had kids or not, liked their jobs or not. He put on no façades. They only knew him as Pleasure, and that was enough.

"Who referred you?" he asked, pulling his aviator shades from his pocket to slip on with one hand.

"MiMi...and Georgia...and Fran," she said. "You're quite the talk over martinis."

His country-club set. Good money. Damn good money.

"Are you available tonight?" she asked.

"Not until very late," he said.

"That's fine. It should make me sleep like a baby."

Pleasure spotted his father walking toward him. "Text me the address," he said, keeping his voice smooth even as his heart rate sped up a little.

He closed the phone and slid it back into his pocket as he walked to meet his father.

"Everything okay?" Tylar asked, placing his arm around his son's shoulders.

"Yeah. No biggie," Pleasure said, as they walked back toward the church steps where the photographer was positioning his mother and her lone bridesmaid—one of her friends from work—for pictures.

Most of the wedding guests had left the church for the reception while he was on the phone.

"So the dog ready to sit on the porch and watch the cars go by instead of chasing them?" Pleasure asked, looking down at the tip of his handmade Italian leather shoes as they walked together.

Tylar tensed a bit. "Well, with all due respect, son, whatever happens between your mother and me, is between your mother and me . . . but yes, this old dog don't hunt no more."

Pleasure slid his hands into his pants pockets. "And with all due respect to you, Dad, remember that she's not just another woman, she's my mother, and so I feel how I feel."

Tylar laughed off his son's subtle threat. "Like you ready for this," he quipped, turning to playfully air-box.

Pleasure laughed, deepening his dimples, as he raised his fists. "Don't get hurt, old man," he warned with a grin.

"Boys," Cara said sharply. "Really? On church grounds? Really?"

They both paused in their fighting stance and turned their heads to look at her before turning their heads again to look at each other in almost perfect unison. Laughing, they shared a hug and continued up the steps.

★ ★ ★

Pleasure parked in front of the two-story brick home and climbed from the silver Ford F-250 that he'd purchased after selling the Corvette. He jogged up the stairs to the massive wood double doors. He rang the bell as he stood with his hands in the pockets of his black track pants. Even at night, the Bridgewater, New Jersey, neighborhood was quaint and cute. On the surface it looked like the perfect place to raise a family in happy suburbia. But these places of seeming perfection hid so much unhappiness. He knew that firsthand.

"Well, look at you."

Pleasure slowly turned, and he was surprised when he saw the woman standing in her doorway as naked as Eve. And she had every reason in the world to flaunt her body. Almost methodically, he took in her assets.

She was a brick house—soft where she needed to be soft (breasts, hips, and ass) and toned where she needed to be toned (abs, arms, and legs). It was clear she was fit and solid and well-shaped. Hers was a body urban models and video vixens paid well to have.

Pleasure's dick was ready to salute the beauty before him.

She took her time stepping back, as one of her neighbors went jogging past.

Pleasure entered her home, turning to finally look at her face. She was a beautiful dark-skinned beauty with features straight from Ethiopia, and her short ebony curls only emphasized that. He couldn't tell if she was twenty-five or forty-five. She was timeless.

Life is so fucking sweet.

"A little back story," she said, picking up an envelope from the back of the sofa and tossing it to him. "My ex-husband supposedly worked from home as a medical transcriptionist."

Pleasure caught the envelope with one hand and felt the bills inside. He didn't bother to count it as he slid it into his pocket.

"My neighbors—my *so-called* friends—sat back and watched him parade a line of cheap young women in and out of my house while I was working this big ass off to pay all the bills," she continued, taking him by the hand to lead him across the living room and up the stairs.

"They said nothing as they smiled in my face and sipped on my wine during many dinner parties," she said calmly as she opened the door to her bedroom—an all-red affair that gleamed with candles everywhere.

"It took me hiring a private detective to finally discover just what he was doing all day that his paycheck wasn't adding up to the hours he claimed to work. Foolish me, I thought he was on drugs," she said before laughing and shaking her head.

She released his hand and moved to the nightstand to open a large gold-trimmed wooden box. Inside were enough condoms to stock a Walgreens. "So I really don't give a fuck if they see me naked as I stroll a big, handsome man into my home for the night," she continued, sitting down on the bed and then lying back with her arms splayed across the crimson satin. "Especially one who I heard should be called…the backbreaker."

Pleasure removed his black sleeveless t-shirt and dropped it to the red-tiled floor as she spread her legs wide and opened the bald lips of her pussy.

"So now that you've gotten a li'l bit of my business, let me get into some of yours," she said. "Are you everything they have made you out to be?"

"Yes." He kicked off his athletic sandals and then took off his pants.

"Commando, huh?" she asked.

Pleasure walked across the room, massaging the length of his dick in his hand. Standing by her nightstand, he reached inside the open box for a condom and tossed it onto the bed beside her before reaching down to rub his hands up her thighs, her hips, across her flat abdomen and upward to massage her breasts.

"I'm Assefa, by the way," she said languidly as she stretched her arms above her head and arched her back with her eyes closed. "And I hope you're worth every cent."

"I am," he said confidently as he crawled onto the bed between her open thighs.

Pleasure sat on the edge of the bed and pulled his sleeveless T-shirt over his head before he shoved his feet into his sandals. The bed dipped as Assefa rose from it. He looked over his shoulder as she began to blow out the candles before she hit the switch to bathe the large room with light. His eyes stayed on her body, loving the way she moved, almost like a panther.

She came to stand before him and reached out to stroke his chin with a smile. "My friends are easily impressed," she said.

"Oh really?" he asked, his expression guarded.

"That was...good," she said, before turning to walk between the open double doors of her large closet and emerging with a white satin robe that she left open. "But it could have been better."

Pleasure's pride took a hit.

Assefa came back over to stand before him. "Listen, Pleasure. Your dick is more than enough, and when it comes to down-and-dirty fucking, you're one of the best," she said, stroking his chin. "But you have absolutely no idea how to make love to a woman—*especially* a grown-ass woman like me."

Pleasure rose to his feet and patted his pocket to make sure the envelope with his pay had not slipped out. To him that was all that mattered. Not her opinion. "I've never gotten complaints," he told her with a shrug.

Assefa nodded as she walked across the room and turned on the light to her adjoining bathroom. The combination of her smooth chocolate complexion and that white robe as she moved about the red room was a sight to see. "Perhaps you have never dealt with a woman who's had good lovers before. Even my slut of a husband was better, and that was with almost half the size dick you have."

Pleasure crossed his arms over his chest. "What makes you think I care?"

"Because you're still here," she shot back quickly as if it was ready and aimed to fire from the tip of her tongue.

"I can easily change that," he said.

"Let me walk you to the door," she offered, coming over to wrap her arms around one of his as they left the room together.

He felt like shaking her off but he didn't.

"You have . . . potential," Assefa said as they descended the stairs.

"Thanks," he said dryly.

She released him with a pat that she might have meant as reassuring but felt condescending to him. As she moved ahead of him to open the door, a draft caused her robe to fly up and expose her shapely legs and rounded ass. He couldn't deny she was top notch, and although he had given her his best pipe work, she was telling him to do better. Be better.

His eyes widened when she waved to someone. "Be sure to tell Ingram that you saw me," she said, slowly closing and tying her robe.

Pleasure stepped through the door, and he spotted two women next door on their porch, shaking their heads in obvious judgment.

Assefa made a show of hugging him close, and that actually made Pleasure smile because of the craziness of it all. "Those jealous bitches were the main ones keeping my ex-husband's secrets and smiling in my face the whole time," she whispered up to him. "You get home safe."

With that she released him and stepped back.

Pleasure jogged down the stairs to his truck and was glad to slide inside and drive away from the drama.

Chapter 14

Assefa

Pleasure dropped his keys and cell phones onto the studded wooden table against the wall directly next to the front door of his two-bedroom apartment in the Twelve50 in downtown Newark, New Jersey. He'd made the decision to move to Newark to make his drive time to Club Trick a little shorter and because the high-rise luxury building was ideally situated for an easy commute into New York or any of the cities in the tri-state area where he did business. The amenities of a concierge, exercise room, and bowling alley were bonuses.

Whenever Kezia and Lola visited him, they liked to tease and call him George Jefferson for "moving on up." That was after reminders that they had helped him become the star stripper that he was—they didn't know he sold dick too. All of their years of friendship had led to them treating him more and more like an annoying little brother they tolerated. And loved.

Pausing by the door, he looked out the row of windows at the inky night sky lit up by the bright lights of the buildings in the distance. Some of his friends at the club told him Jersey City would have been a better move for a similar building with a lower rent and a view of New York. But for now, Pleasure was content.

His mother had decorated his apartment in Tarrytown, but Pleasure had taken the time to pick out everything in this one. He felt he hadn't done too badly with the chocolate, khaki, and red décor with wooden accents. He was especially proud of all the African artwork and sculptures he'd picked out. He felt he was on his grown-man status.

He'd come a long way from his studio apartment in Tarrytown, and he had plans to go even further.

His home was his respite from the world. He never had his friends or coworkers over. He never dared to bring one of his clients there. He didn't even allow his neighbors beyond the door. This place was his and his alone. It was his needed quiet from the noise and the stench of the club. It was his solitude from the women paying him for his time. It was his shelter from his addiction.

Pleasure treasured his home. He was never wary to be home alone. He was glad for it.

Moving through the apartment, he turned on the overhead lights in his gourmet kitchen before washing his hands. His stomach growled loudly. It had been hours since his dinner of chicken piccata at his parents' reception.

The days of ordering pizza or zipping by one of the fast food joints for a burger were behind him. His body was his source of income, and Pleasure was determined to keep it in shape. A year ago he'd cut red meat and processed foods from his diet and got into juicing. That one move had led to him shedding ten pounds, and his muscles were even more defined and sculpted. It was also a change that helped him stay consistently sober since his one and only stint in rehab years ago.

He closed the fridge and decided to shower first instead. He felt sweaty from his sex with Assefa, and he knew his dick smelled of a blend of latex and his dried semen. As he stripped and stepped under the shower spray, he thought of Assefa and her...observations.

Was she just an angry woman burnt by her husband and looking for anyone to dominate to boost her self-esteem, or was he truly the "wham bam, thank you ma'am" king like she claimed?

Most importantly, did it really matter?

A memory of her taking over as he rode her from behind played over in his head, and he had to admit that it turned him the hell on to have someone put in a little work for him. All of his clients let him do all the work and just lay there either scratching his back or damn near passing out as he pumped away to make them cum. That move of her pulling downward on his dick and then twerking her ass as she squeezed the tip with her walls had been bad as hell.

"Shit," he swore at the hot memory.

When he lowered his hands to soap his dick, it was hard, long, and curving to the right. He took a step back inside the marble shower and let the water hit against his hardness until it eased. The memory of her riding him didn't ease away quite as fast.

Pleasure finished his shower, pushing thoughts of his first complainer away as he dried off and wrapped himself in his thick navy terrycloth robe.

He paused just long enough to straighten his bathroom before turning out the light and heading straight back to the kitchen to fix himself a salad topped with strips of chicken and a tall glass of a mix of spinach, apple, and carrot juices.

Pleasure bypassed the granite-topped breakfast bar and headed into the living room, wanting to enjoy one of his rare Saturday nights off from the club. He sat his plate on the large wooden tray atop the chocolate leather ottoman and dropped down on the red suede sofa with a fatigued grunt. After the excitement of the wedding and the reception, plus his travel time and session with Assefa—whom he now called Ms. Insatiable—he was spent.

He flipped through the channels on his plasma TV and settled on a nature documentary as he demolished his salad.

"The mating of lions is very similar to humans..."

Pleasure paused with his head slightly tilted back and his glass raised as he eyed the male lion take the female lion from behind as she lay on her belly in the wilderness.

He thought of Assefa again, especially when the male bit the neck of the female before throwing his head back and roaring as he rutted.

It reminded him of his natural instinct to do the same when she worked his dick.

"But you have absolutely no idea how to make love to a woman—especially a grown-ass woman like me."

Finishing his juice in one deep gulp, he closed his eyes, but he saw nothing but Assefa standing there in her white robe with the material barely closed enough to cover her nipples. *Just hot as hell.*

"Even my slut of a husband was better, and that was with almost half the size dick you have."

He scowled.

"You have...potential."

"Potential?" he muttered, standing up to cross the polished hardwood floors to pick up his trick phone from the table by the door. He looked up into his reflection in the square window over the table. "Potential?!"

He moved across the room to lie on his back on the sofa, his head cushioned by his dreads. Lifting one foot up on the back of the sofa, he felt a slight draft against his privates as his robe fell open and exposed him. Not caring, he used his thumb to go to his list of recent calls and hit Send on his last outgoing call of the night.

It was midnight and he didn't care.

It rang twice, and he was surprised at how nervous he felt. He was even more surprised at how disappointed he felt when the call eventually went to her voice mail. He didn't bother to leave a message.

Tapping his cell against his square jaw, he looked up at the tall ceilings. As much as he tried to focus on anything but Assefa and her judgment, his ego was in control. Sitting up, he dropped the cell phone onto the couch and picked up his glass and plate to carry back into the kitchen. "I'm a *fuck* the shit out of her," Pleasure said with confidence before he turned off the lights and headed to the master bedroom for some sleep.

Club Trick was crowded, and the smell of alcohol, perfume, and moist panties was cloying as Pleasure moved about, going to woman after woman to tantalize them for tips. He had to admit that this particular Thursday night he was mildly distracted, as his eyes kept going to the door and searching the many faces in the crowd for *her*, Miss Prim and Proper Pearls.

Once a month like clockwork for the last couple of years, she'd never missed the third Thursday ladies' night. Never. Not even after he noticed the sizeable wedding band she started wearing on her left hand.

"Pleasure!"

He turned even though he knew it wasn't her. She had never once hollered out to him or even carried on when she gave him a tip. She was always reserved and poised, but her eyes always revealed the heat boiling inside her. Her eyes *always* gave it away.

Moving through the crowd, he felt hands reach out to

stroke his body. He was used to it. He could expect no less dressed in nothing but a pair of leather boy shorts with brass buttons outlining the area over his dick where he could snatch it away and let it *all* hang out.

"It's her birthdaaaaayyyy," a woman of no more than twenty said as she pointed a long acrylic nail at her friend, who was already rotating her hips in the chair as she snapped her fingers to the sounds of "Love in This Club" by Usher.

Pleasure dragged her chair from behind the table before he squatted down before her and worked his hips as he grasped her knees in her jeans and spread her legs wide before dipping his head in just enough to imitate eating her pussy.

Thankfully, her intimacy smelled of some sweet perfume and he said a quick "Thank you, Lord" for that. The horror stories he and the other dancers shared about women and the less-than-credible smells down below . . .

Holding the sides of her chair, he leaned back and rolled his abs, ending each one with a hard hip thrust that made her stomp her feet and cover her face with her hands as she screamed.

He smiled as he rose to his feet. These days he made more money with his clients than he did at the club, but there was nothing like the rush he received when the women all screamed his name or acted like they were near fainting from one of his moves. *I love this shit.*

Pleasure accepted the bills the ladies pushed into the top of his shorts and just winked at them when one boldly stroked his dick print that ran clear to the edge of the boy shorts like he was about to reveal it.

"Damn, he got a big dick," he heard one of them scream to the other over the loud music. He turned and grabbed his thickness, shaking it at them. They all threw up their hands.

The lights flickered twice, letting him and the other dancers on the floor know it was time for another solo dance onstage. Pleasure had long since had his, and even though he knew he was one of the most popular dancers at the club, Vera still had the vets showcased last.

With one last look around the club and at the door, Pleasure danced his way off the floor, disappointed that *she* wasn't coming.

"Mr. Lover Lover . . ."

Pleasure paused on his way out the door of the strip club and reached inside the side pocket of his duffel bag for his trick phone. Assefa's number filled the screen. It had been five days since he called her. He started not to answer her, but again his ego dominated his decision. He was well aware and fine with that.

"Pleasure," he said, using his remote to unlock the door of his silver Ford F-250. He opened the rear door of the double cab and placed his duffel on the seat.

"Good evening, Pleasure. I was returning your call," she said coolly.

"From last week," he slid in smoothly.

"I couldn't imagine what you possibly had to call about," she explained. "I checked the house and you didn't leave anything behind. I paid you. We did the deed. To me, our association was over. Curiosity just got the best of me tonight."

Pleasure closed the passenger door and opened the driver's to climb in. "I want another go at you—"

"That sounds appealing," she said dryly.

He started to hang up on her. In the Rock, Paper, Scissors game of life, ego sometimes won over pride and common sense. "I want another chance to show you just why I live up to the name Pleasure . . . and it's on me," he added, cranking his truck and eventually reversing back from the pale peach building that was peeling in spots to reveal the putrid green paint beneath it.

The line remained quiet for long moments.

"Hello," he said, making sure she was still there.

"Listen, what purpose does this serve?" she asked. "From my understanding, you have plenty of women wanting your brand of sex. Why do you care what I think?"

Pleasure pulled to a stop at the red light. "This is my business, and I am just offering you an exchange of sorts."

"There's more to you than just muscles and a big dick," Assefa mused.

"Trust me, there is," he assured her as he sat back in his seat and tapped the wheel with his long fingers.

"Okay, fine, if you insist," she said with a sigh. "When? Tonight?"

"It can be."

"Be here in an hour."

Beep.

She ended the call.

Assefa liked control. That was clear.

Glancing at the clock on the wood grain dashboard, he knew it would take most of the hour to make it to Bridgewater. He passed on going by his house first.

As he made the drive, his mind wandered back to Miss Prim and Proper Pearls. He couldn't believe that in a crowd of close to two hundred women, he had so clearly noticed her absence. Not that they had ever shared a word or seen each other outside the club, but still it was hard to deny that seeing her every month had become a ritual of sorts.

Pushing away thoughts of her, he turned the music up and listened to the sounds of Hot 97 as he ate up the miles to Bridgewater.

Bzzzzzzzzz...

Feeling his personal phone vibrate against his thigh, he leaned over a bit to pull it from his front pocket. "Yo," he answered.

"Yo, Pleasure, you left already?"

It was Hunter, one of the newer dancers at the club. Unlike the vets before him, Pleasure tried to offer help to the newbies. There was plenty of money to go around. No need to be selfish. He tucked his cell phone between his ear and his shoulder as he navigated the highway traffic. "Yeah, I had something to handle. Why? What's up?" he asked.

"We all were headed to the diner down the street, but go handle your handle," Hunter said, the noise of the club still booming in the background.

At that moment, Pleasure pulled up in front of Assefa's house. "Wish me luck," he drawled, eyeing her porch through the windshield.

"A'ight. Let's hit the gym tomorrow morning."

"Cool. I'll call you." He ended the call and left the phone inside his glove compartment before easing out of the truck.

Just as he stepped on the curb, he noticed her neighbor's curtain fluttering closed. Pleasure ignored it and continued up the steps. He wanted no parts of their soap opera.

The door opened before he could even ring the doorbell. He was surprised that Assefa was fully dressed in a sleeveless maxi dress. She stepped back and waved him in.

"Hello, Pleasure."

"Hi." Without the distraction of her nudity, Pleasure quickly took in the warm brown and rust colors of her living room. He glanced away from the pictures lining the mantel and found her leaning against the back of her sofa looking at him as if she was bored.

He moved over to scoop her up into his strong arms before heading up the same stairs she'd led him up before. The door to her bedroom was open and he strolled right inside to lay her down on the middle of the crimson bed. He stepped back and began to undress slowly.

Assefa sat up on her elbows and crossed her leg with her foot swinging.

He frowned. His eyes shifted down to the foot. It reminded

him of that time he'd auditioned for Vera and sent her into boredom.

Assefa tilted her head to the side as she continued to eye him...continued to wait for more.

Pleasure reached for the waistband of his pants.

Assefa held up her hand like she was stopping him in the name of love. "Because this is a freebie, I am going to do you a favor, Pleasure," she said, rising onto her knees.

Pleasure fought the urge to push her back down onto the bed, fling her dress up above her head, and give her The Dick until she cried for no more.

"Come, sweetie." She beckoned with her hand.

Shirtless, he walked over to her.

"No, you wait. I'll come to you," she said, climbing off the bed.

Pleasure stopped, pressing his hands to his hips.

"See, not every woman wants to be fucked, Pleasure, some want to make love," she said, caressing the contours of his chest as she slowly circled his body. "Some want to be freaked. Slowly and sweetly. It is your job to figure out who wants what and deliver."

His body tingled as she stroked his taut nipples with her fingertips. "Take every moment—every chance—to stroke, caress, and kiss her," she whispered against his skin as she dipped to lick a trail from just above his buttocks and up his spine, ending with a kiss and a suck just below his shoulder blades. "You remove the clothing. You pamper her. You do the work."

Pleasure felt goose bumps race across his skin and he tilted his head back as she eased his pants and his boxers down over his buttocks. He gasped lightly when she lightly bit each ass cheek before she spread them and blew a stream of air up the divide. His eyes opened in surprise and pleasure.

"Kiss and touch every part of her skin. Leave nothing without your attention." Assefa came around the front of him and shifted the clothing over his erection as she sucked the hard groove between his biceps and then licked a trail hotly from one hard nipple to the other. "There is so much more that should happen before you slide this big dick inside a woman," she said, tilting her head back to lock eyes with him as she stroked the length of it from the root to the smooth brown tip before she lightly fondled his tight balls.

Pleasure's ass clenched at the feel of her touch.

"Everywhere," Assefa insisted in a whisper, leaning to the side to place a row of kisses from the side of his hard buttocks and up his rib cage to just below his armpit. She leaned to the left and replicated the move.

Pleasure shivered, fighting the urge to pick her up and toss her on the bed to fuck her hard. He couldn't deny she was schooling him because his anticipation was building.

"And talk to her, Pleasure. Tell her what you feel and convince her of what she should feel," Assefa said, working his pants down until they fell atop his Jordans. "Make love to her mind. Let your words fuck her up too, baby."

She smiled at him and wrapped her fingers around his dick to lead him to the bed. Bringing her hands up high, she caressed his shoulders before bringing them down, her nails lightly raking his skin while she lowered her body until she knelt before him. Hard and curving inches were now above the curls of her hair. She stroked his dick as she leaned in to lick, kiss, and bite the sensitive insides of his thighs.

"And trust me, the longer you pay attention to the little things, the more she will enjoy—and the more she enjoys it, the more you will enjoy it."

Pleasure sat down on the bed as she stepped out of her maxi and revealed she was completely naked underneath. "Damn!" he swore.

She smiled and opened the box to remove a condom. "Now, I'm not saying everyone deserves oral, but for the ones you do bless, take your time to get to know the pussy," she said, opening the foil and bending again to settle the latex on his throbbing thick tip.

"Nah, I don't eat pussy," he protested, his dreads shielding his face, as she sucked the condom-covered tip.

Assefa leaned back. "Never?"

"Nah, I'm good."

She shook her head. "You don't know what you're missing," she said, just before she placed his dick back in her mouth and then used her lips to unroll and push the condom down the length of him.

Pleasure's mouth fell open as she sucked him deeply and slowly. He looked down at her moves. He was near coming and she pulled back just in time for the feeling to ease. "Did that feel good?"

"Damn good," he said.

"So why not make a woman feel that way, too? Hmm?" she chided him.

She licked the hollows of his abdominal muscles as she pushed him down onto the bed and straddled him. For long minutes he was lost to everything as Assefa caressed, licked, sucked, and nibbled her way over his body. The entire time her hot words pushed him closer and closer to the edge. Pleasure lay back on the bed and enjoyed every second of her teasing and tantalizing him with a skill that completely fucked him up.

Pleasure was speechless.

"Remember, make love with your dick *and* your words," she said, spreading her moist pussy lips with one hand as she held his dick upright with the other.

She was no joke.

"I want your dick in me. Do you want to put your dick in me?"

His heart was racing and his entire body felt alive as she

settled her pussy on him and took nearly all of him inside her as she bent to suck his ear. "Oh, your dick feel good, daddy," she moaned with a little soft grunt.

Assefa rode him slow and easy, with her walls tightening on his tip before she dipped her hips again. "Who am I?" she asked, sitting up a bit to look down into his face.

"Assefa," he whispered back, not caring that he sounded like a bitch.

She smiled softly and bit her lip. "What am I giving you?"

"Good pussy," he said, arching his back before he roared like the mating lion as he filled her with his cum.

Assefa sat up and pressed her hands into his chest to ride him faster and push them both over the edge as she came as well. "You're welcome," she told him before she stood and freed herself of his now-limp dick.

Pleasure couldn't muster enough energy to do anything but give her a thumbs-up.

Chapter 15

Assefa

One Month Later

Pleasure felt eyes on him. He closed his lids as he continued his daily five-mile run on the treadmill, but that was disappointing because that shut off his view of the city through the windows surrounding the exercise room. Turning up the volume of his iPod, he stayed focused as he picked up the pace.

That feeling was still there and he knew before he even finished his run and turned off the machine that he would find women looking at him. He was right. Some looked away when he turned and others boldly met his gaze.

He waved and smiled at them all as he wiped his bare chest of sweat before hanging his towel over his neck as he made his way to the locker rooms. He was glad to be free of their stares, smiles, and dreamy eyes.

Pleasure was not in the mood for their adoration.

For the last few days he'd found himself more and more annoyed by the opposite sex. Last night in the club when a woman had snatched off his rip-away front and groped his dick, his first reaction had been repulsion. All day he had avoided the growing number of calls from his clients. Kezia and Lola called him for a night out in New York, and he'd even brushed them off.

"Are you a trainer?"

Pleasure was about to walk into the men's locker room but he looked down and found a cute blond woman with reality-defying breasts looking up at him. He forced a smile. "No, I'm not," he said politely, already pushing the door open.

"You really should be a trainer," she said, reaching out toward his abdomen.

Pleasure stepped back before her touch landed.

Her blue eyes widened a bit in surprise. "I'm sorry, I didn't mean to offend."

"Well, it's not the 1800s and I'm not a slave named Mandingo," he told her coolly before he entered the locker room.

Pleasure knew he had been harsh with her because there were many days when he had enjoyed the flirtations of the women he encountered in the building. He had preened under the attention.

Not today. Fuck it.

Opening his wood-faced locker, he removed his cell phone to check the time. He had six missed calls on his trick phone. If each was unique, at three hundred dollars a client, that totaled close to two grand—his rent for the month. He didn't bother to check the calls and tossed the phone back inside the locker atop his shirt before he took off his shorts and wrapped a towel around his waist. The only thing on his mind was a nice long sit in the steam room.

Once he claimed a spot on one of the cedar benches in the nearly empty room, he inhaled deeply to take in some of the steam that swirled around him until he could barely see his hand in front of his face. When he leaned his head back against the wall, the cushion of his dreads reminded him that he forgot to wrap them. He wondered what effect the steam would have on his locs, but he didn't move from his spot.

The quiet was addictive.

For the last few nights, sleep had been evasive, and when he rose in the morning he felt like a bear awakened during hibernation. He wiped his face with both hands, wishing he could decipher what was bothering him. If he was a woman he would call it PMS, but Pleasure was far from female.

As more men entered the steam room, Pleasure rose, tightened his towel, and left. Back at his locker, he checked his phones again.

"Assefa," he said at the sight of her number.

They had a morning appointment that he'd missed. Of all his clients she was the most thrilling for him. Their time together was hot, sexy, and mind-blowing. She'd even convinced him of the joys of eating pussy, and he had to admit that she was right. He hadn't known what he was missing. Feeling a woman's body shiver as he sucked her clit was a whole other kind of high. She was just as determined to make him the best lover she'd ever had as he was to have her admit that he was the best. That made for good times.

Still he didn't return her call—calls. Numerous calls.

"Mr. Lover Lover . . ."

Pleasure eyed his trick phone but shoved it into his pocket without even checking the Caller ID.

He was his father's son, but he was not his father. Pleasure needed a break from women. If only just for one day he needed not to see, smell, talk to, touch, or fuck a woman.

His mind, his body, and his dick needed a break.

Gathering his things from the locker, he left the gym.

Pleasure awakened with a start.

He sat straight up in the middle of his bed with his heart pounding wildly. Bending his legs, he pressed his forehead to his knees and wrapped his arms around his legs. He shook his head as if to clear it. That failed. Roughly kicking away the sheets, he snatched off the silk wrap he wore to protect his dreads at night. Everything felt like it constrained him.

He spent the entire day holed up in his apartment, avoiding all phone calls and finding a dozen different ways to rationalize why he was trying to mentally check out from the world. Something had him on edge. His temper was short. His patience was thin.

And now his night of sleep was ruined.

He covered his face with his hands and rubbed it vigorously as he yelled out sharply at the top of his lungs. "What the fuck?" he gasped in frustration.

Pleasure pounded his fists into the bed. "Breathe. Just breathe," he repeated into the darkness, fighting for control.

Cloaked by the dark, he took deep cleansing breaths that shifted from shallow and shaky to even and steady. Licking his dry lips, he looked out his bedroom window into more inky blackness broken up by twinkling stars. He focused on the brightness and the distance of the stars. He kept his eyes locked on the largest one and forced himself to just breathe.

And to forget.

He felt embarrassed to be a grown man of immense strength and presence who huddled naked like a child in the middle of his bed. But the truth was he didn't want to go back to sleep. He didn't want to return to that place.

"Shit," Pleasure swore, rising from the bed. He slid his bare feet into his slippers to avoid the coolness of the hardwood floors caused by the central air.

His dreads swung across his back and chest as he quickly moved across the room and down the hall to the kitchen. After a cursory check of his fridge—which resulted in him walking away empty-handed—Pleasure let his eyes adjust to the darkness and made his way to the living room.

Beneath the window and the limited illumination it offered,

he did a hundred quick sit-ups, flipped over onto his stomach, and did a hundred one-armed push-ups—on each arm.

He stood by the windows.

He lay on the couch.

He turned the television on to briefly flip through the channels.

He turned the television off.

He paced.

He stubbed his toe, swore, and paced some more with a slight limp.

He craved a drink. He yearned for a hit of cocaine. He would even settle for some good weed.

He thanked God he had none of them at the ready.

Leaving the living room, he headed back to his bedroom—back to whatever he refused to face. He paused at the open door of his unused guest room. The moonlight from the window landed on his easel.

It was the only item in the room save for the pictures on the walls, and it looked as neglected as it was.

Turning on the light, he looked at his sketches in black frames on the walls. He walked around the room and paused to rest his eyes on each one. He was mildly surprised at the varying memories or emotions each one evoked. The triumphs. The failures. All necessary on the road he traveled called life. *His* life.

The sketch of the garden outside his room at the rehab facility. It was as rough and as unrecognizable as he was in the first days of detox.

A few different fruit bowls. A charcoal portrait of his mother during her visit. The park across from his Tarrytown apartment. A recollection from memories of his first lover, Essie. A rendition of his father surrounded by the many faces of the women who flitted in and out of his life. A sketch of Quinn before the reveal of love.

People. Places. Things.

They all had meaning. They all had been a release.

Graham sat before his easel and picked up one of his pencils. The point was dull and rounded, but it beat a blank. Opening the pad, he tried to remember the last time he had touched a page. The last time he had released all of the emotions simmering inside him as he stripped and fucked his way to avoid it all.

Taking a deep breath, he began to free hand, following his instincts and hoping the skill from all the art classes with Quinn came back to him like riding a bike. As a picture formed before him he forged ahead, his confidence boosted by his anxiety finally fading away.

As time passed, his body became more relaxed and his grip on the pencil loosened. At times, he nodded in approval, and at other times he would bite down on his bottom lip in concentration or annoyance as he fixed an error. He sat back more than once with his head tilted this way or that as he studied his work.

The light against the paper brightened and Pleasure looked up, amazed to see that morning had come and the sun was shining bright. He hadn't noticed when day reigned over night.

Rising from his seat, he stretched his arms high, rolled his neck, and lifted his weight up onto his toes as the kinks of sitting all night finally registered. He eyed the sketch, impressed by his detail and confused by its subject as he looked into the face of Lionel at eleven as it loomed from a closet over a peacefully sleeping boy of six.

It had been years since his...violation had come to turn his dreams into nightmares. He didn't know what seemingly minute comment, touch, or act had subconsciously pushed his feelings about it all to the forefront. Nevertheless, it had shaken him to the core last night because he wanted to forget. He wanted to move beyond it. He wanted not to care. He wanted not to want to kill Lionel.

He wanted it not to be such of a huge part of what formed his manhood.

He wanted all of those things. Wanted them badly. He didn't succeed.

"Why?" he asked, fighting the surge of tears that rose in him.

"Why?" he repeated, his anger and confusion and shame rising.

"Why?" he roared, reeling back to punch the face in the sketch with all his might.

His fist tore the page in half and dented the dense pages of the pad as the easel tumbled back against the wall. Fighting the urge to spit on it, he turned and left the room, slamming the door behind him.

"Pleasure, what are you doing here? Where have you been for the last month? What's going on?" Assefa asked as he breezed past her into her house.

Pleasure turned and eyed her intently as she pushed the door closed. Before she could finish that simple task, he took two large strides across the room, lifted her, and pressed her against the polished wood.

"Pleasure," she gasped just before he moved his hands to the sides of her face and kissed her fiercely until she gripped at his shoulders, drawing the shoulders of his V-neck T-shirt into her fists.

The moan he released was filled with passion and torture. It had been years since he kissed a woman. Years.

He sucked her tongue deeply before lightly biting her chin, then pressed heated kisses down the column of her neck to her pounding pulse point as he jerked her skirt up around her waist and ripped her sheer, delicate panties from her body with one strong tug.

Pleasure knew his urgency could be frightening for her but he couldn't control himself.

He bent low enough to hoist her legs up onto his shoulders and pressed her thighs apart to open her pussy lips and expose her clit to him. To his tongue. To his lips.

Assefa gasped and bit her bottom lip at the feel of him sucking her clit at a steady pace. She pressed the back of her head against the door and arched her back, bringing her hands up to thread through his dreads, massage his scalp, and press his face deeper between her thighs. "Shit, shit, shit," she swore in heated whispers as her entire body came alive.

Pleasure was relentless as he felt her bud swell and warm against his lips. Spreading her legs wider until her knees touched the door and her buttocks lifted up off it slightly, he sucked away between intermittent feather-light licks even as Assefa brought her hands up to press against his forehead to free herself from the sweet agony of his tongue on her sensitive post-climax clit.

"Ah-ah-ah-ah-ah-ahhhhhhhhhhhhhhh-ah-ah," she cried out. "Oooh, ooooh, oh-eee. Hmmm. Yes. Yessssssssss! No-no-no-no. Yessssss."

Pleasure roughly pushed her legs off his shoulders and stepped back slightly to let her shivering body slide down the door into his arms. He set her on her feet and she stumbled a bit, disoriented from the high of cumming. With another kiss to her lips, he began to undress her the way she'd schooled him all those weeks ago—with lingering kisses and caresses to her neck and nape, twin rounded shoulders, her collarbones and pulse points. The sweet and warm valley between the swells of her breasts. And then each of her taut brown nipples.

Assefa sighed, cried, moaned, or just dug her fingernails into his hard flesh with each new spot.

The sounds of her pushed him until every piece and pulse

of her body was explored, pampered, and revealed and she stood before him naked and shivering with stoked desire.

"Pleasure," she sighed almost in surprise as her chest rose and fell with her labored breaths.

He too exhaled deeply out of his mouth as he stood before her as if he was ready to go to war. He needed her. He needed to be in her. He needed these moments. He needed it... and he needed it now.

She stepped up to lightly bite his chin and reach for the edge of his shirt, but Pleasure swiped her hands away. Assefa reached for the waistband of his sweatpants this time and eyed him defiantly with one brow arched as she jerked his pants down around his muscled thighs.

A challenge. Two strong wills. Two lovers built to please.

She stroked his hardness before bending to her knees and taking him into her mouth.

Pleasure's entire body went still at the first feel of her sucking his dick. With a sharp intake of breath, he thrust his hips forward and grasped the back of her head as he fucked her mouth. His butt clenched with his tiny thrusts forward.

Assefa wrenched her head free of his tight grip and leaned back to look up at him as she rose. She opened her mouth to speak but Pleasure pushed her roughly against the door and kissed her again until whatever words of protest she thought about forming dissipated in the heat they'd created.

He picked her up again and hoisted her over his shoulder with a sound slap to her buttocks as he turned to lay her down on the floor right atop the edge of the area rug showing beneath her living room sofa. She brought her hands up high above her head and lifted one leg onto the back of the chair as she spread the other wide.

Pleasure shook his head. He wanted her in his way. Not hers. *I'm in control here.*

He pressed his thick tip inside her as he reached for her

legs and wrapped them around his neck. Tightly gripping her thighs, he clenched his jaw at the feel of her as he filled her heat with his thick width . . . inch by inch, until nearly all of him was planted deeply within her.

Assefa's mouth opened a bit with a hot little gasp that was only just the beginning.

Pleasure was on a mission to prove something to himself and to her.

He flung her legs away roughly and began to make love to her passionately and slightly aggressively. He combined many of his wicked dance moves along with the attentiveness she'd taught him to make love to her fiercely. At times slow and deep. Other times fast and deeper. But always . . . *always* with pleasing her uppermost in his mind.

Time sped by as he continued to pick up the pace of his thrusts. He shifted her body from one position to another. Beneath him. Riding him. On their sides. And a dozen more. Each more pleasing than the last. Each sending her into a mind-blowing climax that made her cries and moans fill the air. He lost count of how many times he felt her walls tighten around him as she came.

And he wasn't done with her yet.

"Yes," she cried out shakily, her full lips quivering.

"You love the way I fuck the shit out of you, don't you?" he asked her, massaging her breasts and teasing her nipples, both of her legs up on one of his strong shoulders while he continued to rotate his abs and hips to send his dick around her walls in tight, delicious circles.

Assefa nodded several times.

"Don't I?" he demanded again.

"Yes," she whispered harshly.

He sucked her calf and brought his hands down to lift her buttocks up off the floor. "What's my name?"

"Pleasure."

"And what do I give?" he asked her, his eyes locked on her face.

"Pleasure."

The student had become the teacher.

Pressing her onto her back, Pleasure pressed his hands against the floor and did push-ups in her pussy, ending each extension of his arms with a deep dip inside her tightness until she was clutching him with her arms and legs and crying out as she came again. He rode the wave with her until he too felt as if his entire body lit with fire as he climaxed.

Assefa pressed kisses to his shoulder as he gave her one last thrust that made his entire body weak. He dropped his head to her shoulder. "Pleasure, that was so good," she said, languorously raising her hands above her head to clap. "You finally got it. That was *the best* I ever had."

Pleasure allowed himself those desired moments to recollect himself before he finally raised onto his elbows and looked down into her eyes, his softening dick still inside her. "The very best?" he asked, his heart pounding in his chest.

Assefa nodded. "*The very best,*" she emphasized, her hands now on his broad shoulders.

He nodded and took one deep breath before he rose to his feet, pulling his dick free from her. "Then our time together has come to an end," he said as he looked about the room for his discarded clothing.

"Our what? What? Huh?" she asked, still on her back on the floor.

Pleasure glanced at her as he quickly dressed. "This one is on me because it's over, Assefa," he said.

She sat up. "No, it isn't," she insisted.

He opened the door and looked down at her one last time, appreciating her body and everything she'd taught him with it. "I don't want to play the game with you of topping myself. Let another man take my crown...one day," he told her cockily.

Assefa looked surprised and even a little hurt, but then her face filled with as much bravado and cockiness as he gave her. "You'll be back," she said confidently.

Pleasure shrugged as if that was a possibility, but he knew as he turned and walked out onto the porch that he would never return...or answer another of her calls.

Interlude

Present Day

*H*is eyes fluttered open. He winced at the brightness of the sun beaming through the many windows of his top-floor apartment. In between slow and labored blinks, he finally focused on the view of the New York skyline. Day two of the bullshit.

Life was moving on at a frenetic pace outside his apartment while his was on pause at the hands of a lunatic from his past. He couldn't deny his fear or shame. He was a man of size and strength, and a woman had overcome him.

Shit. Shit. Shit.

He shifted his frame in the chair and he winced. His body was a mass of tightness and aches. He didn't know whether to be thankful that he was still alive or not.

"Good morning, Pleasure."

Shaking his dreads back from his face, he watched her walk into the living room from the hall leading from the kitchen carrying a plate and a glass of apple juice. She had changed clothes but was still all in black with the mask in place. When she neared him he could smell the scent of his special blend of handmade soap clinging to her skin.

"I loved sleeping in your bed last night," she said, her eyes locked on him. "I just wished you could have snuggled up with me in it, but you were so tired that I decided not to disturb your sleep."

"Sleep?" he snapped. "You drugged me."

"I used to hate getting drugged too," she said, pausing to oddly rotate her shoulders as she shook her head.

"Where, in the psych hospital?" he asked, frowning deeply.

"Yes," she answered simply—almost pleasantly—to his sarcasm. "I know you must be hungry, so I made you breakfast."

The revelation of her lack of sanity didn't surprise him.

"Are you going to loosen the ties so that I can eat?" he asked.

Sitting the plate and the glass on the floor by his feet, she pulled one of his heavy dining room chairs up to sit before him. "No, I'm going to feed you, silly. Don't you want me to feed you?"

He looked down at the plate of grits, egg whites, and turkey bacon. It looked edible enough, but he ignored the ravenous growling of his stomach. "I'm not hungry," he said in a hard voice.

She froze in her motion to sit in the chair. "You always was an unappreciative motherfucker," she said, her voice cold and tight and angry. "Nothing I did was ever good enough."

He watched silently as she picked up the plate and stirred the grits before scooping up a good bit onto the fork.

"And now here we go again with the same bullshit," she said, the fork hitting against the plate with her agitated movements.

He pressed his lips closed when she lifted the fork to his mouth.

"Eat, Pleasure," she warned him, poking his lips with the prongs of the fork as she kept pressing it against his mouth.

Some of the steaming grits fell onto his thigh and clung to his skin, scorching him. Still he did not waver and kept his eyes locked on her and his mouth closed. I'm not going to help this crazy bitch spoon-feed me only God knows what.

She inched forward on the chair and reached behind her to remove her sheathed knife from her waistband. "You going to be thankful for this meal I cooked or not?" she asked, pressing the edge of the knife against his cheek.

He didn't trust her any further than he could see her with his hands tied behind his back. The cold of the knife was all too real and he wasn't confident she wouldn't snap and slice or stab him.

What the fuck did I do to deserve this shit?

Fearing for his life and wanting to stall what she swore was the inevitable, he opened his mouth. He could tell from her eyes that she smiled behind her mask.

Chapter 16

Smyth

2009

For the last hour of his life Pleasure had rushed. In driving. In parking. In walking through the halls to reach the door he now stood before. The rushing stopped. He stood before it as if frozen in time. Frozen by fear of just what he would find on the other side.

God, please . . .

Pleasure lightly patted the door twice before he pushed it open and stepped inside the room only to pause again at the sight of his father lying in the hospital bed connected to monitors with an oxygen mask on his face and his eyes closed.

"Hey, Graham."

He shifted his eyes over to where his mother sat in a bedside chair. She was smiling but her eyes were slightly red and puffy. He glanced at his father again as he moved across the room to bend down and press a kiss to her brow.

"How is he?" he asked, leaning against the wide ledge of the window.

"He did have a heart attack, but he's stable now," Cara said, reaching over to rub Tylar's hand.

Pleasure nodded.

"He's just sleeping, Graham," she said, reaching back to grab his hand with her other one.

He nodded again.

It was hard for a man to swallow, facing his father's mortality.

"He's young and strong and he *will* be fine," she said.

Pleasure looked down at her because her words now sounded like she was trying to convince herself and not just him. He squeezed her hand a bit tighter.

"I'm going to see if the doctor is ready to update us," she said, rising to leave the room.

Pleasure stepped closer to the bed and watched the steady rise and fall of his father's chest as he slept. Futilely, he eyed the different monitors, wishing he knew what they all meant.

The door opened and he looked up as a petite nurse with reddish brown twists wearing dark blue scrubs entered the room with an IV bag in her hand. He gave her a cordial smile as he stepped back from the bed. She looked up at him and did a double take before leaning back a little as she eyed him.

Pleasure shifted where he stood under her appraisal.

"Oh my God. I recognize you," she said, sitting the bag on the bedside table as she glanced at him. "I took home one of your flyers from the bachelorette party and my husband had *me* sleeping on the couch for a smooth week."

Pleasure sharply looked down at his father's face and was glad he was still sleeping.

She swapped out the empty bag for the new one, giving him glances as she did. "He's mad but he could use a stripper lesson," she said, before leaving the room with a little wave and a quick up-and-down look at Pleasure's tall, muscled frame and good looks.

He was glad to see her go.

The door opened again and his mother entered with a soft, reassuring smile. "The doctor will be in to talk to us in a little bit," she said, reclaiming her seat.

"What exactly happened?" he asked, more for distraction's sake than anything else.

Cara shifted uncomfortably in her seat and wiped her brows in a decidedly nervous gesture. "We were...we...I didn't mean to..."

Pleasure's deep-set eyes widened in understanding as his mother's caramel cheeks flushed and she avoided his eyes before breaking into tears that shook her rounded shoulders. He frowned deeply.

"He told me to—"

"Ma!" he exclaimed in disbelief, throwing his hands up in the air. "I'm sorry I asked."

What the fuck were they doing?

Cara turned her back to him in the chair and dropped her head in her hand.

"No, son, I'm sorry I asked."

They both looked over to the bed to find Tylar's eyes on them and his oxygen mask pulled down around his chin.

Pleasure smiled in relief and then turned suddenly to look out the window at the street traffic in a clear move of avoidance as he felt all his emotions surge forward and gather in tears. Tears he refused to let fall.

Losing his father shouldn't have been a possibility.

"You all right, Graham?"

He nodded and turned with a smile as he continued to blink rapidly. His mother was stroking his father's closely shaved salt-and-pepper hair, but their eyes were on him.

"Cara, let me talk to him for a second, baby?" Tylar asked, his voice slightly hoarse.

She nodded and pressed a half dozen kisses to his forehead before she left the room with an encouraging look at her son.

Tylar replaced his oxygen mask and took several deep breaths before moving it down onto his chin again. He waved his hand at the chair. Pleasure took the seat.

"You are my son," Tylar said, shifting his tall frame to sit a bit higher in the bed. "When I was your age I was running wild. Enjoying life. The women. The sex. I didn't give a damn about anything or anyone but what I wanted...when I wanted it."

Pleasure kept his eyes locked on his father.

"I thought the world owed me everything. Hell, that was still true up until a year ago," he said, shifting his eyes to look up at the ceiling. "I hurt a lot of women, son. Your mother included."

"Dad—"

Tylar shook his head and took another few breaths from his mask. "It took me damn near all of my fifty-one years to realize that I was hurting myself too."

Pleasure looked pensive.

"I don't want it to take you fifty years to learn the same lesson." Tylar raised his arm to slide it under his head as he looked at his son. "You're young and handsome and you know it. You're running through women like cheap panties. I knew that. The whole *stripping* thing is new to me."

Pleasure covered his surprise well.

"You got more than my looks, son, you got my ego too," Tylar said. "And I didn't set the best example of how to treat women."

"Fuck 'em and leave 'em," Pleasure said, pressing his elbows into his thighs and folding his hands in the space between his knees.

Tylar shook his head. "That was my motto," he said. "But then I realized I left so many behind that I was alone."

They both fell silent, and nothing but the steady beep of his machines filled the air.

"Don't be so focused on the pussy, son, that you don't take time to find the right one to share your life with," Tylar said suddenly.

"I'm only twenty-six, Pops," he reminded him.

Tylar nodded in understanding. "And before you know it you'll be thirty-six and then forty-six and fifty-six..."

Pleasure chuckled. "I got it."

"I'm just saying time flies, son." Tylar used his mask again. "I got lucky when your mother gave me a second chance. I just want more for you, son. Pussy is easy to come by, love ain't."

Pleasure nodded, letting his father's words sink in.

"Just imagine lying in a bed after a major heart attack and not having someone you love—who loves you back—by your side letting you know she's happy you made it. Imagine that, son."

Pleasure appreciated his father's concern, and it nagged at him that his father didn't even know the half of just how much pussy was a factor in his life and not love. Love was nowhere in sight.

"You make good money?"

He shook his head and laughed. "I do a'ight," he said, jokingly.

Tylar made a face. "You look like me. You should be doing better than just a'ight...make sure your ass not forty still doing that shit."

Pleasure made a face. "I would be dead wrong for that."

"Yes the fuck you would."

The door to the room opened and his father motioned for him to say no more. Pleasure knew then that his father was not going to tell his mother about his stripping, and he was happy for that.

"And don't forget what I said, Graham. Love over sex always wins in this game called life."

"Good evening, sir."

Pleasure nodded at the uniformed door attendant as he held the large ornate door open for him. He entered and crossed the large expanse of the marbled foyer to the gilded elevators with a brief wave to the concierge.

He could hardly believe this had been his home for the last couple of months.

He moved to the small group of residents. Only one of the four elevators was exclusively for the use of the owners of the two penthouse apartments. He eyed the interracial couple standing before that one. The white man in his early forties was Baldwin Grant, a popular and wealthy plastic surgeon catering to discreet celebrities, and the African American woman in her early thirties, Smyth, was his devoted wife.

Everything about him spoke to his well-to-do lifestyle, from the cut of his pin-striped suit and double-knotted silk tie to the beautiful woman draped on his arm. Both cost him well, but the man could afford it.

That's what the fuck I'm talking about.

Pleasure shared a brief glance with her and she looked offended before she clutched her husband's arm a little tighter and looked away as if dismissing him.

Whatever.

The elevators slid open. Pleasure was one of the last to get on. He leaned against the wall of the elevator. The metal showed his reflection. His dreads were pulled back from his face, revealing his lean features. The crisp striped mono-grammed shirt and dark denims he wore could not hide his tall, muscular frame. The clothes were so different from the athletic gear he always wore, but he figured taking college

classes had called for a change in wardrobe...when he wasn't
working or tricking.

The elevator came to a stop on the twelfth floor and he
pushed up off the wall to ease past the other occupants. He
had barely made it inside the apartment and dropped his bag
by the door before the doorbell sounded. He opened it and
stepped back as Smyth Grant breezed in.

"That was quick," he said.

"Baldwin had a conference call and locked himself in his
office as soon as we walked into the apartment," she said with
a shrug before she turned and lifted the layers of her hair to
offer him the zipper to the designer dress she wore.

Pleasure eyed the dark-skinned, slender beauty. Nothing
about her was real except for the deep brown tone of her
skin. Her shoulder-length auburn weave, the hazel contacts,
her double DD breasts, and lipo'ed stomach were all manu-
factured by her husband, but only genetics and the Great
One above could create the skin that was almost as dark as
midnight. She reminded him of the model Alek Wek. Smooth.
Unmarred. Radiant.

Knowing exactly what she needed, Pleasure unzipped her
dress and pressed a row of kisses down her spine. It was his
job as her paramour to know her wants and supply them
without question.

Two months ago, Smyth Grant, a Dartmouth graduate
and heir to her father's makeup company, had solicited him to
be her lover on demand. The position included a stipend and
free use of the apartment she'd resided in before she wed her
husband. Her only stipulation was that he make love to no
other woman during their arrangement. She hadn't even
known he was a stripper when she was initially referred to
him, and so she made no claims on that part of his life. Pleasure didn't bother to fill her in.

Pleasure had been hesitant, but he couldn't deny that her

generous stipend and the rent-free apartment left him with plenty of time on his hands. Not wanting them to become too idle and serve as the devil's playground more than they already did, he decided to enroll in college. Being involved with Smyth had opened up possibilities to him that the hunt for pussy had blocked from his vision for himself. Plus she was decent enough in bed—a bit restrained and seemingly afraid to break a real sweat. No Assefa by any means.

As he unlatched her bra with one move of his finger, Pleasure forced himself not to think of Assefa. It had been a year since he walked out of her house, and he had not been back, just like he said. The blow to her ego—or maybe a testament to the skill she finally acknowledged—had led to her blowing up his phone and even changing her number several times to trick him into picking up.

"Baldwin was asking questions about the apartment," Smyth said, turning to face him.

He took in her ebony beauty and wished she hadn't gotten such large implants for her slender frame. It was all very Barbie-like and not to his liking—not enough to keep his dick from getting hard, but definitely not his preference in women.

"I told him I was renting it out for five grand," she said in between soft whimpers as he massaged her buttocks and kissed her collarbone.

Pleasure didn't give a damn what she told her husband. The ins and outs of their marriage and the lies needed to maintain the façade were not his concern.

"So if he comes—"

"Do *you* want to cum?" Pleasure asked as he swung her up into his arms.

Smyth nodded.

"Good."

With that said, he carried her into the master bedroom and delivered on his promise.

★ ★ ★

Long after Smyth washed up and changed her panties before returning to the penthouse apartment she shared with her husband, Pleasure was sitting on the ledge of one of the many windows lining the apartment in nothing but cotton sleep pants. His textbook was in his lap as he prepared for a test the following day. Because of his GED and his last-minute decision to start school, Pleasure was attending a community college, but he intended to transfer to NYU to complete his bachelor's degree in mass communications.

It felt good to have a goal outside of making a woman cum.

Closing his book, he looked out at the varying heights of the many buildings comprising the New York skyline. His eyes were troubled, reflecting his heart, as he thought of his father. He had called to check on him and his mother said he was resting but stable. Still, he was concerned.

A bright spot in the darkness was seeing his parents united.

Turning away from the window, he looked at the stylish décor of the spacious Upper East Side apartment. It was all very Smyth, with its subdued neutral colors and posh accessories to give it a feminine feel.

He didn't care.

He had given up his apartment in Newark, placed his things in storage, and was saving the money he made from Smyth's stipend and still dancing to grow his already sizeable bank. Stripping and selling dick was not brag worthy, but it afforded him a nice lifestyle and plenty of savings.

Because her husband lived right upstairs and required her at his side for social events, Smyth was hardly ever underfoot and he was left alone in the luxury she provided. And he took full advantage of being in the middle of an existence so different from anything he knew. Wanting to attain that level of life for himself was part of his motivation to go to college.

Pleasure was under no illusions that he could strip and sell dick forever.

Standing up, he stretched his arms high above his head and rose on his toes for as long as he could. Every muscle in his body flexed as he moved. He spread his legs wide and tilted his head back so far that his dreads, now a good length beyond his shoulders, touched his lower back. Lowering his arms, he jumped up and down in place lightly before bending over to touch his toes.

Bzzz . . .

He turned to pick his iPhone up from the pale gold padded window seat. No one had the number for that cell but Smyth, she insisted on that. His trick phone was working, but he kept it powered off with a voice mail saying he was on "extended vacation." Sometimes for kicks he would listen to the messages a lot of his clients left. Most were annoyed, but a lot were playfully chastising about him holding out or playing hard to get.

He frowned when he opened and read Smyth's text.

COME UP.

That was a first. In the two months since he'd moved into the building, Pleasure had never been inside the Grants' apartment. It felt like a major violation to him. *So is fucking the man's wife.*

Shaking his head, he slid the phone into his pocket and strolled across the travertine floor to the bedroom to pull on a long-sleeved tee and his Air Jordan sandals. Grabbing his keys and a couple of Magnum condoms, he left the apartment and walked the short distance down the hall among its elaborate architectural features. The elevator was empty as he rode the four floors up to the top level.

As soon as he stepped off onto a rug that could only be Persian, there was just a small foyer with two front doors facing each other. One was to his left and the other to his right. The door to his left opened but Smyth never appeared.

Is this some Law & Order *type shit?*

He walked the short distance down the hall and pushed the wood door open just enough to peek his dreadlocked head inside. Smyth was leaning against the wall in nothing but a satin robe with tears streaming from her closed eyes, her head tilted back against the wall.

Shit.

Kissing boo-boos—physical or emotional—was not a part of the deal. It was scenes like this that made him avoid a serious relationship.

Shit. Shit. Shit.

He stepped inside the apartment, and the grandeur of it made him pause. The high ceilings, views of Central Park, columns and lit marble fireplaces made the apartment downstairs look low-rent.

Smyth pressed her slender body against his as soon as he shut the door. "I want you to fuck me in our bed so I can think about you when he makes love to me," she said in a whisper against his ear.

"Smyth, this is crazy," he said.

"He's not here. He left. He won't be back," she said, stepping back to turn and walk away. "He's with his white whore."

Pleasure let his head drop. He hated watching soap operas, and for sure he cared nothing about being a part of one.

"I guess he's tired of dark meat," Smyth said bitterly as she turned to face him. "But I'm not."

She untied her robe and let it drape off her thin shoulders, exposing her full breasts and white lace thong that looked brilliant against her skin. "He can have that minimum-wage ho," she said, her diction making the words seem even more crass. "I have you."

Pleasure watched as she swiped away her tears and walked

over to him with a smile that didn't reach her eyes. He had always wondered just why a woman like Smyth would "keep" a man, but now he knew. For her there was power and redemption in not just having a love, but having one stashed right under her husband's nose. If he thought he was smart, she knew she was smarter.

Pleasure was just a pawn in their chess game.

The doorknob rattled.

Smyth pushed past him to silently but quickly slide the chain lock on the door while she motioned for him to get down behind one of the four couches situated around the spacious living room.

Pleasure threw his hands up in the air, his face incredulous, and did just as she bid; she backed away from the door, tying her robe before she sat on one of the sofas.

Just a moment after Pleasure knelt down, her husband pushed the door, but the chain kept it from opening wide.

"Honey, honey, come take the chain off the door," Baldwin called through the slim opening.

"I'm coming," Smyth called out, rising to move to the door.

Ain't this some bullshit.

"So you didn't have an emergency at the hospital again?" she asked.

"Dr. Harmon is on duty. I asked him to check on the patient for me and call if I'm needed," Baldwin said.

Pleasure assumed Smyth would lead him out of the living room as soon as possible to allow him to escape the drama. He frowned when he heard them settle onto the couch.

"So we can finish what we started?" she asked, sounding coy.

"I'm tired, Smyth, I just—"

At the sound of their kissing and moaning, Pleasure fought the urge to calmly stand up and walk out. It took him a moment to notice he could see their reflection in the windows. They hadn't been kissing. It was Smyth on her knees desperately giving her husband head.

Pleasure wiped his eyes with his hand and just shook his head. *I must be a magnet for crazy bitches. Rich ones, poor ones. Black ones, Latina ones.*

He sat quietly on the floor behind the sofa as Smyth gave her hubby the "happy ending" and all, causing the middle-aged man to squeal like a pig. Pleasure was embarrassed for them both. It was a lot more of Baldwin Grant and his six thin inches than he needed to see. Ever. In life.

"Let's go to take a bath," Smyth said, rising and wiping her mouth with one hand while reaching for her husband's with the other.

Soon their footsteps and voices faded, and Pleasure wasted no time rising and walking out the front door, quietly closing it behind him. He had just stepped on the elevator when his phone vibrated against his thigh in his pocket. He didn't bother to pull it out.

It was Smyth playing more games—or better yet, feeling as if she had just made a move to checkmate.

Chapter 17

Smyth

Pleasure had become the headliner at Club Trick a long time ago, but he always insisted on performing during the earlier shift on Thursday's ladies' night as well. Always. He felt he couldn't break their ritual. If she—Miss Prim and Proper Pearls—could continue for all these years to never miss her once-a-month show, then he would hold up his end of their unspoken bargain and perform during that five o'clock hour.

There she is.

He watched her take a seat down at the base of the stage in the middle. As Jamie Foxx's "Blame It" faded out and Usher's "U Got it Bad" began to play, Pleasure rotated his hips to cause his thick semi-hard dick in a neon green sleeve to swing back and forth as he also worked his abs. He moved his body down to the floor, as fluid as that of a snake, as he imitated fucking in a way that would make her never forget him.

The women in the audience threw money on the stage, cheering his movements, but it was her he noticed squirming in her seat as she crossed and uncrossed her legs. He could see her heat in her eyes as she sat and watched him perform as if he took her to a place—a very good place—where desire and passion and hunger reigned.

A place he knew she had yet to explore.

He could tell in the reserved way that she carried herself. Even in the midst of women screaming, hollering, and gyrating, she sat with dignity, only revealing her lust in her eyes or maybe a gentle nibble of her bottom lip.

When she eased money from her purse and held her hand up to him like a schoolchild requesting permission to go to the restroom, he moved away from some customer that he would never remember to dance over to where she sat. He performed for her, wanting to please her. Tantalize her. Turn her on. She tentatively reached out to tuck the folded bill into the front of his thong. He followed his instinct and grasped her wrist to guide her hand to his dick.

"Don't be scared," he told her loud enough to beat out the pounding music as he felt her slight resistance.

He wanted her touch. He wanted her to feel him. He wanted her to get more out of her monthly trips to Newark just to see him.

"You know what? You need a private dance," Pleasure whispered in her ear, liking the subtle scent of her perfume. It intrigued him. "You game?"

He surprised himself. He wanted her to say yes.

"I'm married," she said, looking nervous.

"I don't give a fuck," he told her. And he didn't.

Her monthly trip to find passion let him know that the addition of her husband to her life had done absolutely nothing to alter it. He didn't know this woman, but he knew that. And he wanted to change it.

Pleasure took her hand and he was surprised when she so easily rose to her feet. He massaged circles against her wrist as he led her to one of the private rooms at the rear of the club and pulled her through the curtain. They entered to the sound of Ginuwine's "So Anxious." The lone red light gave the darkness a fiery glow as he sat her in one of the few chairs before stepping up onto the small stage.

Pleasure gave her a slow and sensual dance, his eyes locked on her as he let the combined effects of the red light, the music, and his body tantalize her.

"I love the way you're talking dirty . . ."

What he didn't expect was his own titillation. Not the bravado he put on for the customers. Maybe it was the awareness of her over the last five years or just the sight of her sitting there, all prim and proper, but giving off a vibe that beneath the layers of propriety was a hellcat.

He was caught up too. The real deal. Desire.

Pleasure moved his hips in tight ticking motions in sync to the sudden flickering lights as he worked the custom-made sleeve covering the length of his thick dick and flung it away. He massaged the length of his dick, biting his lip as he looked at her with intensity.

"What exactly happens during a private dance?" she asked when he stepped down off the stage with dick in hand.

Pleasure smiled sexily at her as he straddled her hips and leaned back onto the stage with his dick blowing in the wind like a flagpole. Rolling his hips, he teased the tip just as his eyes locked on her licking her lips like she wished his dick was in her mouth. He wished the same.

He stood up before her, and although he knew he could probably guide it into her mouth with ease, he refrained. "Touch it," he told her. "Come on, you been coming to my shows for years. You know you wanna touch it. Go ahead, I won't tell."

At the first feel of her hand surrounding his hardness, his hips thrust forward and the pulse of the vein running down the side quickened in unison with his heart rate.

They were in the midst of something and he couldn't stop it. He doubted she wanted to. It was five years in the making.

"That's right. Beat that motherfucker." He tilted his head to the side to watch her. It thrilled him to see her, his Miss Prim and Proper Pearls, uninhibited and free. He wanted to push her even further.

"You need to be fucked, don't you?" he observed, freeing his dick from her touch as he dropped to his knees and pushed her skirt up around her hips to open her legs with a guttural moan filled with the fire she stoked in him at the sight of her spread out before him. The sheer, delicate lace bikinis she wore were so different from the demure clothing. "Damn, that pussy smell good."

She shivered as he rubbed her quivering inner thighs, loving the way she arched her back, causing her hard nipples to press against the thin silk of her shirt. His heart pounded as he pulled her moist panties aside to slide his middle finger deep inside her. There was tightness and heat, and her cry of passion made him hungry to please her. To taste her.

"Your husband ain't taking care of this pussy, is he?" Pleasure asked as he spread her legs wider and dipped his head to lick the length of her pussy before he circled her clit with his tongue.

She shivered as she brought her hands up to grip his shoulders. "Do it again," she begged in a hoarse voice.

Pleasure enjoyed the taste of her. The feel of her clit throbbing against his tongue. The sweet smell of her core. The way her body reacted to him.

"Yes," she sighed, her hips jerking with each stroke of his tongue.

Pleasure reached inside the top of his boots and removed the condom he had stashed there to use during his performance. He wanted to be inside her. He tore away her panties and sat back from her just long enough to sheath himself with the latex.

"You want me to fuck the shit out of you, don't you?" he asked her, feeling more of a thrill about sex than he had in years.

"Yes. Please."

"What's my name?"

"Pleasure."

"And what do I give?"

"Pleasure."

His hand trembled as he held his dick and guided the tip inside her, finishing with a strong thrust of his hips that sent his hardness deep inside her. He swore at the tight feel of her surrounding him with heat. He paused, giving him a few precious moments for his climax to subside.

Everything about her and being in her in the red-lit room with some slow jam playing in the background was thrilling to him. Her face was lit up with her passion. Her mouth was slightly ajar. Her pupils dilated. Her nipples hard. Her clit swollen.

"Fuck me."

Those words from her mouth were his undoing.

"My pleasure." He gave her fast and deep strokes before alternating with a wicked slow grind.

He picked her up by the waist and stood, kicking the chair away to slam against the wall as he worked her hips. Pleasure pulled out every move in his arsenal and made use of any available space in that small room as he did as she bid him. With his strength and her flexibility, he switched positions at a mind-blowing pace as she tugged at his dreads and he removed her clothes. Although she let him know with moans and cries each and every time he made her cum, he could feel her walls spasm and the wetness soak him with each release.

"Have you been pleasured?" he whispered in her ear from behind before twisting his hand in her hair to ride her hard.

"Yes," she cried out.

"This dick 'bout to cum," he told her.

He leaned his head back until the tips of his dreads stroked his buttocks as he quickened the pace of his thrusts like a well-oiled piston. Slick and fast. Back and forth.

His explosion was like nothing he'd ever experienced, and that surprised him even as he hollered out with each spasm of his release as he slid his dick out of her and removed his condom to jack his nut onto her trembling butt. All of his senses were alive, and he felt light-headed and electrified from their chemistry as he rose and stumbled back from her.

He didn't have enough fingers and toes to count the women he had sexed and pleasured, but Miss Prim and Proper Pearls had just given him an experience that scared the shit out of him. "Shake it off, Pleasure," he told himself, still weak and trembling from his release and the rush of endorphins.

He looked at her, slumped on the floor, naked and fighting to breathe. Everything about what just happened had her messed up too. He turned on the regular light and quickly slid his thong and sleeve back on, wishing he could get his shit together and wondering why she had such an effect on him. He didn't even know her name.

Needing to be freed from her and the spell broken, he picked her purse up from the floor. "That's two hundred dollars," he said, needing their roles clearly defined again. He needed that line up between them.

Her eyes popped open and she quickly sat up to take the purse and shove cash into his hand. The fact that he recognized and felt pained by her obvious shame was even more confusing.

"Um, thank you. I guess," she said, rising to her feet to

rush into her clothes and shove her torn panties inside her purse as she raked her fingers through her wild hair.

"You're more than welcome. Call me sometime," he said, careful to remind her that what they shared was just that. But then he felt like this would be the last time he saw her because of the line they'd crossed, and he surprised himself when he stepped close to press a kiss to her forehead before he walked through the curtain.

Pleasure headed straight for the bathroom downstairs in their locker room and disposed of the condom he'd left clinging to the tip of his dick. He leaned against the sink and looked up at his reflection. "What the fuck was that?" he mouthed, before shaking his head.

Miss Prim and Proper Pearls had surprised the hell out of him.

And I broke my promise to Smyth.

He had given her his all and he could only hope that Smyth was busy with Baldwin and didn't require his servicing, because he had absolutely nothing left to give her.

Pleasure was surprised to find Smyth in the apartment when he walked through the door. She was sitting on the couch in a beautiful bright red blouson shirt and matching high-waist pants as she flipped through a file. He paused at the sight of her before closing the door and setting his duffel bag onto the floor.

"Hi, Smyth," he said, setting his keys on a foyer table.

She glanced up at him briefly. "How was class?" she asked, sounding more like his mother than his lover.

"Good," he lied. He didn't have class on Thursday evenings, but she thought he did. "I'm going to take a shower and get some studying done."

Smyth shook her head and raised her hand to beckon him

as she closed the folder gracefully and sat back to drape her arm over the back of the sofa. She smiled at him as he crossed the room to reach her, but her eyes were troubled and she looked distracted.

He briefly eyed the folder as he sat on the opposite end of the couch. "Something wrong?" he asked.

She kicked off her black patent leather Walter Steiger heels to place her feet in his lap. "I hired a private detective to catch my husband cheating," she said, lightly biting down on the tip of her crimson nail as she looked past him out the window in the distance.

He said nothing, even though he was mildly curious if her husband's adultery was true or a fabrication of her imagination.

"When I first purchased this apartment, I thought I honestly did not care if I got married or not," she said with a light shrug of one shoulder. "I had seen all of my friends putting up with enough drama that I was content with my beautiful apartment, my career, my inheritance, and a lover here or there to shake out the cobwebs."

He massaged her feet even though she didn't ask.

"And then I met Baldwin, and he just seemed so perfect for me and before I knew it, I was daydreaming about elaborate weddings, honeymoons, and babies." Smyth snuggled down deeper onto the couch.

Pleasure didn't think that boded well for him enjoying the rest of his night alone. He honestly had no desire to make love. He was still trying to recover from the rendezvous with Miss Prim and Proper Pearls. *I really should have asked her name.*

"He proposed. I accepted. We wed," Smyth was saying with sadness. "And now, seven years later, I'm hiring PIs to track my husband because something is not right in our marriage and it hasn't been in a long time—way before you," she added, as if to defend her actions.

"Where exactly is Baldwin?" Pleasure asked.

"Upstairs," she answered simply. She shifted her eyes to look at him. "I told him I had dinner plans, but that was just a ruse to get some privacy to read this report."

His eyes studied her face for some hint of the file's details.

"You wouldn't lie to me, would you?" she asked, choosing as always not to address him by the name Pleasure and abiding by his request to keep his real name just for himself.

"Our relationship doesn't require lies," he lied.

"But I pay you very well not to share your dick," Smyth said. "Is that enough motivation for a man to remain loyal even when a ring and a promise before God cannot?"

Baldwin had been caught, and now she was trying to catch Pleasure.

"More than enough," he said smoothly.

She released a heavy breath and turned her head on the arm of the sofa to look at the file. Tears filled her eyes. "A woman's intuition is never wrong," she said in a soft, bitter whisper.

Pleasure continued to rub circles in the arch of her foot with his thumbs as he massaged her delicate ankles.

"So what do I do now?"

Good question.

She eased her feet from his lap and sat up. "I guess my black ass is not as smart as I thought," she said, tapping her finger against the file.

He eyed her profile.

"I convinced myself that this docile and sweet white man wouldn't do me wrong like the bro-*thas*," she said, emphasizing the last word as if she was in a seventies black exploitation film.

He bit back an amused smile.

"I may not know what to do about my husband and his dalliance," Smyth said, piercing him with her eyes. "But I'm clear on my use for you if you're playing in the greener grass also."

Pleasure shifted in his seat as he remembered the excitement he felt during that hour he'd spent in that room with Miss Prim and Proper Pearls.

She stood up with the file in hand, lightly hitting it against her thigh as she looked around her apartment again. "If I had just stuck to my original plan," she said with regret.

She crossed the room to stand before the fireplace, reaching up to swing open the framed mirror to reveal a safe. She pressed her thumb to the pad on the door, and an instant later, it opened. As she slid the file inside the safe, he didn't bother to try and see the rest of the contents. They were not his concern.

Smyth closed the safe and then the mirror before she turned and left the apartment without saying another word. The door gently closed behind her with a click.

Pleasure let his head fall back and looked up at the gold-trimmed tray ceiling and the elaborate chandelier above. His thoughts were full.

His decision to sell himself to just one woman had helped with his feelings of being overwhelmed by all the women. It had him in a bad headspace for a long time. Being with Smyth had seemed like a win-win.

That time in the red room with a woman whose name he didn't know had reminded him that there was more to sex than just busting a nut.

Standing up, he walked down the hall into the bedroom and retrieved his trick phone from under his boxers in the dresser drawer. Sitting down on the mink comforter, he powered the phone on. He had twenty voice mail messages since the last time he'd amused himself by listening to them. He switched to speakerphone.

"This is Pleasure. I'm sorry, but I am on an extended

vacation. Time to recharge, you know. Check back often to see just when I can be reached again."

Beep.

"Pleasure, when are you coming back so that I can cum? This is Shantee. Call me."

Beep.

"Damn."

Beep.

"This is some real bullshit, Pleasure."

Beep.

"What do you give? Pleasure. What do I need? Pleasure. Call me. Oh, it's Ursula, boo."

Beep.

Message after message after message.

Still, his motivation for checking the messages was for one woman only. He was curious if *she* called. She hadn't.

Beep.

"Plea-sure . . . come out and play."

He went through them all and saved them. He knew his run with Smyth would not last forever.

Chapter 18

Smyth

Seven Months Later

It had been a very long time since Pleasure had allowed himself to think of Lionel. That night last year had been one of the rare occasions he'd even tried to deal with all of his emotions about being . . . violated. He'd never even broached the subject during the counseling he received while in rehab. He just wanted to forget, and most times, he succeeded.

Slowing his truck down, he looked over at the house Lionel's parents once owned. Although it was two blocks over from his parents' home, Lionel had been five or six years older than him and the two boys had not been friends. Pleasure had never once stepped inside, but it had become a house he avoided. The very sight of it reminded him of everything he needed to forget.

Even far beyond the year when Lionel and his parents moved out of town, Pleasure avoided that street. Avoided the memory.

That hadn't worked today. A parade had blocked off the streets he usually took to reach his parents, and he had no choice.

So here he was.

A new family had purchased the home years ago and even changed the color from a powdery blue to a brilliant white, but still the house affected him. He looked pensive, his hands clutched tightly enough at the wheel to snap through it.

He had been weak then. Just a little boy going to church the way his mother said little boys should. He hadn't deserved to suffer from whatever perverted sickness or weakness Lionel had inside.

Pleasure wasn't at all surprised by the tear he felt race down his cheek and fall into his lap. He was crying for the little boy too afraid to speak and for the awareness that his silence had probably led to other little boys being hurt as well. He clenched his jaw as tightly as he clenched his fist just before he pounded it on his dash.

For the first time in years, his craving for cocaine was so strong that he knew he would've relapsed. He would've given up years of being clean to get out of this moment. Out of his head. Out of his pain. Out of his memory.

"Father God," he prayed, turning to a foundation he had long since left behind.

The sound of a horn blaring behind him shook him visibly and he shifted his eyes away from the house and up to the rearview mirror. There was a row of cars behind him, all detoured away from the parade route and just trying to make it to their destination.

He blocked them.

Taking in large, deep breaths, he forced himself to accelerate and move out of the past, figuratively and literally.

Pleasure drove the remaining two blocks to his parents' home and parked on the driveway behind his father's motorcycle. The sight of it made him smile, and he needed a reason to feel good. A picture of his mother and father atop the Harley did just the trick.

You did it. Something fucked up happened to you, but you made it through.

Right?

Climbing from the truck, he swallowed over a lump in his throat and hoped he was right.

"Mr. Lover Lover . . ."

Sitting back down onto the driver's seat, Pleasure picked up his trick phone from the console. He was disappointed that the number wasn't Jaime—Miss Prim and Proper Pearls. She was the only client he was dealing with outside of Smyth. She didn't know that, and that was fine by him. It helped to maintain that line that so often blurred between them.

Jaime had not called. Not for an entire six months. And he had noticed. Even as he enjoyed the lifestyle Smyth afforded, finished his first semester of college with a 3.975 GPA, and even enjoyed a trip to Paris over winter break where Smyth purchased him a suite beneath the one she shared with her husband, still he noticed that she never called. There were dozens upon dozens of calls from women who clamored for some of the "Pleasure Principle."

But her call never came. And he noticed. And he didn't like that he noticed.

Then one night when he was walking into Club Trick, she was sitting there in her car. Waiting for him. He played it cool and cocky, but on the inside he had been happy for her reappearance and even happier when she solicited his services.

"How much?" she asked.

"How long?" he countered.

"The rest of the night . . . if you can," she said.

"Five bills. Midnight," he said, *remembering to make the line clear.*

It had been on ever since. She couldn't get enough of the dick, and truth be told, he couldn't get enough of her.

Somewhere in the midst of that six months that she'd disappeared, she had changed. She was more bold and confident and aware of her sexiness. She was like a butterfly free of the confines of the cocoon.

He knew she had left her husband and there was some drama about a friend possibly sleeping with him. He didn't know the details and he didn't care. All he knew was she had her own place—a town house—and they spent quite a bit of time together. He didn't even charge her when he initiated the sex play.

He hadn't done that since Assefa, and with her that was because he had something to prove. Now he did it because there were times when he just wanted to be with her. He wanted to experience her. Taste her. Fuck her. Make love to her. Be with her.

And that chemistry that blew his mind that first time in the little back room was still there pulsing between them with a life all its own.

He reached the bottom step and then turned to head back to the truck with a smile on his face that deepened his dimples. He unlocked the vehicle and reached for the phone to dial her number.

"Surprise, surprise," she said. "No one else buying up your time today?"

"Just had a cancellation," he lied. "You want this dick or not?"

"I got wet as soon as I saw your number," Jaime countered.

He shook his head. So very different from Miss Prim and Proper Pearls—or at least his preconceived ideas of her.

"I'll be there 'round eight," he calculated.

"Ah. The dicking hour," she teased.

With a chuckle, he ended the call, not bothering to say another word.

Tossing the phone back onto the console, his iPhone—

aka the Smyth phone—vibrated in his pocket at just that moment.

As he answered the call, his mother stepped out onto the porch and waved him over. "Hey, Smyth," he said, raising his hand to his mother.

"I'm at the apartment, where are you?"

"I spend Sundays with my parents, remember?" he said.

"Oh," she said, sounding disappointed. "Baldwin's off doing only God knows what, and I was lonely."

That was a hint and a half for him to ditch his parents and hightail it back to New York.

Pleasure was a little over a month from finishing his first year of college. Between his classes, making time for Jaime, still working at the club, and Smyth's demands, he barely had time to see his parents. He actually looked forward to their Sundays together, and normally Smyth was preoccupied with her husband.

Still, she paid him very well and he agreed to the terms. He was breaking enough of the rules with his trysts with Jaime.

"I'll be there in a couple of hours," he promised, figuring he could get back enough in time to satisfy her, take a nap, and reboot his energy for Jaime later that night.

"Good," she said firmly.

He left all three cell phones in the truck and securely locked the door before finally climbing the stairs and walking inside to share some time with his family.

Pleasure entered the upscale building and barely glanced at Smyth's husband Baldwin as he stood in the hall awaiting the elevator. The man barely spared him a glance as well.

What did take Pleasure aback was Baldwin stepping on the elevator with him and not using the one to the far right reserved for the penthouse residents. Stepping on, he started to reach to push the button for his floor, but stopped when Baldwin pushed it before him.

Pleasure shifted in his stance, towering over the man by nearly seven inches, as he wondered just what was unfolding before him.

"You didn't select your floor," Baldwin said, his black hair raked off his face.

Pleasure looked down at him. "That's the one," he said with a lift of his chin toward the door panel.

He faced forward but he could see in the reflection provided by the metal walls that Baldwin slid his hands into the pockets of his chinos and stared up at Pleasure for a long time.

Am I gonna have to whup Smyth's husband's ass?

The elevator slid to a stop and Pleasure let the other man step into the hallway first. Not out of fear or deference. He wanted to see just where he was headed. His suspicions were soon confirmed as Baldwin walked up to the door and knocked.

Here we go.

Pleasure removed his key from his pocket. "Can I help you?" he said politely, using his most refined voice.

"*You* live here?" Baldwin asked, pointing his finger to the door.

"Excuse me," Pleasure said, and then patiently waited for the man to step aside before he unlocked the door.

Baldwin's blue eyes widened.

"A friend of my parents is renting the apartment to them so I can stay here while I attend NYU," Pleasure lied flawlessly. "There's not a problem, is there?"

Baldwin cleared his throat and rocked on his heels. "No, no. My wife, Smyth, owns this apartment," he said.

Pleasure pretended to look surprised. "Oh, all this time I thought Smyth was a dude," he said.

Just as he suspected he would, Baldwin looked relieved

that the six-foot-nine, handsome Black man before him had never met his wife to distinguish Smyth from Smith.

Pleasure opened the door a bit but held on to the door-knob securely. He had no clue if Smyth was inside or any of her lingerie still was lying about from one of their prior dalliances. "It was very nice to meet you," Pleasure said politely...dismissively.

Baldwin took the hint. "Uh, yes, nice to meet you as well..."

"Mikel," he said, supplying the alias he sometimes used for members of his clientele who insisted on knowing his real name.

"Yes, nice to meet you, Mikel."

Pleasure stood in the doorway, completely aware of his and Smyth's boldness, as he watched her husband finally take his leave. He remained there until he heard the elevator doors open and then close.

Turning, he entered the apartment and shook his head at the sight of Smyth lounging on the padded cushion of one of the window ledges looking casually elegant in a crisp French blue shirt and jeans with flat navy patent leather shoes.

"I just met your husband at the door," Pleasure said, dropping his key on the table by the door.

Smyth shrugged. "Perhaps now I will go and knock on the door of his whore and ask her if she plans to have the baby she's carrying," she said sadly, before turning to look out the window. "Baldwin really shouldn't have *fucked* with me."

Pleasure strolled over to stand beside her, raising his hand to stroke her nape.

"And neither should you."

His hand froze midair.

Smyth looked up at him as she turned to rest her feet on the floor before she crossed her slender legs. "Really?" she asked, sounding bored.

Pleasure stepped back from her.

"Where should we begin...Graham?" she asked.

He felt his stomach clench. He'd never told her his real name. She always gave him his allowance in cash. He'd been very careful to protect that.

She shook her head woefully as she rose from the bench just enough to remove yet another file to open.

Pleasure calmly walked across the room and picked up one of the dining room chairs to carry back over to sit down before her. Smyth was no more than one hundred and twenty pounds but the figurative fat lady was singing, and he owed her this final song without interruption.

"Kicked out of high school for fighting. A GED. Cocaine addiction. Rehab. Stripping at Club *Trick*...in Newark, of all places," she said sarcastically, glancing over at him briefly.

He waited.

"You've been selling yourself for years—"

"That's how we met," he inserted smoothly.

Smyth leaned back and eyed him in reproach.

His look never wavered.

"Thank God you're tested for diseases every three months," she said, whipping the folder back open.

"Does it have my blood type and parental DNA tests as well?" he asked in clipped tones, the invasion of his privacy getting to him.

"Type O. You get it from your father," she answered without hesitation.

He furrowed his brow.

"What was most revealing is Ms. Jaime Pine-Hall."

He looked away, shifted in his seat, and then looked back at her. He was surprised at the tears gathering in her eyes. "Smyth—"

"No, no," she said, holding up one long finger to shake at him in reprimand.

"My husband had risked all of this," she began, waving her hand up and down her length, "and most importantly...

this." She pointed vigorously at her heart. "For a woman with no breeding, no class, and no looks—as far as I'm concerned. They will have their little ugly baby and I have to sit here and either play blind or wait for him to leave me. That's not so hard with his dick and one foot already in the streets."

"You can leave him, Smyth." Pleasure reminded her of another option.

She laughed bitterly and her face lit with fire. It was the most beautiful and vibrant he had ever seen the woman before him. "Don't you dare give me advice on *my* marriage," she spat, flinging the file over at him.

A corner of it hit his chest before sliding down his body and landing on the floor. He picked it up. His life story would not join Baldwin's in the safe if he could prevent it.

"I thought at the very least you would remain loyal since I paid for it, but I thank you for the costly lesson that I've learned. I thank you and I thank Baldwin—my two men— for teaching me that money matters not at all when it comes to you whorish motherfuckers being led by your dicks."

Pleasure bit his lip to keep from reminding her that she frequently spread her legs to two men—basically giving him and Baldwin carte blanche to tag team the pussy.

"My husband didn't care about what all I brought to the table in our marriage, and you couldn't care less about everything I offered you for your loyalty." She swiped away her tears with the sides of her hands. "This is a nasty little circle we all have going on here. The five of us: me, my husband and his whore, and you and yours."

Pleasure was surprised at how quickly she struck his ire by calling Jaime out of her name.

"So that's where you've been spending all of your time this last month," she said. "Ms. Jaime Pine-Hall and her little town house."

She rose from the window seat and walked around the living room, touching items of splendor here and there. "You have a choice to make. All of this"—she waved her arm around the apartment and then up and down the length of her body—"or Ms. Jaime Pine-Hall."

The protectiveness he felt about Jaime both surprised and disturbed him. Theirs was not a relationship built on concern and care. And for her to frame the ultimatum of Jaime versus Smyth was ridiculous.

Or was it?

He thought about the excitement he felt at just the thought of seeing her later. It all was too much like a relationship of sorts, because his gut said "Jaime" without hesitation. *Shit.*

That blurred line again. He had to fix it. Make it clear.

But for the more pressing matter at hand...

"I think we've run our course, Smyth," he said.

"Really?" she said, her shock evident.

"I appreciate everything—"

"Spare me," she snapped, striding to the door.

Pleasure stood up with the file rolled up in his hand.

"You must really love this Jaime Pine-Hall," she said, stopping by the table to pick up his keys and remove the one that unlocked the door to the apartment. "You have twenty-four hours to get out."

And with that she was gone.

Interlude

Present Day

"So you're going to kill me because we didn't work out?" he asked as he eyed her sitting on the floor at his feet, slicing sheets of blank paper with her knife.

She pointed it at him. "Nice and sharp for you, Pleasure," she said.

He flinched instinctively.

"I might just rape you and enjoy that glorious dick you love spreading around the tri-state area," she said, leaning against the back of the sofa as she set the knife down on the floor.

"When does this all end?" he asked, his hands and feet tingling with numbness.

"You ready to die?" she asked.

"I'm ready for you to get whatever it is you want out of this and let me get on with my life."

She spun the knife like a top and watched it whirl on the polished floor. "Your life with her, Pleasure. I was fine with all your other bullshit . . . until her."

He remained quiet.

"*You can't protect her. When I'm done with you. She's next,*" she said with a simplicity that revealed her diminished mental capacity. "*Pow-pow-pow.*"

And for the first time in since his ordeal began, he felt true fear fill him. He would gladly give his life for hers but how could he defend her when he was tied to a chair with a whack job as his guard?

"*I have sat back for almost a year. Watched and waited for this chance, and now it's here,*" she said, rising to her feet to sit on his lap and roughly grab his chin.

She uncurled her tongue and he jerked his head back to avoid her kissing him. Her brown eyes lit with fiery anger. "*You promised me that we would be together, Pleasure,*" she said. "*You liar.*"

"*I never promised* anyone *forever,*" he said truthfully.

WHAP.

Yet another slap that stung.

"*You're going to wish you never fucked with me,*" she whispered harshly.

I already do.

"*You and that bitch can talk about me in hell,*" she said, mushing his face before rising from his lap.

He knew exactly of whom she spoke.

Chapter 19

Jaime

2013

Jet lag is a bitch.

Pleasure slid his aviator shades back into place on his face as soon as the Tahoe pulled to a stop outside his Jersey City apartment. He opened his door and stepped out onto the sidewalk before his driver could even come around to open it for him. As he did wait for the driver to retrieve his leather garment bag on wheels, he smoothed the pockets of the blue linen blazer he wore with a crisp plaid shirt and dark-wash denims. He checked the time on his Piaget watch and brushed his dreads back off his shoulders.

Thirty never looked so good.

"Here you go, sir," the driver said, sitting the luggage on the sidewalk.

Pleasure reached for his billfold and pulled a twenty-dollar bill to hand the man. "Have a good day, sir," he said politely, then turned to walk across the wide sidewalk before the upscale high-rise apartment building overlooking the Hudson riverfront.

He smiled at the white-gloved doorman as he entered the

lobby with its Italian granite and wood finishes. It was a long way from the apartment he'd shared with his father in New York.

Gone were the days of his Jordan sneakers, track pants, and T-shirts. He hadn't worn one of those clinging dick sleeves in at least two years. Stripping was in his past. Too much work for not a lot of money.

He had just flown in from Los Angeles for a one-night rendezvous with an entertainment reporter for a major television show. These days his focus was on the list of high-profile clients he'd established. Bigger bank for the bang. Less miles on his dick.

And it afforded him a good lifestyle.

He rode the elevator thirty-seven levels up to his penthouse apartment—one of four in that tower. Entering his apartment, he paused by the door to take in the sweeping view of New York across the Hudson via the windows spanning from the parquet floors to the nine-foot ceilings. It almost reminded him of his apartment in Newark, but better. Much better.

Unbuttoning his blazer, Pleasure sat down upon his sofa and turned on the television as he browsed through the stack of mail he left before his spur-of-the-moment jaunt to the West Coast. He was barely able to make it through the endless bills before he dropped them and sat back against the sofa. Still, the days of him enjoying his work were fading.

He didn't know if it was reaching the milestone of thirty or whether his father's words of advice of choosing love over sex were finally resonating, but Pleasure was becoming more and more discontented with a life he should have been happy about.

He was paid very well to have sex with beautiful women. A lot of them. But still, only one woman remained uppermost in his mind. For him, one was always elevated above the rest.

Even if he hadn't seen her in over two years.

It was after he chose not to continue his affair with Smyth that he moved into the Bell Towers penthouse apartment and opened himself back up for business. His reasoning for that was twofold. He needed the influx of cash without Smyth's weekly stipend, and he'd discovered that his feelings for Jaime had run deeper than even he knew. That was something he neither welcomed nor wanted.

With that realization, he made very sure that things between him and Jaime ended.

Whether doing immature acts like walking out in front of her mother naked and asking Jaime if she was ready to have sex or boldly giving her best friends his sexy business card and offering them his services to "please," Pleasure had lived in a world where his body desired her but his head wanted to push her away. He wanted her to be the one to tell him to go away because he didn't have the strength to do it.

The antics hadn't worked. Jaime continued to call for him, and fighting the temptation to answer her had been getting too great for him. Avoiding her calls hadn't worked when she sought him out at Club Trick, his old stomping grounds. He saw the hunger she had for him. He felt it too but he knew he had to end it.

She had gotten too close.

Pleasure shook his head, then let it fall back on the sofa. He made a small noise of regret as he recalled the night . . .

When she couldn't afford his rate, he had danced away from her and instead chosen a much older and far less attractive woman to take into one of the private rooms, purposely leaving Jaime and her shattered ego behind. Truth be told, he had just given the woman a dance, accepted her tip, and sent her on her way, not even returning to the floor to continue work.

It took everything in him not to call Jaime and tell her the truth, but he didn't. That line had blurred so many times that now it was beyond repair. The last thing he wanted to do was fall in love back then.

Today?

Pleasure rose from the sofa and crossed the parquet floors to stand at his window and look out at the sun reflecting against the water. He couldn't say that he loved Jaime—he'd pushed back from her before that happened—but after two years he still missed her. Still wanted her. And was even curious about her life.

What became of her?

Reaching into the inside pocket of his blazer, he pulled out his iPhone and dialed her number, not at all surprised that he remembered it well. His heart hammered and he paced a bit as it rang. He felt nervous and unsure.

"Hello."

He stopped pacing and his head dropped as his pulse raced.

"Hello," she repeated.

"Jaime. Hi. It's me. It's Pleasure," he said, shifting on his feet so that he faced the window.

"You have the wrong number," a teenage girl snapped before ending the call.

Did I remember it wrong?

Pleasure's brows furrowed as he double-checked that he had not misdialed. He hadn't. *Shit.*

Sliding the phone back inside his pocket, he felt disappointed.

Maybe it's for the best.

What was he going to say? "Hey, I just wanted to reminisce over how you used to pay me to fuck you?"

Shaking his head and releasing a breath, he walked out of the living room and headed down the hall to his master bedroom. Halfway across the length of it, he turned and retraced his steps. He snatched up his keys and left the apartment.

As he rode the elevator down to the lobby and exited

into the parking garage, he wondered if he had lost just a little bit of his mind. His father's words came back to him. He could remember them well.

Don't be so focused on the pussy, son, that you don't take time to find the right one to share your life with.

Pleasure had indeed become so preoccupied with avoiding love and filling his days with these fleeting moments with women too numerous to count that he had no one to truly share his life with. His dick? Yes.

He unlocked his black convertible Jag and climbed in easily. "What the fuck am I doing?" he wondered aloud as he reversed out of his reserved parking spot and accelerated out of the deck and onto the Jersey City streets.

Pussy is easy to come by, love isn't.

During the entire hour-long drive, Pleasure tried to convince himself that his impulses were not leading him astray. *Fuck it. What's the worst that could happen?*

Slowing down the vehicle, he waited for traffic to pass and made the left turn into the Richmond Hills gated community. He forced his body to relax as he pulled up to the security booth and lowered the window when the portly red-faced guard came out of the booth.

"Good afternoon. Does Jaime Hall still live here?" he asked, squinting his eyes against the sun as he remembered he'd left his shades back at his apartment.

The guard, whose tag read *Lucky*, nodded. "Yes sir, she does," he said. "I can call her and request permission for you to enter. What's your name?"

"Pleasure."

Lucky did a double take at his name before he entered the booth and picked up the phone.

Will she let me in?

Did she remarry?

Does she look the same?

Those and a dozen more questions rapidly flew as he

fought hard to breathe and maintain his usual cool composure. "What the fuck was I thinking?" he asked, his eyes shifting up to his rearview mirror before looking over at Lucky just as the portly man glanced over at him as he continued to speak on the phone.

Pleasure shifted in his seat when the guard finally left the booth.

"Go right in, sir," Lucky said.

Pleasure waved to him and raised his window; all the while his heart was beating so loudly that he could see himself having a heart attack. He couldn't deny that he was pleased and surprised that she'd allowed him entrance back into her life, even if for just a little bit.

As he drove around the curve and enjoyed the sight of the landscaped grounds, he recalled the very last time he had come to Richmond Hills. He couldn't remember the name of Jaime's neighbor who'd called him to her home under the guise of buying his dick but had used him to embarrass Jaime in front of her neighbors and attendees of her husband's funeral.

Pleasure threw his hands up at all the drama that had unfolded behind the wrought-iron gate. It was just like he always said. It was the places of seeming perfection that hid so much unhappiness.

He didn't know all the details, just the little bit Jaime divulged to him in between hot sex and whatever stories the national news reported, but he knew enough that he hated he was involved in all the drama on even a minute level.

A vengeful mistress who betrayed her friend with a lover who turned right around and stalked her when she tried to end things because he broke his promise to leave his wife for her. A text message. Angry friends and neighbors. A suicide/murder attempt. Pregnancy. Lawsuits. Publicity. Book deals. Speaking engagement. Jessa Bell had ridden the wave of her infamy.

"That's right, Jessa Bell," he said as he turned down the final curve in the paved road before reaching the street Jaime lived on. "How the hell could I forget a name like Jessa Bell?"

As he pulled up and parked outside Jaime's house, he looked up the street to the house where drama once lived. There was a white couple sitting outside watching their toddler play, and so he knew Jessa Bell had moved on. Still, after all the hoopla, he knew her actions had to leave a stain on the community.

He climbed from the car and adjusted his clothing before he stepped up onto the sidewalk and climbed the stairs to her front door. He had knocked just once before it opened. Taking a step back, he steeled himself for whatever reaction she gave him.

"Mikel," Jaime said, offering him a smile.

"Graham. Graham Walker," he offered, as his eyes took her in. She hadn't changed a bit. She was still beautiful.

"So your name isn't Mikel?" she asked, leaning in the doorframe as she looked up at him with her arms crossed over her ample chest.

"No," he admitted, barely able to stop smiling.

"It's been a long time."

"Too long," he countered.

She shrugged one shoulder.

"You married?" he asked, his eyes locked with hers.

"Definitely not," Jaime stressed, brushing her long bangs from her forehead to tuck behind her ear.

Pleasure nodded and licked his lips as he gave her a slow once-over that missed not one detail of her curvy body in the strapless maxi dress she wore. The peach color looked breathtaking against her light brown complexion. "You look good, Jaime. Damn good," he said, his voice even more deepened by his appreciation.

Her mouth opened a little and he knew it was a small intake of breath. "Why are you here, Pleasure?" she asked.

He wondered if she felt that familiar hum of their chemistry building in intensity around them like an orchestra's crescendo. "I missed you," he said honestly.

"Really?" she asked in disbelief.

"I missed you," he repeated again, his voice softer.

"Pleasure," Jaime said, pushing up off the frame to eye him.

"I missed the hell out of you," he said with one bold step. Jaime's hand came up to rest lightly against her throat, and he knew from the look in her eyes that she could feel her pulse pounding just as hard as he could feel his. "Pleasure, this is crazy—"

He shook his head as he took another step to enter her personal zone. "This is undeniable. Always has been," he said, reaching to jerk her body up against his. "You haven't thought about me—about *this*—in all these years?"

She opened her mouth but no words came out.

"I'm sorry I came," he said, stepping back from her before he turned to walk away. "I'll go."

"No."

He smiled at the feel of her hand on his arm. Turning, he picked her up and wrapped his arms around her tightly as he pressed his face against her neck and placed kisses against her pounding pulse that caused her to shiver as she released a small cry of passion.

He walked them into her house and closed the door with his foot decisively.

"How much do I owe you?"

Pleasure lifted his upper arm from across his eyes and looked up to find Jaime standing above him with her wallet in hand. "Are you fucking kidding me right now, Jaime?" he asked as he sat up in the middle of the bed with the sweat-soaked sheets clinging to his naked body.

She looked confused. "Did I say something wrong?" she

asked, her naked body barely covered by a sheer black T-shirt that ended mid-thigh.

Pleasure hated that deep in the midst of his hurt feelings, the sight of her made him want to pull her back in the bed and bury himself deep within her until she stuttered.

"What is your going rate these days?" she said with a wrinkle of her nose. "What? A grand? More?"

"This reminded me of the time you fucked me on the floor of your town house and left my dick swinging in the wind after you got your nut," he said, flinging back the covers to sit on the edge of the bed with his back to her. "And then you put me the fuck out and told me to bill you."

"Are you upset?" she asked.

He made a face as he glanced at her over his shoulder before he reached for his discarded boxers and stood to pull them on. He eyed the wallet still in her hand and waved his hand at her dismissively.

"Well, maybe I should pay you for the last one since it's stuck in your craw," she snapped.

"Keep your damn money," he told her, pulling up his jeans with jerking motions.

Jaime threw the wallet at him and it hit him squarely in the chest. "What the fuck is going on?"

Pleasure stood still, leaving his jeans unbuttoned and unzipped, and eyed her hard.

"A man-whore who is mad that his trick *wants* to pay him?"

Pleasure forced himself to step out of his emotions. Their parameters had long since been set, and he was being irrational to be upset by them now. "I came to ask you out. I didn't even have it in my plans to make love to you, Jaime. I came to ask you out. The rest...just...happened."

She opened her mouth in surprise and her lips shaped an "O."

"So *keep* your money," Pleasure told her, reaching down to snatch up his shirt and blazer, his dreads flying wildly as he did.

"Graham, you can't be serious," she said softly.

He paused at the sound of his real name easing off her lips. He liked it a lot. "I was, but obviously I was wrong, so just forget it."

"I am hungry," Jaime said. "You worked up an appetite."

"Is that a yes?" he asked, biting back a smile.

"Are you paying?"

"McDonald's all day every day," he teased, enjoying her company.

"Damn, not even Wendy's?"

He stayed silent.

"Let me wash and change," she said, raising her hand to run her fingers through her short curls. It caused her sheer T-shirt to rise until the twin bald lips of her pussy peeked just below the hem.

"I could use a shower too with your juices all on me," he said, removing his jeans to toss them onto the unmade bed.

She eyed him. "They don't stink."

"Not at all," he agreed.

They shared a light laugh.

"Dinner, huh?" she asked again, sounding unsure.

"Dinner," he assured her.

She nodded, her face still showing her surprise and hesitance. "Okay."

Across the table from each other at a waterfront seafood restaurant, Pleasure and Jaime eyed each other as they enjoyed their meals. He had shrimp and vegetables over brown rice while she dined on scallops in white wine sauce over fresh-made pasta. They reminisced a little over the more fun times they used to share in the days after she left her husband and declared herself free of the rules of what a proper lady should look like, dress like, and act like.

"So you are still in the business?" Jaime asked.

He nodded as he wiped his mouth with his cloth napkin. "I have fewer clients but more...discerning taste."

She nodded but he saw that her confusion about the night still lingered.

"And the interior decorating business you were starting. Did you get that off the ground?" Pleasure asked, fighting the urge to reach across the table and take her hand in his to stroke her wrist—a hot spot of hers he remembered well.

She nodded. "I must admit that Eric's death afforded me a lot of freedom financially, but I stuck to it and the business is doing very well. Thanks for asking," she said politely.

"I remember when you offered to decorate my apartment—"

"Until you sent me a text of this beautiful upscale apartment and just cracked my face because I assumed you lived in the hood in a roach-infested flea trap somewhere," she said, her eyes light with humor.

"I was living in an apartment on the Upper East Side—"

"Pleasure, what are we doing here?" she asked, setting her fork down on her plate with a ding. "What do you want?"

"You," he answered unequivocally, looking at her before returning his focus to his food.

"Me?" she asked with an arched brow as she reached for her goblet of white wine and took a deep sip.

Pleasure sat his utensils down as well and leaned back in the leather club chair to look at her. "Definitely," he assured her.

"So we should overlook the past? Pretend it never happened? Play crazy or stupid?"

"I never lied to you," he insisted.

"No, you just tried to hire yourself out to my friends and

chose to fuck Grandma Moses that night in the club because she had the money I didn't," she snapped, lowering her voice as she drew the eyes of those at neighboring tables.

"I was fighting how I was starting to feel about you, Jaime," he explained. "I never slept with that lady in the club."

"No, but you did screw the same woman—my supposed friend—who slept with my husband and later had his baby and wanted to sue his estate," she said, sitting back in her chair as well as she crossed her legs beneath the table and eyed him as if to say, "so there."

"First off, I didn't know anything about her cheating with your husband. Secondly, I never screwed her, and thirdly, you weren't even dealing with me then, Jaime—"

"Oh, she reminded me of how well you ate her pussy, so trust me, I know far too much of your dealings with Jessa Bell's *slack* ass," she said coldly.

Pleasure wiped his mouth and square jaw with his hand before he leaned forward and extended it across the table. "Are you denying you had feelings for me, Jaime?" he asked, his voice warm and deep. Charming. Alluring. Pulling her in. "As you sit there still mad about something you shouldn't care about if I meant nothing to you?"

Jaime eyed his hand but never reached for it. "Are you done selling dick or am I supposed to set aside days where it's okay for you to fuck other women?" she asked, her tone snide.

Pleasure turned his hand down on the table before making a fist and lightly knocking it against the tabletop before he withdrew his hand. "I'm—"

Her hand slashed the air as she leaned forward. "I'm supposed to believe that your ass reappears after two years and suddenly you want to start a relationship with me—and *only* me—thus giving up your splendid variety of two or three different pussies a week?"

"I'm—"

"I don't believe that...and neither do you," she said, rising to her feet. "And we never will."

She turned and walked out of the restaurant, leaving Pleasure sitting there with his unspoken words still lingering on his lips.

"I'm done," he finally was able to say in answer to her question, but she was gone.

Chapter 20

Jaime

Two Weeks Later

"All of the women over this decade of my life have been a need to affirm that what happened to me—"

"What happened to you, Pleasure. Name it. Defuse it."

Pleasure sat up straight on the sofa and placed his ankle on the knee of the opposite leg. He clasped his hand around the striped socks he wore as his mouth dried at the thought of giving name to his violation. He licked his lips as he looked over at Dr. Templeton and released a short puff of air. "I was molested," he said, surprised as his emotions surged up and nearly choked him. "I was violated. I was hurt. I was touched. I was abused."

Dr. Templeton nodded in approval.

Pleasure fought hard not to cry and he was glad that at least this early in his therapy the doctor didn't press him to do so. That day would come, he knew that, but at least it wasn't that day.

"Finish your earlier thought," the psychologist gently nudged him.

"All of the women over this decade of my life," he re-peated, "has been my need to make sure that being molested didn't turn me gay."

"For all these years, Pleasure, you have been stuck in the same age and same mind-set created by the abuse, and it dictated the actions that you took as a man." Dr. Templeton eyed him over the rim of his glasses. "The work that we will do is to heal that little boy who is still present inside you and move you to a place where he doesn't dictate your life any longer."

Pleasure smoothed his sweaty palms down the length of the tailored slacks he wore with a matching silk shirt open at the collar. This was just his second session, and although there was a stigma in the African American community about seek-ing counseling or even life coaching he knew he had to fi-nally face the demon of his abuse to live his best life possible. That was just as important to him as his money, his clothes, and his lifestyle.

"I think, Pleasure, that a very important step, Pleasure, in you adjusting to a new way of thinking, Pleasure, is addressing your need to be addressed as—"

"Pleasure," he finished dryly as he eyed the therapist across the divide between them.

Dr. Templeton shrugged and held up his hands. "It's not your name given to you by a mother who loved you, but by a woman who introduced you to drugs and later sold you as a whore. If I'm remembering your story correctly from our first session?"

Pleasure nodded. Last week had been all about revealing every detail of his life.

"So, Pleasure, why shackle yourself with it, Pleasure?"

"It sounds really creepy when you say it," Pleasure told him.

"I was hoping so."

Pleasure smiled. "It sounds better coming from the lips of ladies."

"What ladies?" Dr. Templeton asked. "You're still celibate, right?"

Pleasure smiled again. "Okay, Dr. Templeton, let me reintroduce myself to you. I am Graham. Graham Walker."

The elderly white man leaned forward and extended his hand. "Nice to meet you, Graham," he said.

He uncrossed his legs and leaned forward as well to capture the man's hand with his own. "Nice to meet you."

It was Graham's turn for a surprise visit.

He had just stepped out of the shower and wrapped a thick towel around his waist when his doorbell sounded. *Who the hell is that?*

Graham rarely got visitors and liked it that way. He doubted his parents had driven in from Bedford for a visit, but he firmly believed anybody was capable of anything. Removing the wrap he used to protect his dreads when he showered, he slipped his feet into black suede slippers and made his way out of his bedroom and down the long hall to the front door.

He checked the peephole and then opened the door as his heart beat furiously. Jaime stood there all in white with a takeout bag in her hand. "I thought I owed you dinner since we didn't get to finish the other one," she said, tilting her head adorably to the side as she enjoyed a leisurely up-and-down look of his body.

"I finished mine," he quipped before giving her a hint of a smile.

"No, you didn't, that's how I was able to follow you and find out where you lived," she said, leaning this way and that to look past him inside the apartment.

"You stalking me?" he asked, stepping back to open the door wider.

She made a face like "Negro, please." "You hunted me down after two years. You *stalking* me?" she shot back.

"Come in."

Jaime took a step and then paused. "I am not crossing this threshold until you promise me that none of your tricks have been here," she said.

"Come in," he said again.

Jaime let her foot dangle in the air above the threshold as she eyed him.

"You're the first woman to come inside my apartment, Jaime," he reassured her with truth.

She set the foot down and stepped inside. "Wow. This is really nice. Good dick has its privileges," she said as she handed him the bag.

He paused on his way to the kitchen. "Not funny, Jaime," he said over his shoulder.

"I said good dick."

He looked across the span of the kitchen to watch Jaime slowly take in his apartment. Graham had always been a very private person with his clientele, and he allowed himself a moment to see if it bothered him to have Jaime invade his space unannounced.

It didn't. It didn't at all.

Opening the cabinets, he removed plates and tall glasses.

"Is this your parents?" she called out to him.

Looking up from placing the Chinese food she'd purchased onto the plates, he saw her peering at the eight-by-ten wedding photo of his parents that he kept on his mantel. "Yes, it is," he finally said, walking back into the living room with dishes in hand.

"Your father is gorgeous," she said, turning away from the fireplace to look at him. Her eyes dipped to the towel draped around his hips and the outline of his dick against the thick cotton as he stood there.

"Should I get dressed?" he asked, pointing down the hall toward his master suite with one of the plates.

"Definitely not," she answered, coming over to take a seat on the sofa.

"You sure about that?" Graham asked with a cocky smile. "You look distracted."

With one last long look, Jaime turned away. "I'm sure."

Graham went to retrieve the glasses of wine he'd poured, and when he walked back into the living room, he spotted five cheap-looking cell phones lined up on the table between their plates. "You selling wireless service or something?"

Jaime set her purse down on the sofa between them. "Over the last two weeks I have called you from each of these five phones with five different numbers—numerous times—on your dick hotline to see if you were still open for business," she admitted.

"Oh really?" Graham asked.

She held up her hands before smoothing her bangs away from her face. "I sure did."

"And what did you discover?" he asked, his heart pounding with hope.

"You never answered," she said.

"That's funny you used the words 'never answered,' because when you asked me in the restaurant if I was able to give up the business, I never answered then either," he said. "You never gave me a chance."

"Pleasure—"

"Graham," he corrected her.

Her eyes warmed over at that. "Okay, *Graham*, are you done selling dick?" she asked.

He stood up and walked to his bedroom to retrieve his trick phone from its spot in his top dresser drawer. He held it clutched tightly in his hand and looked down at his past as he slowly walked back to the living room. He powered it on for the first time in two weeks. Picking up one of her throwaway cells, he dialed his trick phone.

"Mr. Lover Lover..."

Graham ended the calls on both and then proceeded to rip each of the phones in half with ease, dropping each sign of destruction to the mink area rug on the floor.

"The answer to your question that night is the same as it is today, Jaime," he said. "I'm done. I'm finished with all of that. I want to try and see if all those feelings for you I was running from are exactly what I need. I'm a grown-ass man and I am ready for grown-ass love...with you."

She stood up. "Am I crazy because I want to try to see if it can be as good out of the bed as it is in the bed between us?" she asked, coming over to stand before him.

"Am I crazy to trust a woman who cheated on her husband with me?" he countered.

Jaime reached for his towel and snatched it away to stroke the length of his dick. "So this dick is all mine?" she asked as she rubbed the smooth tip with her thumb.

Graham's eyes heated. "All yours," he promised her.

Six Months Later

"So I get to formally meet the friends," Graham said as he and Jaime stepped out onto the porch of her home. "I am coming out of your closet and I'm not even gay."

Jaime eyed him in his suit as she locked the door and turned to stand at his side. "Considering that the last time we ventured out we ran into one of your ex clients who acted like she didn't see me sitting at that table in the restaurant with you," she said, reaching up to smooth his lapel as they descended the stairs and crossed the street to the home of her best friends, Aria and Kingston Livewell.

"My past was never a secret to you, Jaime," Graham reminded her.

"Yes, but that doesn't mean I want constant reminders of it either."

They climbed the stairs and Graham rang the doorbell as he eyed her. "You look good, baby," he told her, loving the bright red one-shoulder dress she wore like a second skin.

"Wait until you see what I have on underneath." Pressing a hand to his chest, she lifted on the toes of her already high stilettos to taste his mouth.

He touched her lower back and rubbed it. "Do you want to make it to this party?" he asked deep in his throat.

"Hi, you two."

They stared at each other heatedly for a few more moments before turning away with secretive smiles to face Aria standing at the door in a multicolored jumpsuit interwoven with gold thread. She reached for each of their hands and pulled them inside to kiss their cheeks.

"Welcome, welcome," she said. "Come on in."

"Nice to see you again, Pleas—um, Graham," she said, correcting herself.

Graham remembered her from that day in Jaime's town house when he'd offered her and another woman one of his business cards.

"Hey, Jaime," another woman said as she walked up.

And there she is. Graham eyed the tall woman in her mid-forties, with a short natural haircut that reminded him of Assefa's, now standing before them as well.

"Renee Thorne, this is Graham Walker. Graham—"

The woman gave him a cool, assessing smile as she extended her hand. "We've met," she said.

Graham eyed her critically as he took her hand in his. He knew women. After learning to home in on their needs and wants, his instincts were sharp. And he was clear that Renee had no use for him.

The husbands of Jaime's friends came forward and

introductions were made before they all walked into the spacious den together.

The dinner party was already in full swing, and six additional couples were lounging in the den and adjoining kitchen enjoying cocktails and light appetizers. Contemporary jazz music played in the background and everything was very civilized and polite.

"Where's my godchild?" Jaime asked of Aria's toddler daughter, Neru.

"With my mother for the weekend," she answered with a wiggle of her hips. "I packed her little hyper behind up with a quickness and had Kingston drop her off."

Renee laughed. "Trust me, as a mother of two grown children, you learn to enjoy having the kids you adore out of your house," she said.

"Baby talk," Kingston said. "Fellas, right this way."

Graham followed him and Renee's husband, Davin, to the bar set up in the corner with a young white man in a red vest and black tie serving. "Seltzer water and lime, please," he said, turning to look around the room.

He didn't miss the look the men shared, and Graham instantly wondered just what they knew about him. Married couples and those in long-term relationships were infamous for making their pillow talk about another couple's business.

As they began to discuss the latest sports highlights, he looked about the room, stiffening when he noticed a tall and slender brown-skinned redhead across the room staring at him. She lifted her glass of wine to him in a silent toast. Graham couldn't place her, but instinctively he knew she had to be one of his clients. *Probably a one-timer that I forgot.*

Offering her a forced smile, he accepted the drink the bartender offered him and looked over the rim at Jaime as he sipped. Being amongst her friends and neighbors as well as in the same environment as one of the women from his roster of clients did not bode well.

The last six months had really been good between them. The sex was still explosive and hot. They talked and laughed with each other. They discussed politics and current events. They had a lot of things in common, and those things they differed on, they fought hard to convert the other.

Those good times were only broken up by intense arguments following moments when he drew the lingering stare of a woman and Jaime instantly assumed the woman either wanted him or had him. The argument was on from there. He had to admit that it wasn't him Jaime didn't trust. It was the other women. She absolutely refused not to be recognized and respected as his woman.

And even though her quick attitude seemed insufferable when they were in the thick of the storm, he found that he loved that about her as well. She wanted no one else to possess him. Know him. Have him.

He loved her.

Graham Walker was in love. Glancing back at her again, he smiled into his drink. *I love her.*

"Hi there. Long time no see," the redhead said with a conspiratorial wink as she walked past him to stand at the bar. "White wine spritzer, please."

Oh boy.

Once her drink was handed to her, she gave him another hot look before crossing the room to take her spot by her husband's side again.

Graham frowned into his drink and looked at Kingston and Davin as they shared another glance. "Is there something the two of you want to get off your chest?" he asked.

"There sure is," Kingston said, surprising Davin, who choked on the frosted glass of beer he was drinking. "Right this way."

More than curious, Graham followed the men until they reached Kingston's office.

"Did my wife . . . *hire* you?" Kingston asked as soon as he shut the door.

"No," he answered simply, before turning to Davin. "And yours either."

They both looked relieved.

"Those three are thick as thieves, and when Aria mentioned what you do—"

"*Used* to do," Graham corrected him smoothly.

"It's been nagging me. That's all," Kingston said, dropping down into the chair behind his desk. "Aria and I had a rough patch a year ago and . . . I just needed to know."

"Me too, man," Davin added. "You're strutting around here and all the women are sneaking glances and licking lips and all kind of shit when their husbands aren't looking."

Graham actually smiled. "Understood . . . with me *strutting* and all."

The men all laughed.

"We better get back before we're missed," Kingston said, rising to guide them back out of the office and down the stairs.

When they reached the bottom of the steps, the redhead was just walking out of the guest bathroom. She stepped in Graham's path before he could follow the men back into the den. "I definitely need to give you a call and make an appointment," she said.

"I'm out of business," he said, attempting to sidestep her.

"Hello," Jaime said, walking up to them to place her hand on the small of Graham's back.

The redhead did not miss the subtle hint. She instantly stepped back. "Cheers to you," she said, raising her drink in a salute before she walked away with one last look at Graham over her bare shoulder.

"You are determined nobody else gets this dick, aren't you?" he asked before taking another sip of his seltzer.

"Glad you know it," she said, taking the glass to have her own sip before she walked over to rejoin her friends.

Graham hated to check his watch when they hadn't even been there for a solid ten minutes, but the crowd of mostly forty-something couples was not his speed. He had outgrown the steady bass of the club, but sitting around discussing the latest TV shows or the newest wonders at their jobs was a mindfuck for him—and not in a good way.

He walked onto the porch with his drink and looked out at the tranquil neighborhood. He'd much rather be on Jaime's couch—or his—watching a movie or catching up on the latest news.

"Renee, would you check the chicken for me?"

He looked over his shoulder in surprise, and through the blinds covering the window he saw Jaime, Renee, and Aria moving about the kitchen. "Why didn't you hire a caterer?" Jaime asked.

"Because I'm no Jessa Bell with a need for the absolutely perfect dinner party."

"Do not bring up *that* bitch."

"Yes, she's gone, and this last year has been fucking fabulous without her living in Richmond Hills."

"Can you believe she opened a business to help women catch their men cheating?"

"Skanky pot meet skanky kettle."

"*Exactly.*"

The ladies all laughed.

Pleasure turned from the window and moved down to the other side of the porch to try and avoid eavesdropping.

"Now why would I need a caterer when I have my two best bitches to help a sister out," Aria said, using tongs to move string beans from the oven roaster and onto a platter.

"Well, this bitch could've saved the work, ordered in, and enjoyed dessert with my man later," Jaime said.

Graham turned to walk back into the house.

"Your man?" Aria said distastefully.

Graham froze.

"Yes, my man," Jaime said with a sharp edge to her tone.

"Do you think it's the best idea to try and make a man-whore a husband?"

Graham flinched.

"Who said anything about getting married?"

"I hope the fuck not."

Graham's jaw clenched as he sat the glass on the chair and descended the stairs. He didn't stop until he climbed into his Jag and eventually pulled away without looking back at Richmond Hills at all.

Chapter 21

Jaime

Present Day

Is that the last time I'm going to see her?

That had been two days ago. Those two days hadn't seemed like forever until the last twenty-four hours of it was spent in the hands of some lunatic claiming to know him and once love him.

Graham's head hung lower than it had during the whole ordeal.

She had called. He hadn't answered.

Now he was facing death. He would never get to tell her he loved her. Never even get to tell her how her flip comment to her friends had stung him to the white meat.

"God's will *always* will be done, motherfucker, no matter how much you run and hide."

Graham closed his eyes as tension radiated across the breadth of his shoulders. He was sick of her. Sick of being tied up. Sick of not knowing when, where, and how it all would end.

Just sick of the shit.

"We were meant to be, and we will be, whether here on earth or burning together in hell."

He raised his head and eyed her as she tilted her head this way and that while she crouched lower until their eyes were level.

"I knew from the first moment we—"

"Fuck you," he told her coldly.

She jumped to her feet quickly and snatched up his face with a tight grip on his chin. "You said fuck me when you ran and hid from God's plan like a little bitch."

Graham's eyes widened a bit.

"God's will always, always, always will be done."

It can't be.

"You thought *He* wouldn't lead me right back to you?"

Not her.

"Quinn," he said, more a statement than a question.

"Try again, motherfucker," she snapped.

Graham sat up straighter in his chair. "You try again, bitch," he said coldly.

She whirled again and pulled his cell phone from her back pocket. "No, the bitch is Jaime," she snapped. "And a begging bitch at that. 'What did I do?' 'Why are you mad?' 'Answer your phone.' 'Call me.' 'I love you.' Whine, beg, whine. Dumb bitch."

Graham's gut clenched. Jaime had texted that she loved him? She'd never declared that to him before. And he had held back on his own feelings for her.

Now this bullshit.

"She never has to beg me for anything," he stressed, wanting to push her to reveal herself. "When she wanted me, she got me... *Quinn.*"

"You swear you're so fucking smart... but I'm smarter, you dick-whore," she snapped, turning to fling his cell phone across the room and into the fireplace.

"Not smart enough to know when a man doesn't want you," he volleyed back.

She froze for a few tense seconds before she reached behind her for the knife and unsheathed it to point at his chest. "It doesn't matter what you want. It never did," she said, cocking her head eerily from side to side as she also rotated her wrist.

"Your crazy is showing... *Quinn*."

"Maybe if I take away the one thing you love so much, you could love me instead, the way God wanted it?" she asked.

Her voice was so low that he had to read her lips to be clear on what she said. As he did, his heart filled with fear for Jaime. "Hurting her won't make me love you," he said.

She rocked her head three more times—right, left, right—before she lowered the knife to aim at his dick. "You don't love her any more than I thought you loved me," she said. "*That* is the only thing you love."

Graham's instinct was to close his legs to protect his dick, but he couldn't because the binds had his legs spread. His *privates* exposed. Unprotected.

She reached up with her free hand and snatched off the ski mask to throw at his chest.

Graham eyed her. He hadn't really believed he was right until he looked into the face of the one woman from his past who he had loved like a sister. The one woman whose ties to him were not based on sex. The woman he really hoped it would not be.

"Why are you doing this, Quinn?"

"God's will be done," she said, using her thumb to stroke the carved wooden handle of the knife.

"Don't be mad at my dick... Quinn."

"Yours ain't the only dick I've seen, trust me," she said with a giggle that quickly escalated to a full out laugh that was high pitched and inappropriate. Maniacal.

Graham was looking into the face—the poster child—for crazy. He felt a true chill to his bones.

Gone was the woman he thought he knew.

She raised the point of the knife to her own throat, pressing it so that she pierced the skin just enough for a dot of blood to emerge as she ended her laugh with a whimper and a tear fell down her cheek. "Why don't you understand? Why don't you get it? What is wrong with you?" she asked, her face truly incredulous.

Graham kept his face blank. "Wrong with me?"

She raised her free hand and lightly smacked her palm against her forehead as she closed her eyes tightly with a grimace. "I told you I loved you, and you fucking moved. Changed your number. Said fuck your friendship. Fuck your pussy. Fuck everything," she said, with another chuckle that was more tears than joviality. "You took everything I offered you on a platter and shitted on it before you kicked me to the curb and ran like a scared little boy."

Graham hardly recognized the woman before him. He watched, almost in fascination, the disturbing swings in her mood and her affect as she continued her tirade of how he'd denied her love. She became unhinged right before him.

"But God is so good because he led me right back to you *again*," Quinn said, turning to ram the knife into the back of the sofa as she ran her fingers across her scalp and grabbed her hair into her fist. "God knows what is in my heart. He knows our destiny. Nothing could keep us apart. Even when they locked me up in that place...that...that bad, bad place I figured out if I just played along they would set me free and we could be together."

Graham felt a moment of sadness. This woman was nothing like the friend he once had. This woman standing before him was her truth, and the woman she'd presented to him was a façade. She hid her crazy well.

"You don't even appreciate everything I did over the last

year to find you. Like pretending to give a fuck about what book your mother's book club was discussing." Quinn reached for the hem of her shirt and jerked it over her head and down the length of her arms. "But you don't give a fuck that it took me months pretending to be her friend just to keep up with your life. Just to know where to go to find you. To watch you. To see you."

Graham stiffened, not giving one solitary damn about the sight of her breasts in the sheer white bra she wore. This woman had latched onto his mother like a tick or a leech. "My mother better be okay," he warned her even as he felt his threat was futile.

Quinn eyed him with wide eyes. "I never hurt your mother, Pleasure. She likes me. She really likes me," she said, with an odd lilt to her voice. "I'm sure she told you about her new friend Janice."

Pleasure's shoulder slumped. She had. He'd had no idea his mother had invited crazy into her life because of him. His parents had heard of Quinn but they'd never met her, and it would be no hard feat for her to pretend to be somebody else.

"See, when she actually led me right here to you, when she dropped a package off at the front desk, that was nothing but God." She kicked off her shoes before she worked her hips back and forth as she took off her jeans. "You were back in my life again. I would sit outside your building and play in my pussy while I dreamed of lying in your bed with you. For months. I love you so much."

This crazy bitch stalked me.

"And for the longest time not one woman came to your apartment. No one," she said, kicking away the jeans like they offended her. "You fucked plenty of women. I know. I followed you. But not one ever came to your apartment. I was special because I knew where you lived, just as God wanted. Only me. Just me. Until that bitch."

He shook his head a bit in disbelief. "You were the only woman I didn't want to hurt, Quinn," he lied. "I fucked everybody else, but you were the only one I cared about."

In nothing but her sheer lingerie, she came over to stand between his open legs. "Liar," she snapped harshly, spittle flying from her mouth and landing on his face. "And that's why you are going to die, because you were made for me and *only me* but you just won't be obedient."

"If I didn't care, I—"

"Shut up with your lies!" she screamed, the veins in her neck distending.

And then she smiled and laughed a little as she turned this way and that before him. "I paid good money for all of this," she said, smacking her ass and reaching up to squeeze her breasts. "Me and God used to laugh at how you didn't even recognize me."

He leaned back from her.

"What's the matter, Graham, feeling fooled again?" she asked with a light laugh. "Even now, you think you know, but you don't. Like I said, you so fucking smart you dumb."

He frowned deeply.

"Best surgeries and hormones a man can buy, ain't it?" she said, pulling down the front of her panties to reveal a small keloid-covered scar on her shaven pubic area. "I finally became the woman God meant me to be. Hallelujah!"

Graham went still as stone.

"Allow me to reintroduce myself. I am Quinn, formerly known as Lionel, bitch. Did you miss me?" she asked. More high-pitched laughter filled the air.

What the fuck?

Graham went numb. He had to. If he reached for his first emotion at the mere mention of Lionel, he would let anger and hatred push him to hurt himself to try to get free to hurt him. Or her. Whatever. None of it had ever made sense, and now he was really lost.

Quinn was Lionel?

Graham hadn't seen any signs of his molester in the person before him, but he continued to study Quinn's face, looking for some sign that what she said was true and not just more of her crazy. *But how would she know about Lionel? No one knows.*

"When my parents moved, I thought that day in the closet was the last time I would ever get to be...close to you."

Graham's eyes filled with menace as a coldness that scared him began to chill his body. It was awareness that he was capable of murder. Without the restraints and the last of the drugs inhibiting him, he could easily snap Lionel or Quinn or whoever's neck in half and then drop the dead body to the floor with less care than a hunter gives its animal prey.

Quinn lightly stroked her scar as she walked across the floor to stand in front of her reflection in the windows. "All my dreams came true," she said in hushed tones with a sad smile, as a tear raced down her cheek. "I always knew I was meant to be a little girl and look at me now. I put every bit of that insurance money from my father's death to good use. What you think?"

Graham was releasing short and heavy breaths in a valiant attempt to release the angry pressure building inside him as he lowered his head and glared over at Quinn until his expression was vicious.

Quinn looked over her shoulder at him. "My parents had no right to choose for me whether I was a boy or girl. They had no right to cut my hair and shove me in boy's clothes because I had a dick and a pussy," she said, her eyes glinting with her madness. "It was my body, and God blessed me to be able to choose. I was one of the lucky ones."

"After what you did to me, do you really think I give a fuck about anything concerning your worthless-ass life?"

Graham chewed out, his chest heaving as he strained against the ties until his feet and hands felt numb.

"Oh, cry me a fucking river," Quinn snapped in annoyance. "Boo hoo fucking hoo. I touched your dick and made you touch mine. Big deal. You try having your cousin force you to suck his dick—*and swallow*—for a year straight before he finally decides my ass was better than my mouth for another two."

"So because your cousin made you his fuckboy, that gave you a right to mess with me? Huh?" Graham roared, his heart pounding loudly like furious stomps on wooden steps.

Boom. Boom. Boom. Boom.

Quinn swiped away her tears and laughed. "I shoulda made you my fuckboy when I had your little soft ass in that closet," she said with a taunting and malicious glint in her eyes before she licked her lips with the swiftness of a lizard's tongue.

"Try me now," Graham warned ominously.

She laughed. "I don't want you. You are no longer a part of God's plan for me. So you gotta die," she said with simplicity and a shrug of her shoulders.

"I can't tell if you've been stalking me since I was six."

Quinn laughed as she walked back over to him. "Is that what you think? Man slut, please. There were plenty of little boys before and after you. You were not on my mind until after I got my surgery and the Lord saw fit for us to meet again. And at a gym of all places. Once I recognized you, I just knew that it was fate and that you were the man I prayed to the sweet Lord above about. You didn't see me but I saw you. I followed you. I watched you day after day until I found just the excuse to be near you."

Graham tried to maintain his grasp on sanity by fitting the puzzle pieces together. The clues he'd missed.

Quinn suddenly joining his art class.

That husky quality to her voice back then.

The pills he used to see her taking.

Her anger at him being a sexual escort.

Hatred burned his gut and tossed reasoning out the window. "You sick, twisted bastard, your father shoulda dumped the nut that made you down your mother's throat and saved the world from your sick bullshit—"

Quinn raced across the room and snatched the knife from where she'd plunged it into the sofa to turn and quickly slash it through the air.

Graham cried out as he felt the sharp blade pierce his skin. He looked down at the superficial wound as blood trickled down his chest.

"It's time the world was free of your bullshit."

He looked up just as she raised the knife with both hands high above her head, her mouth twisted with rage and her insanity.

"Graham, enough is enough. Let's talk."

Both Graham and Quinn looked toward the sound of Jaime's voice just as she breezed into the living room using the key he'd given her months ago. He'd never thought he would regret that so much.

"Jaime, baby. Run," Graham screamed.

"Two for one," Quinn said in a harsh whisper as she turned and took off at a full run toward Jaime. "Will you look at God?"

Jaime's eyes quickly took in Graham's naked and bound bloody body in the millisecond just before Quinn brought the knife down aimed at her heart. She quickly sidestepped her with a cry. The knife lodged into the wall and Jaime roughly pushed her, sending the half-naked woman crashing against the table and to the floor with a solid grunt.

"Jaime. Untie me," Graham begged, his eyes on Quinn, who struggled to rise to her knees as she clutched the front of her head.

Jaime did as he bid even though her face was filled with

fear and confusion. "What the fuck is going on, Graham?" she asked as she tried with trembling fingers to undo the ties.

"Just hurry and get me free. Hurry," he urged her, watching as Quinn rose to her feet and pulled the knife from the wall even as she stumbled back and forth. "Hurry, baby."

"I'm trying. It's tight. I can't. God please, please, please," she said, her breaths coming in pants. "What the fuck? Oh my God. Oh my God. Please."

Quinn came racing across the room with her sights set on Jaime.

Graham felt the tie around his wrist loosen a bit. With a grunt of power and strength, he snatched his arms up to tear through the ties just as Quinn stopped and swung the knife down toward Jaime's bent head.

Graham reached for her wrist.

Jaime screamed and tumbled back onto the floor, scrambling to move away from them.

Graham felt the blade swipe across his forearm, but he captured Quinn's wrist and twisted it until she cried out and the knife fell to the floor. He wrenched her arm behind her back and brought his hand up to tightly grip her neck.

I shoulda made you my fuckboy when I had your little soft ass in that closet.

Graham felt like he'd been pushed back into that closet nearly twenty-five years ago when he didn't understand that he was being violated. He was not to blame. All he knew was he didn't like it. He didn't want it.

I shoulda made you my fuckboy when I had your little soft ass in that closet.

His hand tightened around her neck.

"Graham, let her go. Graham."

He heard Jaime, but her words barely registered as he felt trapped back in a time in his life that had forever changed him.

"Graham. Please. For me. Please, Graham, for me."

Jaime reached out for him, and before her hands even landed on his bare back and upper arm, the fine hairs on his body stood on end. And when her touch landed, goose bumps raced across his skin in awareness.

No other woman had that effect on him.

"Please," she begged again.

And for no one but Jaime would he honor such a huge request.

He kicked the knife away and released Quinn to shove her away from him roughly. "Call the police," he said, his voice still tight with anger.

Quinn collapsed against the back of the torn sofa as she fought to take in large gasps of air. She slid to the floor and lay there with her chest heaving, looking up at him with malice still in her eyes.

"You're lucky you *look* like a woman," he said, knowing he was being crude and snide.

"Look like a woman?" Jaime asked, coming over to wrap a blanket around Graham's waist.

"It's a long story," he said, sitting back down on the chair and leaning into Jaime as she came to stand beside him to stroke the side of his face. He never once took his eyes off Quinn, just waiting for her to make a move and give him a reason to send evil straight back to hell.

The Postlude

Two Weeks Later

Graham stood on the rooftop of the apartment and looked out at the Hudson River through his aviator shades. Taking a deep breath, he shifted back and forth in his shoes and shook his head at having to leave everything behind.

Last week professional movers had already packed up his entire penthouse apartment and moved everything into storage. He hadn't stepped foot back in the apartment since the moment the police restrained a screaming and kicking Quinn and escorted her out of it. He'd said good riddance to both Quinn and the apartment filled with haunting memories of her crazy. She was charged for her crimes, denied bail, and placed on a psychiatric hold. *Bye, you delusional bitch.*

In the last two weeks, he had met with Dr. Templeton on six different occasions. He couldn't deny he needed to be able to talk it through with someone skilled and equipped to guide his steps through a mental minefield. They were currently addressing his anger at his mother, whom he blamed for taking him to the place where he was abused. A place where he should have been safe—a church. With the ultimate person to keep him safe—his mother. *Yeah, we're getting through all the bullshit in me.*

And there was more.

He turned at the sound of heels against the pavement surrounding the rooftop pool. He smiled at the sight of Jaime looking exquisite in a flowing one-shoulder pantsuit with a slight breeze blowing her bangs back from her face before she brushed them aside as she did by habit. His heart swelled with love for her.

"Hello, Graham," she said, holding out her hands to him as she neared.

"Hello to you," he said, taking her hands in his and pulling them around his back as she bent his head to taste her lips.

Sweet, intimate touches deepened without hesitation. They both felt that same familiar pulse of energy surround them in the bubble they created whenever they were near each other.

Jaime leaned back first and reached to wipe her gloss from his supple lips. "You're not making this easy, Graham," she said, trying hard to smile but failing as she closed her eyes and tilted her head back to shake it as if to clear it. "Why are you so *damn* fine?"

He was glad for his shades as he blinked away his own tears before they fell. "There's more to me than that," he said lightly, having made that discovery for himself of late.

"You're right. You are smart and funny and deep, and you are the most amazing lover. You are strong and good and... and... you are leaving me," she finished sadly. She reached to stroke the neat edges of his locs and then the side of his handsome face.

"I need some time alone to get my shit together and—"

"And I need to decide if I can ever get past your past," she finished for him.

He nodded as he rubbed her wrist with his thumb. He

loved that the beat of her pulse pounded against it. "I love you, Jaime. I swear I love the fuck out of you," he told her fiercely.

"I believe that," she said confidently. "And I love you too."

"I know that," he said, his heart swelling.

He pulled her close and lifted her up against him to hold her close as he pressed a dozen kisses to her face and then her lips before he set her back down.

"Until we meet again?" she asked softly, forcing a smile even as a tear raced down her face.

Graham nodded and stepped back from her. Blowing one final kiss to him, Jaime turned and walked away. He watched her until the door to the rooftop closed behind her. It took everything in him not to stop her. Go to her. Kiss her. Proclaim his love for her.

Now was not the time, and he wondered if that time would ever come.

Don't miss any of Niobia Bryant's thrilling books in the Mistress series, now available at your local bookstore!

MESSAGE FROM A MISTRESS

Through good times and bad, longtime friends Jaime, Renee, Aria, and Jessa have shared just about everything. But all hell breaks loose when Jessa texts them a shocking revelation: she's been sharing her bed with one of their husbands. To make matters worse, she refuses to name which husband she's been cheating with. And all three wives have reason to worry...

MISTRESS NO MORE

Jessa Bell shocked the hell out of her three best friends when she announced she was having an affair with one of their husbands—then refused to say which one. She's been reveling in watching them self-destruct. But now, Jessa's ready to confront the ladies, reveal the truth, and move on. But she'll soon find out revenge isn't just sweet—it can be deadly...

MISTRESS, INC.

Shunned by her former friends, Jessa Bell is still being propositioned by married men—and decides to start a business to help wives catch their cheating husbands. But when more secrets about her past are exposed, it's going to be tough for her to stay on the straight and narrow—even if it spells disaster for her future...

Don't miss Grace Octavia's latest novel in the
Southern Scandal series,

His Last Wife

On sale now!

Chapter 1

"Put more of that cheese on my plate." This directive murmur that edged on the possibility of a growl came from the cigarette-blackened lips of a woman in an orange jail jumpsuit whose stereotypical back-braided cornrows and decidedly mean mug announced that not only had she been incarcerated for a very long time, but that this was likely not her first incarceration and it wouldn't be her last.

Six feet tall with a wide back and muscular arms, she was standing toward the middle of a rowdy line at a metal food service counter in the gray-walled cafeteria at the Fulton County jail. All around was a mess of loud, trash-talking female inmates in various stages of eating dinner and wide-eyed guards with their hands on their guns.

"I can't do that!" This uneasy response that was dipped in fear came from the Vaseline-coated lips of a woman whose orange jumpsuit was hidden beneath a white apron; however, this inmate's stylish two-strand twists that only had three inches of gray at the roots made it clear that not only had she just gotten to jail, but also that she didn't plan on staying and still wasn't clear about how life had led her to that place. Indeed, like half of the other women in the jail, Kerry Ann Jackson had maintained that she was no criminal. But that didn't stop officers from putting her in handcuffs and placing her behind bars for allegedly tossing her ex-husband off the roof of a downtown Atlanta skyscraper.

"You better put more that cheese on my plate, bitch!" The murmur coming from the black lips was definitely now a growl.

"But I already gave you the serving. One scoop. That's it," Kerry tried to rationalize, pointing to the soggy pasta shells on the growler's plate. Kerry was standing behind the service counter, holding a one-cup serving spoon over the pan of pasta shells and processed cheese that was supposed to be macaroni and cheese. The kitchen manager had given her one instruction: "One serving spoon per inmate. You fuck that up and you're back on the toilets."

"You think I'm simple, bitch? I know what the fucking serving is, but ain't no cheese on mine." She slammed the tray on the counter in a way that made the soggy noodles shake in the soupy yellow cheese sauce on her plate, and all eyes to the front and back of the line looked over at the spectacle. Guards chatting nearby craned their necks to get a look.

Kerry was ready to disappear. If the pan of artificial macaroni and cheese surprise was big enough, she would've jumped right in and swam to the bottom to escape. Drowned herself in the yellow paste just to avoid what could happen next. And it could be anything. Anything. She'd been in holding at the jail for three months and in that time she'd seen women spat on for less. One woman got stabbed in her right tit for chatting up one of the female guards who'd been sleeping with another inmate.

"Problem, Ms. Thompson?" a youngish white male guard with tattoos up both arms said, approaching the confrontation from the back of the line.

Cornrows looked at him through the corner of her eye and spat, "Nah—none at all."

The guard looked at Kerry. "You okay?" he asked rather politely. He'd been working at the jail for over five years, and in that time he'd seen Thompson and her cornrows come and go and stir up trouble in the jail each time.

"I'm fine," Kerry lied nervously.

"Move it along then, Thompson." The guard nudged Thompson in the back with his index finger.

After taking two steps, she looked back at Kerry and mouthed, "You mine."

Fear shot through Kerry's veins like electricity and she would've tried to run right out of that cafeteria had it not been for a whisper in her ear from the inmate serving green beans beside her.

"Girl, don't mind Thompson. She all talk. She'll set shit off, but if you buck up at her, she'll back off," she said, dumping green beans onto another inmate's plate. She was Garcia-Bell, a Latina with a short black buzz cut and beautiful long eyelashes that looked out of place on her mannish face. She was one of the two friends Kerry had made since she'd been locked up—the other was the inmate who'd gotten stabbed in the tit. "I told you that you can't let these chicks see you all scared. Bitches feed on that shit in here. They like dogs."

"How am I supposed to seem like I'm not scared when *I am* scared," Kerry whispered, watching Thompson continue to peek back at her as the guard forced her down the line. "I'll just be glad when this is all over and I can get away from these people. When I can go home. See my family— my little boy."

"Don't we all," Garcia-Bell agreed, scooping out another serving of green beans. "Don't we all."

★   ★   ★

Most evenings after dinner, Kerry didn't go into the recreational common area to watch soap opera reruns on the outdated projection television with the other inmates. Instead, she'd head to the library, pick up a book, and sit at one of the tables in the back of the room where volunteers taught GED prep classes. There, she could read and think and pretend none of this was happening to her.

But Kerry didn't do that the day after the incident in the cafeteria with the macaroni and cheese. To avoid a confrontation with Thompson, she went straight to her cell and climbed into her bunk, vowing to stay there until the lights went out and later the sun came up. Maybe tomorrow would be different. Maybe Thompson would've forgotten their spat in the cafeteria. Maybe Kerry would wake up and be away from this place altogether. Tomorrow she'd be sitting on the back deck of the Tudor off Cascade drinking margaritas with Marcy. Tomorrow she'd be driving up I85 in the old Range Rover with the windows down and air conditioning on. Music blasting, open road in front of her. Going to wherever she wanted. Tomorrow she'd see Tyrian. Jamison. Home.

Kerry lay back in her bottom bunk and looked up at the picture she'd tucked into the spring beneath the top mattress. Two faces smiled down at her. A man and a boy with the same brown skin, dark eyes, and pug noses. They were standing beside a large wood sign that read "East Lake Golf Course." The boy, who was a little taller than the man's waist, held a golf club in his hand. The man's right arm was draped around the boy. Both looked proud.

A tear left Kerry's eye and rolled back toward the pillow beneath her head. She closed her eyes tightly and tried to go back to that day she'd taken the photo. It was Tyrian's first golf demonstration. She and Jamison had already been divorced by then, but that day was peaceful. Agreeable. Tyrian woke up that morning so nervous and anxious and excited he wouldn't stop asking his mother questions.

"What if I lose? What if it rains? What if it snows? What if I faint? What if my coach faints? What if no one comes? What if too many people come?" he listed so intensely Kerry wondered how a six-year-old could come up with so many worries.

"And what if everything is perfect? Just perfect?" she'd said, placing his clothes on his bed. "Have you thought about that, my little worrywart? What if everything is wonderful and everyone has a great time?"

Climbing from beneath his bed sheets, Tyrian looked off to consider like he was much older and wiser. "Okay," he said after a long pause. "It could be perfect. You're right, Mama."

Kerry winked at Tyrian, kissed his cheek, and said, "I'm always right."

And she was right. While her ex-husband was usually late to Tyrian's practices at the golf course and had gotten into the habit of using his recent victory in a tight race for mayor of Atlanta as an excuse to be absent from most of Tyrian's scheduled events, he was waiting outside the golf course, right by the sign, when Kerry and Tyrian arrived. Sitting in the backseat of his mother's truck, Tyrian squealed with the delight of a six-year-old-son when he saw his father standing beside the sign.

"Daddy's here! Daddy's here already! He really came!" Tyrian cheered, tearing off his booster seat's seat belt before his mother could pull into her parking space and turn off the engine.

She was about to tell him to wait for her before he hopped out of the truck and bolted right to the person who'd become his favorite as of late, but she decided to let it slide that morning. All of the other little golfers unloading from their parents' cars had both mother and father in tow. She knew Tyrian wanted that, too—for his parents to be together like everyone else's. And at that moment, he was just ecstatic that his life would look like all of the other kids' that day.

"My big boy!" Jamison said, gathering his son into his arms after the boy had jumped out of the truck and run to his father standing at the sign. "Man, you're getting heavy. I'm not going to be able to pick you up much longer!" Jamison laughed. The phone in his pocket was already vibrating with other things he needed to do, but he didn't reach for it. He promised himself he wouldn't. Today was about Tyrian.

"Hi." Kerry's greeting was flat and uninspired when she'd gotten out of the truck and walked up carrying the golf bag Tyrian left behind.

Jamison looked over at his first wife. "Good morning," he offered, smiling.

"Good morning," she added to her greeting.

A few parents walked past with their little golfers straggling behind, waving at Tyrian. The whole time—just seconds, really, but to the exes it felt much longer—Jamison and Kerry eyed each other for signs of anything new. Kerry had recently cut off her long, black permed hair and was wearing a short natural Jamison thought made her look younger and thinner. Maybe she'd lost weight, too. Jamison was wearing a new expensive watch. He had the collar on his old gold fraternity golf shirt popped up to hide a hickey on his neck, but even with the carefully planned disguise and brown skin, and two feet of distance, his ex-wife could see it.

"Think we need to get to the clubhouse. I'm sure they're starting the demonstration on time," Kerry said dryly.

"Of course. Of course," Jamison agreed and then added, "Hey, can you take a picture of me and Tyrian?" He pulled his phone from his pocket and stretched to hand it to Kerry.

"Okay," she said, taking the phone.

"Cool!" Tyrian cheered, standing beside his dad.

The three organized the perfect shot in front of the sign and just before Kerry was about to take the picture, Jamison added one of Tyrian's clubs from his bag.

Kerry held up the phone and took a few shots. In the background, a new spring had the grass a bright green.

Once all were satisfied that the moment had been captured, Kerry was about to hand Jamison the phone when it rang and a familiar name came up on the screen—Val.

"Here," Kerry said, rushing to give the phone to Jamison.

"Wait, Mama! You get in the picture!" Tyrian posed with a big smile. "We can take one with all of us."

Kerry and Jamison looked at each other. The phone was still ringing with Val's name on the screen.

"Oh, we can't do that," Kerry said, handing the phone to Jamison. "There's no one to take the picture."

"I'll take it!" A fourth voice cut into the conversation suddenly.

Behind Kerry was a young man in a Morehouse College golf shirt, holding what was clearly an expensive camera in his hand. A bag with "FOX NEWS" stitched into the top flap was hanging over his shoulder.

"It would be an honor to take a picture of our new mayor and his family," the man said.

"Thanks, brother," Jamison said, flashing his practiced public smile. "We'd appreciate that. Hey, what's your name? I love meeting my Morehouse brothers, you know," he added, reaching out to shake the young man's hand.

"I'm Ricky Johnson—a new reporter with FOX NEWS Atlanta," he said. "Good to meet you, Mayor Taylor. You're doing us Morehouse men proud."

Kerry reluctantly got into the picture, standing behind Tyrian's shoulder opposite Jamison.

In minutes, the image would be featured on the FOX NEWS main website. The caption: *An awkward moment at East Lake Golf Course this morning when Mayor Taylor takes a picture with his ex-wife, Atlanta socialite Kerry Ann Jackson, and six-year-old son, Tyrian.*

The bottom bunk where Kerry lay remembering her past rattled with a thud. She quickly opened her eyes, ready to react and jumped up, hitting the top of her head on the bottom of the upper bunk.

"Owww!" she let out, looking at a boot on the floor beside her bed that was no doubt the source of the rattling. Her eyes left the boot and nervously forged a path up the orange jumpsuit to the face of the kicker she was certain had come to pummel her.

"Damn! Calm down, boo! It's just me!" Garcia-Bell held out her hands innocently as she laughed at Kerry's head bump and fearful eyes. "What? You thought I was Thompson coming to kick your ass?"

Kerry rolled her eyes and looked out of the cell past Garcia-Bell. "Where is she?" She sat up.

"Probably somewhere starting more shit with someone else. You in here hiding out?"

"Basically."

"Well, what was you gonna do if I was her? This ain't some dorm room. She can see your skinny ass right through them bars," Garcia-Bell said, pointing to the open cell door as she took a seat beside Kerry on the bunk.

The mattress above them was bare. Kerry's first cellmate, a white woman who'd stabbed her boyfriend five times in the head, had bonded out.

"Guess I don't care," Kerry said. "If I'm going to get beat up, what does it matter if she does it in here or out there? I'm still getting beat up."

"It would be worse in here. No one around. It'll take a while for the guards to get here," Garcia-Bell explained. "Plus, Thompson got a lot of enemies. You never know if someone might want to sneak some licks in if she starts something with you on the yard."

Kerry looked off and laughed a little to herself.

"What? What's so funny?" Garcia-Bell asked.

Kerry's mind switched from inside the walls of the prison to outside where her world was so different. A simple word like "yard" could mean so many other things, none of which included a tiny outside space with nothing but dry, depleted dirt and female prisoners fighting fiercely over turns to use deflated basketballs and rusting gym equipment.

"That word—'yard'—it reminds me of where I went to college," Kerry replied, not knowing if she should mention her alma mater, Spelman College, if Garcia-Bell would've heard of the historically black college or knew what the term meant there. In 1998, Kerry's time on the "yard" included watching her best friend Marcy step with her sorority sisters, sitting on the steps in front of Manley Hall, chatting with her Spelman sisters and professors about images of black women in the media, the future of the black woman in politics, and, of course, black love. There, she was a third generation "Spelman girl," was called "Black Barbie," and had dozens of Morehouse brothers from the college across the street chasing after her. There, she met Jamison.

"You gonna have to let that shit go—all that shit from outside—who you were, who you thought you were—if you gonna make it in here," Garcia-Bell cautioned. "Ain't no tea and crumpets behind these bars. In order to survive, you gonna have to knuckle up."

"Knuckle up?"

"Fight, Kerry. You gonna have to fight. Ain't nobody ever taught you how to fight?"

"You mean, like actual fisticuffs?" Kerry said, watching a group of prisoners who always stuck together walk by her cell.

"Don't ever say that word again, but yes, that's what I mean," Garcia-Bell confirmed, laughing.

"No—no one taught me how to fight. Who would? Who taught you?"

"My ma," Garcia-Bell said as if it should've been obvious.

"Please. The closest Thirjane Jackson came to teaching me to fight was how to keep the mean girls in Jack and Jill from talking about me behind my back," Kerry said.

"Jack and Jill? Like the nursery rhyme?"

"Yeah. It was a social club my mother made me join when I was young," Kerry said. "Had to be her perfect little girl in Jack and Jill."

"Well, you far from that now. And thinking about that out there ain't gonna do nothing but get you caught up in here."

"That's the thing, Garcia-Bell, I don't plan on getting caught up in here. I'm not staying here."

"Hmm. You keep saying that, but then I keep seeing you in here."

Kerry had already told Garcia-Bell all about her case—about how she ran up to the rooftop of the Hyatt to find her ex-husband that gray morning—she knew something was wrong, knew something was going to happen. There was a woman up there. The woman was the one who threw Jamison over the edge to his death. Not Kerry. Kerry still loved Jamison. In the hotel room where they'd been cuddling just hours before, they'd talked about getting remarried. Kerry would be his third wife—after he divorced his second wife.

Garcia-Bell already knew the whole story. Like everyone else in Atlanta, rich and poor, young and old, black and white, criminals and non-criminals, she wanted to know how in the world the city's fourth black mayor who'd come from nothing and promised the people everything ended up split wide open with his guts and everything hanging out and his face crushed beyond recognition in the middle of Peachtree Street during morning rush-hour traffic. She'd even heard this very version of events from Kerry's mother when Thirjane Jackson had been interviewed by a reporter with FOX NEWS. But she let Kerry retell it all a few times anyway. She felt Kerry needed to.

"Well, one day you're going to come looking for me and

I'm not going to be here. I've got people in my corner root-ing for me. It's going to work out. I believe that," Kerry said.

"People?" Garcia-Bell struggled not to sound cynical, but it was too hard. "By that you mean your ex-husband's widow? The one who's supposedly going to bust you out of here and help you find the killer?"

"Yes. I do," Kerry replied resolutely. "I told you she knows I didn't do this and she has proof. It's taking her a little time, but she's helping my lawyer build my case and soon, everyone will know the truth. I'm innocent."

"Sure is taking her a long time."

"These things take time. You know that yourself."

"Well, there's long and then there's loooonnnng," Garcia-Bell pointed out.

"What's that mean?"

"Nothing." Garcia-Bell stood up, ready to leave. She didn't want to hurt her friend's feelings. Since she was a teenager, she'd been locked up for some reason or another and she knew the worst thing in the world was knowing the one per-son on the outside who could do anything about her case was doing absolutely nothing. She didn't want to put that on Kerry.

"Come on, spit it out," Kerry pushed.

"It's nothing. It's like I said—it's taking a long fucking time."

"But you know the situation. You know Val can't just bust me out of here," Kerry pleaded in a way that sounded like she actually coaching herself.

Garcia-Bell pointed to the top bunk. "White girl stabbed her old man in the fucking head five times and she bonded out. Ain't got no kids. Ain't have no job. They got a fucking confession out of her. She home." She pointed to Kerry. "Ain't nobody see you throw your husband from the roof. You got a child. A career. And you say you innocent. And you rich. You mean to tell me that woman and that lawyer she hired to get you out of jail can't even get you out on bond? Come on, girl. You ain't stupid. I know that."

"It's not that simple," Kerry said.

"To me it is. You said it yourself: y'all hated each other. Then your ex-husband threw her ass out on the street after she had a miscarriage, and you and the broad got all chummy just because you gave her a couple of dollars so she could get a hotel room. Then your ex-husband ends up dead when she was still married to him and she got all his money and is living up in his house and running the business you partially own. But you think she rushing to get you out of jail? You believe that?" Garcia-Bell paused and looked at Kerry with a friend's concern in her eyes. "Please say you don't. I mean, maybe you want to believe it because she the only card you got to play, but *wanting* to believe it and *actually* believing it— that's got to be different things."

Tears returned to Kerry's eyes. A lump in her throat obstructed any response to Garcia-Bell's damning assessment.

Garcia-Bell sighed and cursed herself inside for opening her mouth. "I'm sorry," she said, bending down to look at Kerry. "Look, don't stay in this cell. Get out until lights out and if you need anything, you holler for me." She looked into Kerry's eyes and kissed her on the lips quickly before walking out.

CONNECT WITH THE AUTHOR

Websites: www.NIOBIABRYANT.com
                                               www.MEESHAMINK.com

Email: Niobia_Bryant@yahoo.com

Automated Mailing List
(For incarcerated readers):   CorrLinksReaders@yahoo.com

Twitter: www.twitter.com/InfiniteINK

Facebook: Search for: Niobia Bryant | Meesha
                                               Mink

Pinterest: www.pinterest.com/infiniteink/

GoodReads: http://www.goodreads.com/niobiabryant